SEEP

J. Eric Laing

This is a work of fiction. Names, characters, places, and incidents are either products of the author's imagination or are used fictitiously, and any resemblance to actual persons, living or dead, business establishments, events, or locales is entirely coincidental.

The book may not be reproduced in whole or part, by mimeograph or any other means, without the permission of the author. Making or distributing electronic copies of this book constitutes copyright infringement and could subject the infringer to criminal and civil liability. Sandwiches preferred cold.

Copyright © 2007 by J. Eric Laing
All rights reserved.

For Diana

Chapter One

"The last of the chickens is dead," Walter announced, coming into the kitchen from the backyard.

The man seated at the breakfast table stared at the cupboard-clean plate before him and said nothing, ignoring the boy entirely. Walter was content to return his father's discourtesy. He threw his empty egg pail into the corner, brushed his hands on his shirt and sullied the kitchen floor with his muddy boots as he crossed to the sink.

The boy peered from his family's kitchen window to count the men as they toiled beneath the sun. Only six remained. The old men had been dying off one by one as if their lot had brokered some Faustian deal, exchanging the last of their days to see the new funeral parlor finished. Too long in the tooth for such work, their struggle had become the subject of much ridicule and jest back in town. Even from the outset of the construction crew's very first loss, the irony of the matter did not escape them. Nor did it elude young Walter Petry.

He pondered how the supposedly wise could be so thick. Walter had heard the jokes. He found them funny.

So distant from the boy, the men looked like insects scrambling here and there. *Just like stupid bugs. Ants,* he mused. And, much like ants, it was clear they worked in concert, sharing some grand scheme, some greater goal, something more than just the building that drove them. Walter thought for a moment that he'd grasped that elusive something. Then, like a quail startled from the brush, the thought exploded, replaced in a flash with a bizarre image—a scarecrow constructed of offal. But then his mind cleared. The thought was gone as quickly as it'd come over him, leaving him shaken and nervous to have gotten so close to understanding something that had been eluding him for so many days now.

The boy shivered in the heat and changed his wandering mind's course, imagining a great stick in his grasp, his god spear to poke the old men cruelly. Or perhaps his subjects needed squashing. Either way, he rendered them lifeless one by one. As he did, Walter marked each death with a harsh thrust of his sweat-damp head and a satisfied grunt. He made his little macabre dance complete by mashing down his foot, entertaining the notion that some of the men were caught helpless in the hole of his worn boot sole. Their pitiful stabs and sad punches into his wool sock would not save them. Walter would smear them into the floorboards like so much spilt jelly.

The boy knew these men and they knew him. Had any of them truly been present in the Petry family's kitchen, they would have hardly cowered beneath the threat of Walter's boot. These were the town elders, the founders who had towered above all other men, much less boys such as Walter. Had they been there, their words would have no doubt been kind, still and calming, and Walter would have called them sir in the respectful manner to which he'd been raised.

Captured there in the distance, however, the men remained the tortured subjects of Walter's demented imagination. He grinned as his fancy suddenly pounced on the idea of using his magnifying glass on them, just as he might an ant hill. Not to spy them better, but to focus the sun into a pinpoint beam, incinerating, bursting them into flames, mouths, ears, nostrils, and eye sockets all blazing with jets of fire. Then he would turn on their construction, reducing their meticulous labor to cinder. Walter wondered if he would need to strain to hear their insignificant cries. Most gods would, he imagined. More than likely their tortured voices would be too puny to move his ears, although it would be a disappointment if it worked out that way.

The boy, only eleven in years, had been at his game for some minutes when his father finally came around.

"You say the chickens, they're all dead?"

"Dead," Walter reported once more in a voice near as lifeless. His eyes remained fixed on the horizon, on the hard working old men.

"You sure?"

"Yes, sir," Walter confirmed. "As stone."

Despite his father's doubt, Walter was certain. After all, he'd snapped the rooster's neck with his own slender hands. It'd come down stricken ill with the same strange sickness that had slowly killed the hens, was killing the old men, his mother, and a good portion of the town. But it wasn't the bird's suffering young Walter had wanted to end. He simply despised being in the sick creature's company any longer. Besides, he'd never cared for the ornery cock to begin with. It'd forever been in the habit of pecking the back of his ankles, his Achilles tendon, and of late, even more so. Plus, what good was a rooster without hens?

"I don't think we should eat it. It had the pus," Walter

said.

The man nodded silent agreement. The almost imperceptible, far-off pounding of roofing nails being driven echoed over the field, a steady *lub* and *dub* caught in the vacancy of his pause.

"Probably was a stupid idea to eat them hens, too," Walter added.

Though true, it was a poor choice of words to toss out as casual as the chickens' feed. After all, eating them had been his father's idea.

"What of your other chores then?" the man pecked at the boy.

"I heard you prayin' earlier," Walter said, his tone accusatory. The man said nothing. "Are they building that out yonder for mother? In answer to your beggin' and bargainin' with God?" Walter asked, casting a nod towards the old men that still held his attention.

Bill Petry rose and followed his son's gaze where it wandered out the window. "How the mighty have fallen," he muttered. "No, son," he eventually answered after a moment more. "They don't build churches in these parts. It ain't in their nature."

"I know that," Walter said.

The man thought it sounded like 'a hate,' as he would call it, and it was. Ugliness sprung forth from his own flesh, from under his own roof, and the spell of it racked him. Motionless in body but tripping over himself in mind, the man dressed the boy out like a slain buck, wildly splattering the walls with his child's blood, cramming flayed hide and offal down the kitchen sink, skinning his rage-whitened knuckles in the effort.

Fortunately for the both of them, that murderous act was only one more of the father's ever-increasing hallucinations. Before he could look back to Walter the man regarded his own hands to confirm the backs were unscathed, the palms clean of blood. He sighed with silent thanks.

The father and son faced each other in the kitchen, a heartbeat throbbing in their ears as much as the distant hammers pounding on and on. Just as all seemed lost, as though the man might very well make good on his madness, a small bird lit on the sill unexpected, a frail bundle of feathers cocking and craning to see into the home before flitting away. In that fleeting distraction the man found the presence of mind to physically shake himself free from his fevered dementia. It was merely the briefest respite.

Walter startled back as though gut kicked by a mule, when, without warning, his father began to repeatedly throw himself into the wall, as if overtaken with the throes of some violent palsy. The fine china that was kept stacked on a high shelf and rarely used—the mother's prized collection—were jostled from their haven and several large dinner plates along with a gravy boat crashed to the floor exploding into shards. This did not stop the man, however, even as one of the dishes struck his brow, splitting open the flesh into a little, red, ragged frown. Unfortunately, even in the self-inflicted flagellation meant to stave off the rage, to vent it elsewhere, the man saw in himself his ailing wife. He'd been forced to tie the poor woman to her bed upstairs when she'd behaved similarly. For her sake there'd been no other way.

Even as far gone as he was, the man had a scarce bout of clarity. He realized the boy would never be capable of doing the same for him now; of that he was certain. And the man needed no gypsy. He could divine his own fortune. He also knew he would hurt the boy. He would kill him.

So then, the man, the father, Bill Petry, found himself in a place of unbearable helplessness and torment. He now understood the terror he'd seen in the eyes of the calf he'd found last winter. A poor creature, torn and twisted, cruelly tangled up among the strands of a barb wire fence, dying in pain, its meager faculties unable to fathom its circumstances. He was now that calf. The discovery was too much. The last the man knew was the anguish that clamped his breast as his worn heart finally caved. He swayed twice before racing headlong to the floor, felled like a tree, dead even before his blood-drained face smacked there with a sickening crunch.

Walter sat down cross-legged by his father and stroked his hair. "I got your days, just like you promised," the boy whispered in his ear.

Walter's first thought was to carry his father's body upstairs and place the corpse beside his mother in the bed the two had always shared...*for how many years?* They'd told the boy many times in the past, but he couldn't say with any real certainty now. Perhaps that would calm her ceaseless caterwauling. *Worse than a wounded cat in heat*, he thought. *As sure as sunrise, it couldn't get no worse.*

No matter. The body was too much for the boy to do much else with other than drag, inch by grunt-inducing inch, across the kitchen floor and out the back door.

Walter sent the body rolling down the back steps,

flopping and flailing before coming to rest, arms akimbo, one hand tucked behind the back and the other on the hip with the thumb caught in a belt loop. His expression had all the appearance of striking a bargain with Saint Peter, what with dead eyes staring up into the bright blue day. Walter hadn't bothered to close them. Looking down on the body lying there in the short grass, Walter considered doing his father that courtesy now, but then decided it really wasn't important. That much accomplished, the boy became disinterested with fretting over it anymore. He decided to have his breakfast.

His mother's rants echoed above him as he methodically chewed his bread at the table. Her inchoate blathering rose and fell, as steady and irritating as crows harping on a wire, but never faltered completely. Nor did the old men take any break from their roofing. Walter wondered if perhaps he could drag the body—or, better yet, roll it across the field—to leave it in their hands. After all, they seemed rather obsessed with the disposal of the dead.

It would have been far easier to bring the old men to him, of course, but then they would discover his mother's condition. That simply wouldn't do.

If his family still had their horse then Walter could have hitched up the wagon. *Stupid dead horse,* Walter thought. He spit dryly to the kitchen floor to punctuate his disgust. He couldn't recall the old paint horse's name. He tried for a moment then gave up. *What did it matter? It was dead too.* Seemed like years gone by now. It had only been three weeks. The horse, like so many other horses around those parts, had been the first of the family's paltry assortment of livestock to go. The sickness had fevered the creature, but not killed it. Walter's father had seen to that. He'd been forced to put the horse down after it crippled itself bucking wildly in the barn out back.

Paint Brush. That'd been the horse's name. *Good old Paint Brush.* His father had said he'd butcher the animal for stew meat. Times were that hard. The old man had gotten wildly drunk and hung it from the barn rafters and taken a cleaver to it, but other than mutilating the carcass and howling obscenities into the night, the man had done nothing more.

...

Walter was still too far off from the old men for them to take any notice of him while still close enough to home to catch his mother's continuous raving. This, even after spending a good piece of the morning rolling his father through the knee-deep, brown and brittle grasses of the field.

Just after he'd started, he'd had the idea to strap down his father's arms by tucking them into the man's belt to make the going easier. But, like a drunk too easily distracted, Walter had only gotten as far as securing one limb before getting back to rolling the body along.

The boy was taking a break and using the corpse as a seat. The sun was just shy of being directly overhead. The body was still warm. Walter sat watching the men but wasted no more energy considering anything more about them. His thoughts were not elsewhere. His mind was not preoccupied; it was a blank. A horde of deer flies had found him and were tearing at his flesh, raising hellacious welts on his exposed face, neck, and arms. Walter offered no more resistance to their attack than did his dead father.

Then, in an epiphany, like someone who'd only in that moment remembered he was late for an important engagement, Walter leapt to his feet and hurried back along the path of flattened grass he'd made that morning.

...

Even before dusk the turkey buzzards had made the forsaken corpse, found easily enough out in the middle of the field where it lay sprawled out like a defective and fallen scarecrow.

Walter sat at the kitchen table once more. With no lights on or lamps lit he was quickly slipping into the shadows as the ambient light from outside fell away. The sounds of construction had ended unnoticed some time ago and had been replaced by the repeated calls of a lonesome whippoorwill. Walter's shirt was sopped through with sweat and his throat burned anew with each breath like a stoked fire. There was no one to bring him a glass of water from the faucet—so close, but all too far—to douse it.

Although his mother had been quiet since finally succumbing to sleep a few hours prior, Walter was convinced the woman yet railed and wailed in the room above him. This was the fuel that fired the boy's current obsession. As he'd been doing for the past nine hours, Walter turned over the singular thought on his mind once more. It was a simple matter of two choices, use the butcher knife he toyed with to cut his mother free, or slit her throat to bleed her like the spring pig.

Walter hadn't settled his mind either way as he rose from the kitchen table with knife in hand to ascend the creaking stairs.

Chapter Two

Two months before the first sign of the darker days to come found Caleb Sweet walking the length and breadth of the small town as part of his late-morning constitutional. Spring was in full blossom elsewhere in the world—of that old Caleb was certain—but in this tucked-away corner that he and his brother had carved out for themselves, it was easy to imagine the arid heat would hardly ever give birth to anything other than more dry earth and dust.

And soon enough, I imagine, I shall return to it myself.

It was a hard, unforgiving place. Those who suffered to live there—farming as best they could, and struggling to see livestock thrive—had little to no worry that others would come seeking to depose them. This was an abandoned place, they'd decided upon arriving, if indeed anyone before them had ever laid claim to it at all. None had. It was a land free for the taking primarily because it could be counted on to take more than it returned.

It was just the way Caleb Sweet would have it.

In the street ahead a commotion could be heard through the open doors of the general store. A lanky man, along with a reed of a boy and a mange-mottled ghost of a dog—little more than hide stretched over bones—spilled out onto the plank sidewalk. The man, the general store's middle-aged stock boy, Avery Stolks, held the dog tight on a short length of rope. Not leashed by its neck, however, but caught up fast just above the heel crook of a hind leg. Avery was doing his best to kick the dog even as the boy kicked in retaliation at Avery. This all while the wild-eyed dog hopped and yelped and struggled, tangling the rope between the legs of the man and boy. Each time Avery connected his foot with the dog, the poor creature howled. And each time he did, the boy managed to get in a kick to Avery's unguarded shin. The outraged stock boy cursed them both with every exchange.

Caleb paused to check the time on his pocket watch. *Twenty-one past ten in the AM. Stupidity, it would appear, has gotten a late start on the day.* He turned about to regard the curious faces gathering as the spectacle gained momentum. A few folks gasped as the three spilled off the walk and into the street—a cloud of brown dust kicking up all about them—and Avery went down first on his backside and then onto his back. He maintained his hold on the rope, however, despite the boy now getting a firm hold of him by his hair. The dog began twisting about wildly and wailing for all it was worth.

"Leave him be! Let him go!" the boy shrilled.

"I'm gonna tan ya, you runt!" Avery yelled, before quickly changing tack and screaming for someone to get the boy off of him.

Caleb sighed. He pushed the watch back into its place, snug in his vest pocket, and crossing to the three, produced a pocket knife. With a flick of his wrist the long thin blade snapped into place.

Only the dog was aware of the old man as he came to be over them. Caleb's boot settled on the rope. He caught it up with his free hand and severed it in three fast strokes. Still lassoed, but otherwise freed when Caleb lifted his boot, the dog darted off down the street, tail-tucked and without another sound. Caleb Sweet brought Avery Stolks to his feet, lifting him by a twisted ear like a schoolmarm might a truant.

The lanky Avery danced a marionette's tiptoed prance as he caterwauled in protest and pain, "Lemme be goddammit! Lemme be!"

Caleb threw the man off. "Avery Stolks. Son, what on God's green Earth are you doin' beatin' on dogs and children?"

When Avery didn't answer and only rubbed his ear instead, Caleb turned his attention to the boy. He didn't recognize the child by name and, worse, he wasn't even sure if he knew to which family he belonged. The boy didn't speak, either. Unlike Avery, he did meet Caleb's hard stare, however, even if only for the briefest moment. He began dusting off his clothes then as he shot Avery his dirtiest look. Caleb stepped back from the growing dust cloud and snorted to contain his amusement.

At the doors of the general store, the manager, Clarkson, spoke up. "That dog has been snatching foodstuffs all week."

Caleb stayed on the boy. "That'd be your dog, son?"

"No."

"No?"

"No, sir. No that ain't my dog." He scrunched his little face. "I jes' didn't see it right the way he was beatin' on him."

"And I got 'em good this time, didn't I?" Avery said, spitting a wad of foam and grit.

"Go to hell, Avery Stolks," the boy said, getting riled once more. "You go to hell and you stay put. You sorry, dog-beatin'—"

The boy stopped short when Caleb raised his palm with a terse, "Tut-tut."

Avery grabbed his opportunity to chide the boy. "You's is what needs a good tannin', ya runt, you." He turned then to Caleb beseeching the elder with hurt if not vengeful eyes.

But Caleb's scowl suggested it was Avery who was on the verge of getting disciplined. Caleb meticulously wiped the blade of his pocket knife between his thumb and forefinger twice-over before folding and putting it away. "Avery," Caleb said in the calmest of voices, "don't you have some honest work to do? I mean, besides makin' a fool of yourself, that is?"

Avery held fast for as long as he dared and then with a smack of his palms to his dusty dungarees he sulked off back up onto the planks to return to the general store.

"No, no you don't. Not in here," the manager, Clarkson, said waving Avery off as he approached him at the double doors. "Git yerself out back and git cleant up. And be quick about it, too. I pay you to dust the shelves, not…dust the shelves."

Caleb addressed the manager. "Give the boy a raisin cookie or jerky or such, won't you? Put it on my account," he said.

The man nodded once and worried the salt and pepper stubble on his chin with his thick fingers. It amused Caleb to no end to see that Clarkson would rather not have treated the boy. But the manager really had no choice. Only a few folks in town were privy to the fact that the general store belonged to the Sweet brothers, the largest of several such secret holdings. As Caleb liked to say, folks can't begrudge what they don't know.

"There's a good lad," Caleb said with a pat on the boy's shoulder to send him back into the store. "Off you go now." While Caleb had spoken to the boy, his hard gaze had stayed on Clarkson. The man knew his place and went back inside to do as he'd been told.

The boy turned away. "My daddy's right. Damn this godforsaken town." He spat air to earth. "Damn it all to hell." And with that the boy stormed off down the street following in the hazy wake of the dog.

"Hmm. Now don't that beat all…."

Caleb told himself he'd not fret over the matter, but the boy's words haunted him the rest of the morning all the way up until his routine lunch at the saloon with his brother.

Had folks really come to be so miserable? Even if they had, it was no cause for his concern. No cause at all.

The Sweet brothers met at noon in the saloon just as they did most days. Wallace was already seated with a shot of bourbon, the small glass just at his fingertips but as of yet untouched. Looking up, Wallace greeted his brother Caleb with an almost wounded smile.

"I'd ask what you're eating," Wallace said, "but by the looks of you I should think it's the other way 'round."

"What's that then?" Caleb said, dragging his chair along the wood floor to the other side of the table and taking a seat.

"I say, what's eating you, little brother?"

The Sweet brothers were in their winter years, although both still enjoyed remarkably good health as they always had. They were the town's founders and considered themselves the dual fathers to every man, woman and child who walked its streets. Not everyone shared in their self-appointed patriarchy, however.

But for a hint of perfume, the saloon smelled of sawdust and the sour of spilt beers. It was dimly lit and for the most part quiet. The player piano was idle as was the nickelodeon fortune-telling machine. Along the expanse of green felt of the billiards table a few pocked and faded balls were fanned out but there were no players threatening to set them in motion with one of the numerous crooked sticks equally at rest in their nearby rack.

At the bar was one other patron, Curtis Toole, the town's lonely grist mill operator. As he was known to do about every other month or so, Curtis had come into town to drink until his courage was fortified enough to proposition one of the saloon's two prostitutes, Claudette or Mariel. He preferred the younger and more attractive Mariel. In fact, he was in love with her. He usually spent his time with Claudette, however, resigned in his belief that Mariel was far too good for a lowly mill laborer. Both women were at a table at the end of the bar pretending to play cards while they giggled between whispers and flirted with the still-nervous miller. Curtis ordered another drink. The Sweet brothers called out for bourbons and steak. Earl Hodges, the saloon's proprietor and sole barkeep, saw to the Sweet brothers first.

Wallace had only finished half his meal when he pushed the remaining bloody hunk of beef aside.

"Caleb," Wallace began in the practiced tone his brother knew all too well, the tone that foreshadowed a lengthy bit of speech. "We need to do something to shake this town up a bit. Get people in a better frame of mind. Now we both know it was a bleak winter. Cold as a witch's hard teat and just as dry. The result of no snowfall to speak of has meant a spring drought with crops wilting in the—"

Caleb interrupted. "We'll sink a new well in town. Six inch pipe. That and, I dunno…throw a fair or some such."

Wallace wasn't prepared to hear his brother agree so readily. "A fair? Well…I suppose that'd be…."

"Blue ribbons for best hog, steer an' the whole gamut. Have us some music. Food. Drink. Sponsored by yours truly, the brothers Sweet. "

"A fair. Yes. Yes…precisely."

From across the room, Mariel, the younger of the two whores squealed out. "We're goin' have a fair? Yippee! What fun!"

Wallace lifted his bourbon. "See, little brother. Things are looking up already. To us."

Caleb lifted his bourbon and clinked glasses in salute. "To us."

...

The night sky was denied its usual majesty by a canopy of lights strung back and forth the full stretch of Main Street. It had been wisely decided that the event would be a night-time affair—to better avoid the heat—and so the festive lights had been the next good idea.

A band of local musicians—an accordion, two fiddles, a tambourine, washtub drums and two guitars—gathered momentum following each break, growing more and more boisterous as the hard cider and whiskey in their veins stoked their playing. Multiple singers came and went to accompany the ad hoc band dependent mostly upon who knew best, or was moved the most by, the moment's song. Some voices proved better than others. But even those who warbled off-key or stumbled through forgotten lyrics brought smiles and lifted spirits in the revelers.

Some old soul said, "I ain't felt this alive in ages." Several others agreed. Another joked that it was only the firewater talking. "Then give it room to say its peace," another bellowed. There was plenty of laughter to go around with that line and more.

A diminutive red-faced man took to the planks then and began to stomp out a dance that quickly caught on. Soon a dozen or so, both alone and in couples, were spinning and stamping their feet on the band's makeshift stage.

Avery Stolks saw this as his best if not only opportunity. He took a long and last pull to drain his flask before sauntering over to a covey of young women gathered off to the side. They were a plain and pinch-faced lot for the most part and then there was Betty Peters, a quite comely lass—as the old men and women were wont to say—with the company she kept making her even more so. They tittered and shied at his approach. This only served to embolden the man.

Tipping his brand new Stetson before tucking his thumbs behind an equally new sterling silver rodeo-sized belt buckle, Avery coughed twice looking for his voice. He'd been reading a book on attracting women. Following that tutelage he'd planned to sound assured and confident. He did not. Stumbling and mumbling with a mouthful of whiskey marbles, he finally managed to spit out a request to Betty Peters for a dance. The young woman was nearly fifteen years his junior and far too attractive, most agreed, for the likes of a middle-aged stock boy.

Why not? No one else is asking, Betty thought morosely even as her girlfriends giggled and ribbed her.

"I'd be delighted, Mister Stolks," she said and quickly added, "But probably just the one, Avery." The words hadn't finished leaving her mouth before Avery caught her up by the arm, and, with a bit too much gusto, whisked her off to join the fun.

The remaining girls were mirthful at first, teasing Betty behind her back as they watched her dance with Avery. But after one pointed out the lack of prospects remaining for their hands, they fell silent and sullen.

The moon was on the rise when Wallace Sweet finally took the stage to christen the town's new well. He went on to announce that Sterling Peters had won the blue ribbons for both best hog and steer. As everyone applauded and congratulated Sterling, Colonel Rembrandt Warren Hawkins, the town's venerable Civil War veteran, jested loudly that Sterling only won best hog by default since the Colonel had donated his best sow for the barbeque spit. Sterling conceded and offered to give the good Colonel the ribbon to add to his already abundant collection of war "festoonings."

Little Walter Petry thought that hilarious and he tightened his grip on his father's hand and looked up into his face to appreciate his father, Bill, laughing along with him.

"There's goin' to be a pie eatin' contest!" Walter exclaimed to him.

Wallace Sweet heard the boy and boomed to all in reply, "Why yes there is, young master Petry. Yes, there is a pie eating contest. Starting in just a few minutes, in fact."

The crowd murmured with an excited buzz.

"Can I be in it, Daddy? Can I? Please? Please? Please?"

"Why? You think you're goin' out-eat yer ol' man?" Bill shot back with a devil's grin.

Walter's eyes grew. "Really?"

"Oh fabulous," Abigail Petry sighed. "Now I just have to wonder who's going to have all the pleasure of scrubbing blueberry stains outta you two's dungarees."

"Don't you worry none. We promise to bring home the prize, Mama," Bill said with the grin growing into a broad smile.

"You'd better," she said and then broke into an expression of mischief herself. "Probably don't even know what the prize is. If there even is any."

"Yay! Let's go!" Walter hollered and then darted off to lead the way.

The town was small, but, with very few exceptions, every man, woman, and child was in attendance and so that made for more of a crowd than folks were used to. Walter weaved against the current of a posse of children madly in pursuit of a thieving dog, a roasted chicken leg dangling from its mouth. Past that obstacle he wormed his way between the crushing hips of a group of women gathered for the counting of the 'Guess How Many Glass Beads' jar. With the pie stand in sight, Walter only paused long enough to look over his shoulder to confirm his father still followed. They exchanged grins and Walter spun about to press on.

That was how he came to run headlong into Caleb Sweet. With their collision, the old man took the boy up by both shoulders. Walter couldn't believe the old man's strength.

"We meet again," Caleb said, his glassy eyes twinkling above the chasms of his yellow and brown teeth. "I don't believe I caught your name the last time we met, young master...."

Wallace Sweet, standing behind his brother, stepped forward and spoke up. "Now Caleb, you know Bill and Abigail Petry's boy. This here is none other than young Walter Petry."

"Walter? This is little Walter Petry? I say, all grown up. Look at you. Last I recall you were no more than a pea just shucked from the pod."

Walter nodded dumbly.

Bill Petry caught up with his son. "Hullo, Sweet brothers. Caleb. Wallace."

Wallace extended his hand and Bill took it after a slight pause. "Bill," the old man greeted him as he would an old friend, shaking the elder Petry's hand vigorously. "And where is your lovely bride, Abigail?"

"My *bride*? Why she's..." he looked around ineffectually. "She's...she must be coming along."

"Mister Petry," Caleb said, his hands still holding Walter firm. "Did young Walter here tell you of our remarkable encounter a few weeks back, I wonder?"

"*Remarkable encounter*? No, I don't reckon he did. Which remarkable encounter would that be?"

Walter felt the blood rush from his head and his stomach rise. He was awash in a sudden wave of wooziness. Caleb turned him about to face his father as the old man went on. "Oh yes. You've raised quite an impressive young man here, Mister Petry. Quite a young man. Very impressive. The kind of strong blood this town needs, I might say. And I do."

"Yes, he's a fine boy, to be sure. Although I'm not quite certain what yer on about."

Caleb looked down to Walter. "Let's just say he knows right versus might. Don't you, young Walter?"

Walter found his voice. "Daddy, we gonna miss the pie eating contest."

"You? Miss the pie eating contest?" Caleb chortled. "Now how could that come to pass when I just happen to be one of the judges. Right this way, gentlemen. Right this way." Caleb, still with one hand on Walter's shoulder, parted the crowd with the other to lead their way.

As Bill and Wallace nodded a polite departure, the latter noticed Abigail just off in the crowd over Bill's shoulder. She had been watching them discreetly from a distance, it would seem.

"Missus Petry," he said even though the space and the bodies between them conspired to be too great to be heard over. He tipped his hat and she nodded with a slight smile in return before feigning an excuse to abruptly turn away.

Above the din someone shouted, "I win! I win!" To which a great cheer of jubilation went up even as the music and dance drove on.

…

It was exactly a month to the day following the fair and

for the most part folks had finally finished talking in earnest about it.

Avery waved a hand at the dust motes dancing in the air around his head. "She definitely smells like flowers," he said, speaking more loudly than he needed. "And not just her hair. I don't think it'd be any perfumes, either. Likely just her natural smell, you ask me."

His boss snorted. "I didn't. And I'm tired of tellin' ya, Stolks, you need to leave that poor girl be. You're near twice her age and a damn sight too ugly to boot."

"Ugly?"

"U-G-L-E-E. Ugly. And kindly do shut up about the girl. I done heard enough. I'd heard enough near 'bout three weeks gone by now."

"Yeah, well, you just got yerself dis-invited from our wedding," Avery said. "Now whatdaya got to say 'bout that, ya damned sourpuss?"

Clarkson and Avery were alone in the general store. The slight flurry of the usual morning business was complete and there probably would be little more until well close to evening. Avery was pretending to work, standing atop a step ladder, needlessly rearranging stock. It was his common ruse. He would perch there near to the door in hopes a woman might come in and he might better peer down her dress. Clarkson was at the counter, swatter in hand, engaged in and losing his never-ending battle against the flies.

Their banter was cut short when Noreen Bradwell came in with her gingham-covered egg basket in the crook of her arm. Clarkson braced for the chain of children that usually followed and was pleasantly relieved to discover the woman came unaccompanied.

"Good morning, Missus Bradwell, ma'am," he chirped.

From above, Avery Stolks leaned over as far as he dared even though Noreen was a woman no longer in her prime.

Noreen took the basket from her arm. "I have these eggs...good eggs...fresh eggs. Very fresh," she whispered, gently depositing the basket onto the counter.

Clarkson kept his practiced smile, although a hint of sourness crept into his voice. "Now, Missus Bradwell, you know we stopped takin' in eggs. There just ain't any demand to speak of really. And they're hard to keep fresh and—" as he spoke the woman became distracted and began pirouetting, hands on high, chasing after the array of golden dust motes glistening in the sunbeams where they cut through the room here and there.

Clarkson and Stolks exchanged expressions of confusion. Stolks made a little 'drinky-drinky' pantomime as he mouthed the same.

"Missus Bradwell?" Clarkson inquired softly. But the woman only cooed and gurgled something like an infant as she kept at her mindless pursuit, spinning and grasping at much of nothing.

Clarkson, his eyes still on the woman, began uncovering the eggs. As he did, Stolks gasped and swore under his breath. Clarkson looked up to find Stolks wide-eyed and pointing wordlessly down into the basket. It was not filled with eggs as promised, Clarkson discovered then, finally looking at the uncovered contents himself. Tucked in the red checkered gingham folds were fingers, dozens upon dozens of fingers. Children's mostly. Here and there among those small digits were some larger ones, as well. Reaching in, Clarkson delicately lifted out a larger specimen, thick in nail and knuckle—a man's finger, no doubt—with a gold wedding band still binding its ragged stump.

"Oh my," Noreen said, stopping mid-dance to beam her joy at Clarkson for his discovery. "How wonderful. Simply wonderful," she said, clapping her hands. "A golden egg."

It was too much. Avery Stolks stepped backwards off the stepladder, crashing down into the shelves and onto the floor.

Chapter Three

The trouble had taken root around the first of summer and soon enough Main Street resembled a hobo's wrecked smile, pocked and blackened. Within weeks, the hardware store, barbershop, dentist's office, and the penny arcade had all been devoured in a glut of arson. Some of the nervous populace, unsure of anything better to do, fell to prayer for the first time.

All that June, thick with maddening debate, endless speculation, and a few rounds of fisticuffs, no three men among them could settle upon a satisfactory explanation as to the who, the what, or the why of their problem. The town hall and saloon soon became the most dangerous places to be. Home again and tossing in their beds, they would likely find themselves by the morning dun railing against their own previously passionately defended arguments. Facts and rumors would be weighed anew over toast and breakfast sausage as weary husbands and bleary-eyed wives talked in circles covering over and over again the same well-trod ground all in pursuit of some answer. They were as the wooden ponies of the carousel, for all their effort they would get nowhere. Eventually silence would descend upon them to be disturbed only by the tinkling and scrapes of the knives and forks working at their plates.

The trouble defied rational explanation, although that was disputed as well.

Few truly appreciated the dentist—the first victim of the arson, or arsonists—and some went so far as to hold grudges for his none-too-gentle touch. This was widely agreed upon and might have supplied motive enough except for the subsequent destruction of the hardware store and barbershop; two deeds which proved far more puzzling. Debts were being erased by the debtors, or so those proprietors and the like were quick to accuse. That is, until the afternoon of the penny arcade fire. Following that blaze it was agreed that the cowardly deeds were mindless acts without purpose as could be understood by rational men. The twisted, blackened bodies were lined on the street. Even after someone finally thought to cover them with linen sheets they still smoldered with a lingering stench as if refusing to be concealed.

The bloodshot-eyed sheriff argued that the arcade fire was nothing more than misdirection. Right off, more than a few supported the habitual drunk's theory. In fact, that line of reasoning gathered support and held a good deal of water with a majority of townsfolk until the even stranger goings-on began to come to light.

Besides the bizarre and terrible tragedy of the Bradwells, there were whispers of rape and assault and bizarre fits of madness. A rumor of further murder spread regarding a young prospector recently come to town and then vanished. Speculation worried all as to what or who might be struck down next. Families became violent to their neighbors and some even to their own kin. Soon enough the whispers evolved into hurled shouts and screams.

As the days became hotter, blood spilled out into the streets from the saloon almost nightly.

And then the funeral parlor and the Giles family's barn were set ablaze on the same moonless night. The Giles's fire was unsettling even for the most steadfast, as they were counted among the town's first settlers, and were both respected and beloved.

Folks feared to leave their homes. Some of those who did packed their wagons and left those abodes behind for good.

But of all the charred mounds and burnt-out husks only the funeral parlor was being rebuilt. That it was the old men suffering the labor of the new construction didn't come across as so peculiar to the townsfolk. After all, the funeral parlor was a business much more in demand of late, with four having died as a result of the fires, as well as the other mysterious and not so mysterious deaths stacked atop those. And, of far greater relevance, the business was owned and operated by the Sweet brothers, the town's founders. The town's owners, the disgruntled said. The feudal lords of the land. The two men they all paid their taxes to.

The construction crew was far too short on days for the task they'd set before themselves, with a few being far too sick as well. Some of the other townsfolk even made jokes that the work was killing them. But that was no matter. The old men were content to play deaf to the morbid jests made at their expense by those certain, less respectable, persons. The old men couldn't afford to let such foolishness stay them. No time to waste while time was wasting. That had become their mantra. Caleb Sweet, the younger of the old brothers, had coined it.

They'd begun the project nearly two months earlier with nine men but then three died in quick succession. The first to go, Mitchell Stevens, was struck in the temple when a roof beam got away from the crew. He hit the ground as dead as the lumber that had killed him. The next, Horace Wells, suffered a heart attack. Horace might have survived his faltering heart had he not snapped his neck in the subsequent fall from the funeral parlor roof. In the saloon—where Prohibition had long been a failed experiment—a new joke suggested the funeral parlor itself was drumming up business. The third death on the construction site was attributed to heat stroke. Although, in truth, Norris Bridges was so ancient a stiff breeze could have snuffed his candle.

Work on the funeral parlor continued despite those untimely losses, since the Sweet brothers, Wallace, and his younger brother, Caleb, still moved breath in their lungs. By the time the construction would be completed in a scant few days, more of the crew would succumb and the funeral parlor would be left to a sole-surviving Sweet brother.

So then, when it finally opened its doors for business, the new Sweet Brothers' Funeral Home would be christened by laying the recently departed brother to rest. The service would be two pallbearers short, however, as only the remaining old men and a few others would attend.

But that milestone had yet to be passed.

Caleb Sweet was supposedly a staunch atheist, but, all the same, he often acknowledged a higher power by taking the Lord's name in vain. Those moments of indiscretion were usually kept to hushed whispers, muffled asides meant to be heard by nary a body, not even his brother.

Teetering his old, aching bones atop the funeral parlor roof, Caleb was letting the distraction of nearly being finished get the better of him. He was through with meticulously tapping the roofing nails in. He was spent. He was ready for the work to be done, if not entirely, then at least this day's worth. He was racing the fading light. For the last row of shingles he'd begun driving the nails with single blows. Sloppy, dangerously wild blows. Nearly finished, he thought. Nearly finished. As the sweat filled his eyes and skewed his sight, he brought his hammer down and missed the mark. Instead of the roofing nail, he struck his thumb with a resounding smack. The blow was so forceful the thumbnail split in two places and a splatter of blood issued from the tip of the digit as though it were an angry spitting viper.

"Goddamn!" Caleb screamed to the heavens.

The work came to an abrupt halt as the other old men craned their stiff necks to the commotion.

"Damn it! Damn it! Damn it to hell!" Caleb cursed again, letting go his hammer and shaking his mangled thumb in the heat. More droplets of blood were slung about as Caleb baptized the new funeral parlor with his blood and blasphemy.

The offending hammer skittered down the shingles and would have gotten away to fall to the earth if another of the old men hadn't caught it. "Careful there, Caleb. Crack somebody's skull," he said as he did.

But all Caleb heard was the howling of his thumb.

Way out across the field, opposite the town and the nearly completed funeral parlor, others were disturbed by Caleb's outburst as well. His tirade fell upon them like an unexpected strike of lightning, and so the wake of turkey buzzards startled and broke off from the corpse they'd been tugging over. But the disturbance was short-lived and no threat, and so, with just a few lazy flaps, they'd roosted once more on Bill Petry's husk and were back to jostling one another for the choicest portions. But not before being noticed, however.

"What all do we have here then?" the man who'd caught the hammer said to Caleb with a nod out to the field.

"Buzzards," Caleb replied none too amiably. He went on muttering and nursing his finger, sucking it like a babe.

"Aye, for certain that," the man said. "But what is it there they got themselves a fussing o'er?"

"Probably dead calf or such," Caleb said. He didn't even bother to look.

"What's all the hullabaloo?" another man, Wallace, Caleb's older brother asked as he eased himself over the crest of the roof to join them.

Caleb answered, "Did my thumb something fierce." He held it out for the other two to appreciate. It was a mangled knot. Wallace whistled his appreciation for the damage Caleb had done himself.

"Some buzzards over yonder," the other man said to Wallace. "Got themselves something big by the looks of it."

"A calf," Caleb said, still not even bothering to confirm his speculation with a second look.

"Ya don't say." Wallace turned himself around and, out of an odd and old habit, pushed the brim of his Stetson back and replaced it with a calloused palm over his eyes to better spy across the field. What's more, he did this despite there not being any glare from the soft diffusion of light that remained of the setting sun. After a few seconds of fruitless squinting he took out his spectacles and put them on. By this time the other man, Thompson, had climbed up to join him for a better look.

"Yup," Wallace finally said and put his spectacles back in his dungarees, pulling his hat back down.

"Well?" Thompson asked. "You know my eyes aren't so good. What is it?"

"Can't rightly say. Better take a break and get the rest of the crew together and head on over there. Look it over proper," Wallace said, beginning to carefully make his way down.

"Head over there?" Caleb said. "Fer what? Some heat-bloated calf?"

Wallace kept his eyes on his way. "Day's done. Besides, you ought to know that considering the current state of affairs we need to look into such as that. And, unless Bill Petry has taken to dressing up his livestock, it's no calf them turkey buzzards are dining on. Wearing blue it is."

"Och, no," Thompson said.

"I fear it so," Wallace said. "Fear it so."

Caleb shook his head. He'd been ready to have this day finished as well. "Best we get the shotguns from the wagon."

They crossed the field slowly, one following the other like a funeral procession, which was apt. None of them eager to reach the corpse first. They'd seen more than their share over the years and even more so of late. In fact, if it hadn't been for the insistence of Wallace, a few of them wouldn't have bothered with it at all.

Wallace spoke over his shoulder when they were still a good piece away to confirm to the others what they all expected, "It's Petry all right."

Even if they hadn't been in Petry's fields, some of them would have recognized the dead man by his clothes, threadbare denim shirt to match his dungarees.

Caleb took his thumb from his mouth and spat out a cottony froth of crimson. As his eyes followed the bloody spittle to the ground he spotted a stone, near about the size of a pecan, and retrieved it. Putting his hand to Wallace's shoulder to pause the man, Caleb stepped forward. Although well into his sixties, Caleb Sweet's arm was yet strong and his aim still true enough. The stone had hardly an arc to it and struck the largest buzzard with a resounding whump. The thing loosed a startled cry as it was knocked onto its side. Where they'd previously been indifferent to the approaching men, the other birds became alarmed and took flight. After a moment spent scrambling to find its feet, the wounded buzzard limped into the air to follow its brothers.

One of the other men, jealous that he didn't have something to hurl at them as well, and knowing Wallace would not appreciate a shotgun blast due to his chronic tinnitus, satisfied himself by casting aspersions after them instead.

"Yaw, yaw! Git on now, damn ya sorry eyes!"

Two others grunted their satisfaction with both the stone and the anger.

The buzzards knew fear, but knew hunger far better. They did little more than a lazy circle before settling down in a small copse of ash trees that ran along the field's near edge. They could wait.

"I want no part of it," one of the old men, Joseph Miller, said. "Got no truck with the dead what with things being as they are. I got family." He slapped his hands together three times. "Done for the day. See you bright and early on the job come Monday." He turned and marched back through the tall grass the way they'd come.

Wallace sighed and moved ahead once more. The rest were just beginning to follow as the unmistakable scream of a woman rose up. There was no doubt that it came from the Petry farmhouse. There was no doubt that it was a scream of terror.

Chapter Four

The four men on horseback discovered the creek several miles inland from where it spilled down from the mountains. It was a stubborn and steadfast gully coursing across the arid plain like a thin trickle of blood escaping a shaving nick or worse, a wound sliced through the baked-hard, brown land. Where the waters eroded the earth down into the quick, revealing the dark red loam beneath, the creek took on a crimson hue.

The men were fortunate. Normally the creek would have been little more than inches deep, mere feet in breadth if that. But the snows that for so many months previous had been held up in the high country were finally melting off. That, and the ferocious thunderstorms the men had ridden through some three days prior now fed the gully, filled it.

Two of the men clambered from their mounts and stumbled down into the churning water, inebriated with thirst. The stout one of the four only rose up in his stirrups to better survey the horizon as his horse shifted beneath him, restless on a hobbled hind hoof. There were no tributaries or deviating branches as far as his best eye could make in either direction, only that singular vein gouging its way over the flats, disappearing into the heat. More importantly, there was no sign of riders in pursuit.

He turned his attention back to the creek. No doubt it kept up for the dozen or so miles on to the open water, commingling with the gulf there, or so the stout man reckoned. Since they'd come from the other direction, riding down from the high country, there was no certainty of that, however, only logical speculation. He was sure as well that they'd find civilization where this creek found the ocean. And considering the surrounding desolation, it would be some meager populace, too isolated, too hardscrabble, to be concerned with the wanted men of other territories.

They were the Evers Gang.

Two of the four, Dale and Merritt Evers, were so clearly brothers that over their forty odd years they were all too often mistaken one for the other. They weren't twins in strictest biological terms, yet still eerily identical. Not only sharing in outward appearances, gaunt and forever hungry looking, but also calm and stoic from earliest childhood, the brothers might just as well have been the same man. Even the trail had seen fit to weather them in much the same way. Faces etched and carved with craggy lines deeper than would be expected, the exposed skin burnt the color of tanned hide. In fact, the very same drawing had been used for each of their reward posters.

Evan Evers, on the other hand, the third and youngest of the Evers brothers, seemed to be everything Dale and Merritt were not. Leaning to the portly side and easily excited, Evan lacked his brothers' quiet demeanor, didn't share their even keel. He'd been known to pull his gun without using it, a sure sign of his hot temper, and more so, one night Evan had brandished the Colt in a pool hall and made good on his threat, killing a dentist who'd had the audacity to put his hand on Evan's thigh under the card table. To his credit, Evan was also the most intelligent of the brothers. And this by what the eldest, Dale, would begrudgingly admit to be "a good sight."

"Think it's safe to say that we gave them regulators the slip," the fourth man, Gale, said as he rose up from the water. He was no relation to the three, but he felt he'd wormed his way into their close-knit fold. "Ain't no way they gonna catch up to us now." He filled his hat with water and showered himself with it. "A man can breathe again!" he howled and spluttered water into the sky.

I'm breathing. Lord Almighty but I am breathing, Merritt thought, but made not so much as a sigh.

Dale couldn't help but be pleased that they'd finally found their way down from the cold, high country and nearly crossed the arid flatlands. Likely they'd soon have whiskey. And women. He almost smiled. He looked over to Evan who he thought looked like an engorged tick, purple-faced and swollen, pinched snuggly into his saddle. How Evan had kept the weight on while the other three of them wasted away over the past weeks was a mystery. Probably had some jerky or better hoarded away. No matter, Dale pushed the concern aside and dismounted thinking to join his brother Merritt and their partner Gale in the water.

Evan stroked his mare's thick neck and drew his Colt. He fired three times but the third shot—the round that ripped into Gale's face—was unnecessary. The first shot had missed entirely while the second exploded the unarmed man's heart killing him even before he crumpled to his knees onto the creek bed. The water had held him up in place long enough for Evan to let go the third round, however, and so for perhaps the sake of sheer ugliness he took it.

Merritt was still scowling when Gale's body beached on the bank downstream. He preferred a tad more warning when Evan decided to kill the man standing next to him.

"Still got water enough down there to baptize me too?" Evan called down from up on the lip of the gully. He'd holstered his sidearm and dismounted. He let go the reins allowing his horse to limp over and join the others where they'd wandered and found their way down to the water's edge.

Merritt looked to Dale, but the latter only half-shrugged and rolled his eyes. *What was the point in making a ruckus?* They'd known this was coming. Not that they'd ever discussed it, but still, they knew. Now there were only three ways to split the haul instead of four. *What was to argue?*

"I get his guns," Merritt said in an ugly voice as if expecting a fight and spat in the direction where the nickel plated pistols and bandoliers lay on the sand where Gale had removed them before going into the water. When neither of his brothers disagreed, he settled right off and let his defiant demeanor go.

"We ought to be having meat tonight," Dale said.

"Yup," Evan agreed as he sat and pulled his boots free. "Hungrier than a spider in a walnut."

"Got more horses than we need now," Dale said as he watched Evan's mare favoring its lame hoof. He looked to Evan for some sign of protest.

"Lucky for Gale," Evan said.

"Enough talk," Merritt muttered back over his shoulder as he went after the dead man's gun belts.

A few hours later and Merritt was soaking his aching bones in the creek, limp in his dead man's float, oblivious that he was bathing in the release of Evan's bladder. Evan couldn't be bothered to wade past him and besides, he was amused that Merritt was ignorant of the offense. The three had made camp and eaten their fill of the rump of Evan's mare. As he'd chewed, Evan had remarked, "Good horse." His brothers weren't sure whether he meant the animal had been a good mount or a good meal. Maybe both. The two briefly eyed one another in silence and left it at that.

Following their supper, as dusk gave way to night, the brothers took advantage of the stream once more to bathe and clean-up.

"We sure we ain't rushing into things here?" Dale asked as he scrubbed the cookware with water and red loam while Merritt and Evan relaxed in the gentle current. No answer. Off in the dark, some creature had found Gale's corpse and was going at it, eating and doing its best to drag it off to do more of the same. The men ignored it. Eventually all eyes fell on Evan.

"Spent us near three weeks clambering 'round up yonder throwing them sons of bitches off," Evan said. "Don't see how that's any kind of rush." He let his head slip under the water and did his best to eavesdrop on his brothers. But they were quiet. Maybe they agreed or more likely were too wary of him to speak now. The night had come on cold and with it the chilling water was no longer a comfort.

Evan came up out of it in a sudden flurry, splashing madly to make dry land. He whooped and shuddered as he did. Whatever was making a meal of Gale was startled by the big man and gave a yelp and a growl. Perhaps there were two of them. Maybe more.

"I told you to take that horse further out from camp," Evan said as he dried by the fire. He was referring to his own dead mare and speaking to Merritt who'd put the poor lame creature down. "Now those damned things are going to keep us up all night wanting to get at it, too."

"Nah. They'll fill up on that yappy bastard before long. If not, maybe we'll go ahead and toss another body out there to 'em," Dale said, his voice dried leaves on a hot wind.

"Oh yeah," Evan agreed with a sneer, "maybe."

Twenty odd minutes later Evan spoke up again. "We'll follow this on to the open water," he said, nodding to the creek. It splashed and gurgled like a living thing as a chunk of eroded bank broke away almost as if to answer. "Pretty good chance there'll be something there. Town. Farm or two. Probably not much else way out here in this godforsaken no-man's land, but that's all the better."

Dale and Merritt listened intently taking turns nodding their agreement to Evan's counsel.

"If it is a town, we shouldn't rush right in. Best to come in under the cloak of darkness. Hole up at one of the outlying farms until we know better how it is things stand. What kind of law they got about. Never know but them regulators might've somehow got there ahead of us."

"Ain't seen no track," Merritt said.

Evan shook his head. "If they knew they was heading there to cut us off you think they'd put out right ahead of us? Course not."

"It's a good plan," Dale said. He rolled away from the fire and the two of them.

The conversation was finished.

Chapter Five

The woman was alive. Her wailing alone was testament to that. The pool of blood she writhed about in suggested that she wouldn't stay that way much longer. She was wound up in her own gore-stained bed sheets. She'd somehow managed to get one hand free and used it to claw terrible gouges into her other arm in an effort to untie it as well. Despite the knot's simplicity, however, she'd lacked the mental faculties to loosen it. Her ankles—well out of her reach, although that apparently would not have mattered—remained securely fastened to the bedposts as well. The moment Wallace found her he was reminded of the coyotes that gnawed their limbs off to be free of the snare, their eyes just as wide and wild.

The source of so much blood wasn't her clawed arm. It was a well that bubbled up and over from the woman's bare abdomen, like an oil seep upon the earth. On the floor at the bedside, Wallace spied a singular footprint. Odd, the old man considered, since he was sure it could only have been made on purpose. The boy, it appeared, had climbed atop his mother and dipped his foot into her wound. Wallace knew it was the Petry child's print because the woman said as much. *What a thing for the boy to do.*

The woman realized she was no longer alone.

"Don't hurt my boy," she whimpered. "He didn't mean no harm. He's a good boy. Don't hurt my boy."

So then she wasn't as far gone as her torn up arms implied. Not as far gone as her son.

Wallace did his best to reassure her as she kept up her

pleas. In as calm a voice as he could muster he told her that he and his companions had only come to help. They were no danger to her or to any of the Petry household.

"Please let them help," he soothed.

As he paused uncertain whether the deranged woman would let him aide her, and, as he scolded the others to come close, Wallace glanced once more to the small footprint. Long, thin, wisps of blood trailed off from the toes like paint trailed from a flung brush, falsely suggesting the boy had some demonic disfiguration. He had a silly thought. *Had the boy climbed like an imp from his mother's sliced belly?* Wallace shuddered and wondered where the child had gotten off to.

"Check that closet," he barked to no one of the men in particular. "Search the house for the boy! His name's Walter." Wallace didn't fancy being stabbed or shot in the back by the little beast.

"Please don't hurt him," she whispered again and again. "Please don't hurt him," she chanted.

Her eyes refused Wallace's. Her vision was focused on some faraway place beyond the ceiling of the bedroom, beyond the clouds above the home, beyond the infinite domain of the heavens.

"You think he done his old man?" Caleb wheezed. He'd been sucking on his swollen thumb like a child still and had only taken it out long enough to ask his question. When Wallace looked back to him he raised an eyebrow and shook his head. Caleb thought it was in answer to his question and so he added with a shrug, "You never know."

"Please," the woman said, "don't hurt him...."

As the men waited to see who among them would reply

to this, the woman gave way, collapsed, spent, perhaps entirely.

"James," Wallace called to one of the hesitant men, "give me a hand here. You others look around. Find the boy." He watched the woman for any reaction, but she remained still, probably finding peace in search of death now. *That or she's playin' possum*, he thought. Neither one was a comfort.

As James did as he was told, staying to tend to the woman, Thompson and the other man, the foreman Goodman, took to searching the downstairs. Caleb decided to move off down the upstairs hall to search out the boy. He was tired, his thumb ached mightily. He didn't want to be bothered with this woman, with Wallace's orders, with any of this. He didn't want to be here at all.

He eased down the long hallway with his shotgun resting in the crook of his arm as though he waded through uncertain, murky waters, each step slow and deliberate. Only his eyes were quick, darting about, betraying his nervousness. The floors creaked unforgiving even to his lightest footfall, calling out, *here he is. Here is the intruder*. Caleb's eyes pinched all but closed. His worn, tobacco-stained teeth clenched and ground. He pushed on.

He knew all too well the true reason for the creaking floors. Why, in fact, the whole house creaked and sagged, from the foundation to the roof beams. After all, he and his brother had led the construction of it some twenty-two years earlier.

In the spirit of community where all pitched in to build his neighbor's home or business, the Petry farm was but one of many that the brothers Sweet had overseen. They'd played their roles first as town founders and now as governing elders. And part of that oversight was to see to it that the construction was done barebones, as quickly and cheaply as possible when and wherever it could be gotten away with. If five wood joists or studs were called for, four were used, and those secured with only two nails, not the needed four. Every corner was cut. Every shortcut applied. The skimping wasn't just to save costs and resources, but also to ensure the work was for the most part finished in but a day or two. This became the norm whenever the benefactors were the poor, the young, the old, the ignorant, or the otherwise powerless. Of course not all men were equal and so neither were their homes. As a result, most members of this agreement would put in many times the labor they received in turn.

 For year after year, to a man, however, they each and every one shut their mouths and were thankful for whatever the community—the Sweets—saw fit to bestow upon them. By the young town's third decade there were at least three dozen homesteads that had weathered far more rapidly than should have been the case. Homes that had seen fifteen to twenty winters looked as though they'd known fifty or sixty.

 The Sweet brothers' final residence hadn't been among that sorry lot. Some years ago, a mere eight years after the town had been founded, the brothers pulled their combined weight and had another home built, this while their first was still arguably the best in town, and while the town hall itself was in dire need of repair. The Sweet brothers' second residence was by far the largest in comparison to all others. Some would say luxurious. Even while several families with children had to make do with whatever meager shelter they'd built alone by their own hands, they'd been expected, in the name of the community, to share in constructing the brothers' sprawling lodge. By the time Sweet Wood was all but completed, more than a few men had become put off by the gross inequity of it all. They threw down their hammers refusing to participate further. Sadly, none had the spine to do any more than that. Their dissension was of no matter, it was done.

For their transgression, those men, those families, were labeled traitors to the community. And so the townspeople splintered and fell into camps. Bad blood took root and a rancor set in that infected it from that day forward.

Caleb thought no more about this now than he had since the last time he'd walked this floor some twenty-two years gone by.

But he did search his recollection for whether he knew where the attic access might be. If there was a mad boy on the loose, there was a good chance the child had taken refuge up there even despite the heat. Caleb knew all too well that to those ill in the mind, concerns such as food, thirst, and damning heat, were all but trivial. As this madness would have it, ironically enough, it was the trivial or entirely unimportant things that seemed to hold sway. A grown woman walking the town square stark naked in search of her lost doll. A butcher carving off his own thumb merely to be rid of a blister. These things Caleb had recently seen. He shook the troubling images from his mind's eye. *Focus*, he told himself.

He worked to picture the boy. *William was it? No, Walter*. Caleb hadn't seen the boy in a long while, since the night of the fair, what with the Petry family keeping to themselves even more so than others. Prior to that the boy only came into town with his father on very rare occasions. He must be ten or eleven, Caleb reckoned. He recalled the encounter with the boy and Avery Stolks. *Old enough then to be as dangerous as a man if he was sick. Sick and clearly armed with a knife, or maybe worse.*

Caleb wished that they'd had time to discern Bill Petry's cause of death. It would be good to know right about now if the man had been shot.

There was a commotion downstairs. A crash of shattering glass or crockery and what might have been cutlery. Caleb rushed back to the banister. He held there, uncertain, cautious.

In the heat, with his heart pounding as if to open the door of his chest and escape him, Caleb found comfort in letting his finger stroke the shotgun's trigger.

"Cat! Just a cat!" Thompson called up unseen from somewhere in the kitchen below.

"Cat," Caleb mused under his breath. He chuckled with relief and longed for a drink of water. He hadn't realized how parched he was. His mouth tasted of metal. *Panic will do that to a man*, he told himself.

In the master bedroom Wallace set aside his shotgun and was leaning over, working on getting the woman's abdomen bound. He checked her pulse and thought her dead when suddenly she bolted upright and nearly caught hold of him with her teeth. Her free hand raked his neck furiously. Wallace stumbled backwards, tripping over James as he went, and nearly fell to the floor. She clawed out at them repeatedly as though feral. The binding held.

Though enraged, the woman tired almost instantly and after a few seconds she gave up and sank back down. Exhausted once more, she cried like a small child for being unable to bring them into her grasp.

Wallace gave her some time, hoping that perhaps she'd pass out again. He tended to his clawed neck, checking it in the bedroom's vanity mirror, but this time her eyes stayed open. They followed him. Wallace was grateful that he'd decided to leave untying her for last.

"I know who you are, you Sweet," she hissed. "Damn your eyes and tongue, I ain't dead yet. What are you doing here? Why have you come for me? Don't think you'll be taking me to your parlor. I ain't dead. You see that, don't you?" Drained of so much blood her pale countenance belied her angry rant.

As she railed on Wallace tried in vain to soothe her. Still, he kept his distance, not making any physical contact. James, even more cautious, refused to come any closer than where he stood sentry-like at the foot of the bed.

From out in the hall Caleb heard some of that commotion as well, but not realizing the scare his companions had been through, thought little more of it. He listened only briefly, and, not quite able to make out what the men were saying—and tired of the woman's rant—he chose to ignore them.

A short-haired calico sauntered into Caleb's view at the foot of the stairs. No doubt the cat that'd rattled Thompson. It considered Caleb only briefly and then pretended to be completely disinterested with the intruders. Nor did it seem to care that its mistress was still crying out, carrying on in her disturbed state. The cat only looked around lazily with indifference and wandered off just as it had come.

"Never you mind no cat," Caleb called down to Thompson. "Find the gun cabinet. See if anything looks to be miss—"

He cut short his point when the ceiling creaked and sprinkled his sweat-dappled face with fine, gritty soot. As he looked up, he spied the wood slats there ever so subtly shift to have weight put upon them. Another sprinkling—this time silent—cascaded through the still air.

Caleb almost sounded his alarm for the others. He went so far as to suck in the breath needed to holler for them to come quick, he had the boy. The child, the mad thing that'd stabbed its own mother, likely killed its own father, was hiding in the attic, cornered with no place to run. But then Caleb thought better of it. He'd seen the things people with the madness had been driven to in their heightened states of rage and terror. Caleb let his breath ease away, and then, much like the cat, he moved off as though nothing of the discovery concerned him.

He passed down the hall and found his way to the attic access in the last bedroom. Appropriately enough it was the boy's room. The small drop-door at the middle of the ceiling was closed. So were the windows. Three fly corpses, dry as a spider's last meal, rested on the sill. A thin layer of golden pollen coated the sill and the fly remains. Caleb would probably have failed to notice the pollen but for 'Walter' being written in it. *So the windows had been closed a good while*, Caleb deduced.

The room spoke to the family's poverty: a dresser, weather-beaten footlocker, cane fishing pole, a rusted coffee tin of marbles. Next to the door jamb a small pair of worn cowboy boots accompanied two balled socks. The boy's sagging little box spring bed had been shoved out into the middle of the room from the far corner, the floor scratched as though it'd gone against its will. Caleb chose not to move the bed back out of his way. He hoped he was still on the sly. Even though he certainly didn't need the boost to reach the access door's pull cord as the boy had, the noise of moving the bed would certainly give him away.

His discretion proved futile. Caleb grimaced and paused when the bedsprings croaked under his weight, sending up the alarm all the same. He lost his balance on the tired springs and shifted his feet quickly, stupidly, only to fall back landing seated on the bed. He nearly dropped his shotgun. If he hadn't been heard before, there was little doubt of it now. A cloud of what must have been dust—*or maybe more pollen*, he thought—billowed up from the mattress to tickle his eyes and nose. The old man froze. He held his breath and sat dumbly on the bed waiting for any sign that the boy was on to him, was on the move once more. Nothing.

He managed to get his feet. The thick twine cord hung motionless inches from Caleb Sweet's less than steady hand, its knotted end stained in the unmistakable dark umber of dried blood. The old man stayed his hand long enough to allow a moment of doubt to catch up with him.

Who is truly the prey in this hunt?

As if he'd not known it before, the air suddenly became incredibly hot and weighed down on him. Fat sows of sweat lumbered down his face, his torso, tickled the thin of his back, sought out the hollow of his withered thighs. He imagined the heavy air was pressing the very last bit of fluid from his body. Looking back to the closed windows, he was lost and simple. His head pounded. The silence screeched nails on blackboard. The glass in the panes was thick and seemed caught in the swirling stages of a slow, syrupy melt. The world beyond distorted. If he remained, Caleb knew he'd soon enough become just another dried husk like the flies on the sill.

He considered that perhaps he was suffering a stroke. Dizziness forced him to all but fall down from the bed. *No, it was no stroke. He was beguiled by a spell or curse.* He was sure of it, knew this place had damned him, but he had no will to fight. He went to the window and balanced there waiting for his senses to return. An eternity of minutes passed.

Caleb traced his index finger along a split in the warped sill where the wood had known too much of the sun. His yellowed fingernail ran the length of the groove and where that slot narrowed to the point of catching it Caleb gritted his teeth and pushed on. When the knuckle popped, he braced the finger with his swollen thumb. With the newly applied pressure the thumb began to bleed once more. After a moment, the caught fingernail tore free and ripped half of the entirety down to the quick. The nail thick from age, the deed had taken some effort. The result was nearly as bad as his thumb, so that now Caleb had two painfully mangled digits, thumb and forefinger.

Blood issued both from the ragged nail stump and thumb and pounded onto the floor as loud as great sweeping strokes upon a kettle drum. Caleb took up humming a favored battle hymn to match the cadence.

His thoughts darkened. *This house would burn so easily. These people may very well be the criminals who razed our funeral parlor.*

Caleb nodded to the idea that it would be only fair to offer the same in return. The boy in the attic would have no hope. *Smoke and flame, a withering, pain-filled death.* Caleb was surprised the notion hadn't come to him sooner. Like a thing of its own accord, his wounded and freshly bleeding hand crept down into his dungaree's deep hip pocket and crawled about amongst its few contents in search of his box of matches.

Crouching on all fours in the attic above him, young Walter Petry had spied Sweet through a crack between the ceiling slats as the man had maimed himself. That had been very entertaining. But if the old bastard wasn't going to do something more of the same Walter just wished he'd be finished then and go away.

Chapter Six

As a young Colonel in the war he'd struck an imposing figure, four inches over six feet of lean muscle, all too often a gleaming saber held on high to punctuate his commands. His battlefield uniform was bold to the point of garishness. A full chest of colorfully gleaming medals which, along with highly polished brass buttons, readily winked with captured sunlight, teasing the distant snipers' squinting eyes. Golden braids fell from the Colonel's broad epaulettes and more gold embroidery serpent-circled his sleeves, ran stiff the full length of his trousers. He kept his broad-brimmed hat adorned with an ostrich plume, an affectation borrowed from the habits of another similarly gaudy officer he'd met but once, and then only in passing. And, as if all that weren't enough, the Colonel's mount, Jubilee, was a wide-eyed, terrifying beast of sleek black, nostrils seemingly forever flared and more often on two legs than four.

In witnessing him, the soldiers of both armies on the field were convinced that battle instilled in the Colonel no fear, no alarm, no doubt. For certainly no man could embody such a commanding appearance, call down such attention upon himself, not if he trembled to the sound of the distant cannon, quaked to know the bugler's rally.

It was all a lie, however. A ruse. Like the raised hackles of a barking lapdog, Colonel Rembrandt Warren Hawkins's extravagant appearance was merely a display, the threat bluff of the coward. Far more flight than fight, he kept well behind his lines, well beyond the enemy's reach.

No matter. Those days were the stuff of history books, being some sixty-five years gone by now. Well out behind his farmhouse, on a patch of ground where his wife rested, a good-sized pecan tree now mingled its roots with the bones of his once upon-a-time handsome black steed, Jubilee. His homestead was one of the few that the Sweet brothers had had no hand in. The Colonel was not lacking for funds, and he did abide by a calling to his Lord, God. So then, he'd no call for their dubious charity. Besides, he loathed the brothers, both for their occupation as handlers of the dead, and for the command they held over the local populace.

He sat alone in his bedroom in a shaft of the day's last light, an open footlocker at his feet. The Colonel's battle dress uniform was long faded, the material stiff to the touch when he lifted it from its musty hold. The stench of moth balls lingered as he shook the trousers out. This brought more water to his already damp eyes. The medals, boxed separately beneath the folded garments, were dull, their once colorful ribbons cracked. The brass buttons of his jacket were no longer shiny, but now tarnished to the color of deep and damp earth. No amount of effort from the Colonel's arthritis knotted fingers would rediscover their hidden luster. He shook his head as he let them slip from one hand to the other like sand escaping to the bottom of an hourglass.

Lastly, the former officer came to his cavalry saber. For years after the war he'd kept it proudly over the mantle, but with the passage of winters came a paranoia of thieves, and so some time ago he'd stowed it away. The effort to pull the rusted blade from its scabbard ached his joints, nourished his melancholy. Finally it came free, however, sliding out much like one of the old man's dry, rasping breaths.

...

Colonel Hawkins's farm was quiet when the Evers brothers finally approached. Quiet, but well-illuminated. Jack-o-lantern-like, the two-storied farmhouse glowed from every window as well as the front double doors. The latter being inexplicably thrown open wide. The barn just out back was illuminated as well. Although its doors and gable entry were closed tight, the abundant light within escaped through its many tilting gaps. On the whole it was a strange spectacle for so isolated a place. It made the brothers apprehensive. They'd remained a little ways out to size things up. Evan paused to check his pistols, confirming full cylinders.

No animals were to be seen or heard. The fields were in neglect. There'd been no discernible effort towards agriculture, such as tilling or planting, attempted in quite a good while. The land was thick instead with the dead and dried remains of mostly cheatgrass and carpetweed. Here and there stood a stray stalk of corn, lonely remnants of some previous season's plantings.

"Why don't we just ride up, introduce ourselves real friendly-like?" Dale suggested.

Evan shook his head and ran a palm over his horse's muzzle to calm it. Refusing to be soothed, it champed and stomped. Having been the recently-deceased Gale's mount, the animal wasn't accustomed to the far heavier man's abundant girth and additional saddle bags. That and it was an older horse, already exhausted, nearly spent from the last hard weeks in the high country. From the moment Evan had heaved himself into its saddle a few hours earlier, Merritt had been keeping an eye on the beast, wondering just how long this one would last. *Not long,* he imagined.

"Why don't you give the horse a rest? Sneak up there like you so good at and see what's to be seen," Merritt suggested to Evan.

Evan ignored him for a moment, and then looked to Dale who only nodded.

"Yeah, fine. Beats sitting out here like three little chicken-shit owls," Evan said. He dismounted with a grunt and heavy thump to the Earth. The horse, glad to be rid of him, whinnied and had to be reined down. Once it settled he passed the bridle to Dale. He adjusted his gun belt. "Guess I'll mosey over and go see what's for dinner," Evan said.

The way he walked off with so casual a stride, it appeared as though that was his exact plan. After he'd covered half the distance, however, he drew his gun and tucked down into a creeping gait, hugging the shadows effectively and moving with a grace and silence that belied his size.

Evan avoided the house, it was too well lit. Instead, he made his way to the barn, circling out broadly and back around to keep it between himself and the house for good measure. Evan disappeared around the barn and minutes passed. Dale and Merritt held their watch without any noticeable concern, the latter scratching beneath his hat at the back of his head and sucking his teeth in disgust at the unexpected tick he dislodged there. At first he'd thought it was a wart or similar skin protrusion. After a moment of scratching, however, Merritt freed the parasite from its fleshy mooring and, realizing what it was, ripped it out. He glanced at the swollen thing caught between his thumb and forefinger only briefly before flicking it away. In the dark as they were, he'd failed to notice that the tick's head had torn free and remained deep in his scalp.

Evan appeared once more from the corner of the barn he'd crept around and was heading back.

When he finally reached them he was as breathless as if he'd run a quarter mile. He hoarse-whispered between pants to them while collecting his tired horse's bridle and his breath. "This ain't…any run of…the mill…hayseeds. Got 'em a Pierce Arrow. In the barn," he reported with a stabbing thumb back over his shoulder to the barn.

"A what?" Dale asked.

"Automobile. Nice one. In the barn," Evan said. He pulled himself with great effort back up into the saddle. "Emerald green," he elaborated with a toothy grin as though such a detail greatly mattered, his eyes glistening as much as his sweating brow.

"What do we care about some goddamned fancy jalopy?" Merritt said and spat.

"We don't," Dale answered before Evan could.

"Well my sore ass cares," Evan argued. "How about that for starters?" The two ignored him. He went on, "Generator plus a windmill further out back. One of them Delco light plants hooked with a line of batteries," he said.

"Did you see anybody?" Dale pressed, his voice thick with impatience. Evan would get no chance to respond.

Suddenly there was a commotion from the one structure all three brothers had overlooked, the outhouse. Nestled between a pair of poplar trees on the side of the house opposite the barn it had been easily missed. Its door flew open so violently it thwacked against the side of the small building and bounded back. The withered and bent frame of the old man burst out from the dark, stopping the returning door with the same hand that'd thrown it open. As the venerable, retired Colonel stepped into the light that blazed from his nearby home, the Evers brothers shared quizzical expressions to find Hawkins attired in his once-glorious battle dress uniform. He adjusted the sword dangling from his belt and then the Colonel donned the ostrich plumed hat that'd been tucked beneath his free arm. Much like the man himself, however, the feather was broken and limp. It fell down comically across his face and he blew twice to move it off. When that failed he snatched it free and threw it to the ground in disgust. Evan couldn't help but laugh.

Dale and Merritt scowled to silence their brother, but it was no matter. The three horsemen were in the shadows a good ways off and the old man's ears were as dead as his crops. Oblivious of them, he marched off to the barn without a moment's pause.

"Deaf as a goddamned post," Evan chuckled. "Probably blind and crazed as hell too, judging by that wonderful getup." He paused and wiped his mouth. "I want me that sword." Evan shifted forward and would have started to ride ahead, but Dale's hand shot out and seized his horse's reins. The worn animal was all too satisfied to stop.

"Hol' up," was all Dale said.

Across the large front yard and around the corner of the house, the old Colonel strode with purpose to his barn. As he opened it and went inside the sound of a horse whinnying and much thrashing about quickly followed.

"You forget to mention they got 'em a horse?" Dale said to Evan.

Evan only scowled with impatience. Another moment more and he'd slap Dale's hand away. Peeved, but too weary from the trail to ride Evan further, Dale released the reins as the Colonel appeared once more. The old man led a saddled and swayback dun mare that even in its decline still possessed something to imply that it once was a remarkable animal. In his other hand the Colonel carried a sloshing five gallon drum. The weight of it doubled the old man over and made his labored going slow. Oblivious to his spectators, he led the horse to the house and up the steps, coaxing the unsure animal inside.

"What'd I tell you? Old coot is crazy. Watering his horse in the house," Evan said. "What're we waiting for?"

Neither brother replied. Instead, Dale nodded to draw their attention back over to the barn. Evan suddenly caught the crackling sound of fire when he did. This followed by smoke, first smelled, and then seen, rising white and ephemeral like spirits in the dark.

"Old nut set the barn on fire...." Evan clucked. Under his breath he slipped out a string of profanity.

Dale and Merritt shared knowing glances, but said nothing.

Two loud percussions, like enormous champagne bottles exploding, emitted from the quickly growing blaze and were immediately followed by the lights both there and in the home going dark.

"The batteries," Evan said needlessly. Dale nodded.

Now it was the flames within that kept the barn partially illuminated, while, inside the house there was the glow of hurricane lamps, one of which stood out prominently in the front parlor window.

"Well, you two get your way with the car. Happy? Bet you your last dollars I'm fetching me that sword before it's too late for it too," Evan said.

Merritt was perplexed. "Too late?" he asked.

"This here ain't no accident. The old man's done. He's burning the place down. What do you think that can was for?" he said referring to the five gallon fuel drum.

Dale didn't wait to hear more. Much to Evan's dismay and irritation, Dale spurred his horse forward, bolting to make for the house.

"Oh, so now…." Evan began, but Merritt didn't wait for Evan's complaint. He took off as well, leaving Evan behind. The abrupt turn of events made Evan so angry he toyed with the briefest flash of shooting both of his only kin in the back. His horse grunted beneath him and spun twice before giving in to Evan's harshly goading spurs and mad bridle yanks. Mouth sore and haunches bleeding, the creature stumbled and almost lost its footing before relenting in its protests. It rushed the fat man off into the dusty wake of his brothers.

…

The men had left, finally. With them, however, they'd taken Walter's mother. The man in Walter's room, Caleb

Sweet, had stood there beneath Walter as the boy spied on him from the attic. But the man did nothing. Caleb Sweet merely stared out the window dumbly for nearly a quarter of an hour before one of the other men screamed his name a magical three times to shake him from wherever he was. Walter knew then that Caleb was sick.

As Caleb began to walk out of the room he paused, however, and, with the odd twitch and pop of a windsock in a wild wind, threw back his head and shot an all knowing eye to Walter's hiding place. Walter could no longer see him, thankfully, but he knew he'd stopped before leaving the room. Walter was sure he knew the reason. He was the reason. The cat caught at the cow's milk pail, the boy was certain he was had. Maybe the demented men would hang him in a noose of a widow's hair and bury him face down like he'd heard once was the way to be rid of evil. That, or skin him. Or break his every bone. But there was none of this. Caleb Sweet ran his hand over the pate of his bald head where hair once grew, sweeping it down to his neck where the hair grew all too much. After a few moments of this he strode away with heavy boots. His steps echoed off down the hall, down the stairs, and, without pause, out of the house. This day Caleb Sweet would trouble Walter no more.

Just the same, the boy waited until well after dark to reveal himself. At the window sill Walter played with the blood and the fingernail Caleb had torn free there. Walter lost track of time for a long while and so when his mind finally did return to him he had to think hard to remember where the blood and fingernail had come from. Once he recalled Caleb Sweet's visit, the boy gave the incident no more thought.

He stole his way through the house. Even though he knew the men had gone, Walter crept along with more stealth than the family cat stalking a mouse. The house was quiet now, yet Walter still was sure some remnant of his mother's voice haunted the rooms.

She'd wailed and swore with great venom at them when the men took her. At least until they'd gotten the gravely wounded woman downstairs and into the wagon they'd fetched from their construction site. *She either died or passed out*, Walter thought. Either way, she lay as still as one of the Sweet brothers' grave stones as the men bore her off. Walter had peeked through the attic vent and watched as the small group moved off over the field to the place where his dead father lay. They didn't retrieve the body as he thought they might, however. Instead, they argued. Bitterly. Caleb even struck Wallace and with that the two had to be pulled apart. Eventually, after much dusting of clothes and angry gestures, the small procession was on its way once more.

Walter nodded knowingly at the heated exchange. The old men were most definitely sick with the pus, the madness. Or perhaps they were afraid to touch his father's corpse for the fear of it. Probably both. No difference. The worms would have Walter's old man whether he lay out in the field or down in the earth in one of the Sweet brothers' cheap, pine boxes. *This way would just be all the quicker.*

Walter assumed they were taking his mother to town. There, or maybe the cemetery. He didn't care. In fact, he was glad she was gone. She was crazy. She would have killed him. Even tied to her bed she had her powers, her wicked ways. She'd driven his father mad. Walter had seen that for himself. She would have done the same to him. He wondered if he'd killed her. He thought perhaps he'd tried. His hands and clothes were bloodied as proof. Or, maybe not. Maybe he'd tried to save her. He couldn't be sure. He couldn't quite remember what had really happened.

But she was gone. Of that one thing the boy was certain. And after he decided he was glad she was gone, Walter went to his parents' room. He stood in the doorway a long while before moving over to the blood-splattered bed. He sat down on the floor beside his own little bloody footprint, now dried, and traced it with a trembling finger.

He cried then for his mother. He cried until his eyes swelled red and streaming snot smeared the sheet after he'd pulled it down to bind his quivering shoulders and arms. He wanted his mother there to hold him tight, to rock him gently with whispers of, "Be at peace."

Downstairs in the parlor, the cat lifted its head, listening momentarily as the boy cried, "Mama, Mama, Mama, Mama." The boy was still weeping when the cat nuzzled its head back down and returned to sleep.

Chapter Seven

Evan caught up with Dale and Merritt easily enough, even on his frazzled and exhausted mount. The two brothers had ridden up to the house's large front stoop like a pair of devils broken loose of hell's bonds, but once there, they'd become subdued. Without speaking, they each knew the other's mind; *let Evan go in there and drive this hare from his hole.* Or, in this case, it was more on the mark to say they were dealing with an old snake. Slow to strike, perhaps, but venom just as deadly. They'd seen the "farmer" was armed not only with his cavalry saber, but pistols as well.

And Evan knew his brothers' minds. While he may not have been attuned to share in their seemingly telepathic link, he was more than bright enough to make up for it after riding in their wake for so many years. They might *ride* ahead of him, but they would never *be* ahead of him. Or so, at least, ran the strong current of Evan's certainty.

As he and his mount thundered up beside them, Evan longed to chastise his elder brothers for what he would've deemed cowardice had they been other men. Experience assured him, however, that they were simply more willing to let him take the bullet and they the reward. He hated them. He feared them. But he knew, now as always, the only way he could be more alone in this hard world would be to kill them. In moments of weakness, or perhaps strength—he had never satisfied himself on which of the two it truly was—he wished things were different between the three of them.

"What, ya worried he kept an old artillery cannon or two with him to boot?" he taunted. "Fine, let little brother Evan handle the scary old war coot." As he dismounted he mumbled, "Pair a piss ants."

He tossed his reins over to Dale. The brothers quietly backed their horses off as Evan pulled his pistols and mounted the steps to the porch. Dale and Merritt were several long paces into the shadows by the time Evan stood atop the porch, backlit in what meager light still escaped from the hurricane lamps somewhere beyond the home's open double doors. Evan paused there and looked back to Dale and Merritt. He could see nothing of them. But for the snorting and stamping of their horses, for all he knew they'd left him behind yet again. Off in the barn the fire caused another small explosion followed by a collapse of some interior structure, most likely the hay loft. It wouldn't be long now before the whole thing came down. He wondered briefly whether, if it collapsed towards the house, it would fall close enough to catch the home ablaze along with it.

Evan curled his face up in disgust. The brothers couldn't make his expression out, however; such details were lost, swallowed in the blackness of Evan's silhouette.

A shrill yell suddenly erupted from behind Evan.

"Captain, hold that line by God!" This followed by a horse's terrified scream and the pounding of iron shod hooves striking the floor. It was clear to Evan that the old man and his horse were just inside in what he would discover was the dining room. Evan shouldered his way through the open front doors and headed to find them as though pushing his way through a crowd. He preferred to only offer his profile as a target. As he quickly neared the dining room's archway, he smelled the kerosene. Where he hadn't noticed it before—since he had been holding his breath unconsciously—the smell was suddenly overwhelming and began to burn at his eyes. Too late he realized the rug beneath his feet was soaked in the acrid fuel. His boots squished with each step. Still, Evan pressed forward. He knew, judging by the now destroyed auto out in the barn, that this man had money. And he knew this type. They didn't trust their money to bankers. Evan wanted both that money and that cavalry sword. He wasn't about to let the old man deny him. Evan braced and turned the corner, guns leading the way.

It was a sight that defied reason, beguiled sanity. The room's furniture had been thrown aside, and now, where the great dining table had been, atop his nervous steed—a swayback as long in the tooth as himself—sat the old Colonel, arrayed in his battle dress uniform as they'd first seen him, but now with his saber in one hand and a lit and uncovered hurricane lamp in the other. The ends of the horse's reins were clenched in his teeth. More kerosene dripped from the old soldier as though he'd ridden out a thunderstorm. Colonel Hawkins was facing Evan when he entered, and the old man did not seem in the least surprised by the portly gunman's sudden appearance. The Colonel shouted something unintelligible, the words garbled and lost in the reins fast between his teeth.

Evan's guns were trained on the Colonel, but he realized that to pull a trigger would mean to send the burning hurricane lamp crashing to the fuel-soaked floor. For a heartbeat Evan was indecisive. His pause was irrelevant, however, for the old man was not. For his last act in life, Colonel Rembrandt Warren Hawkins violently threw the lamp at his horse's feet, instantly tearing open the gates of hell beneath him.

...

Of late, one of the more disturbing facets of nightfall in the little town had become the marauding pack dogs. In the beginning, they'd only attacked small children or the elderly left unattended. Two such children had disappeared in the course of four short nights causing folks to wildly speculate over their fate. When a third child's body—or a grisly portion of it, at least— was actually found on the fifth night, wolves or coyotes were immediately and without question cast as the culprits. A party of armed men and teen-aged boys was formed to patrol the night streets to eradicate the problem. Residents were nervous and angry, but satisfied that the matter would be quickly resolved. Then, when Regina Spencer, who worked the counter of the feed and grain, was horribly mauled on her way home from work one night shortly thereafter, she lived long enough to warn the others, to frighten them.

These hadn't been feral animals. They were what just a few weeks earlier had been domesticated farm dogs, sheep and cattle dogs, old women's lap companions. In her final shudders, Regina Spencer spoke of how the dogs neither growled nor barked nor made any other of the "expected behaviors or signs of their kind."

"Took me up quiet as a man would his Sunday pot roast," she whispered near the end.

As the townsfolk who were still of their right minds gathered in the town hall to discuss the matter, a dozen or so came to realize that their own missing canines were not isolated concerns. They each recognized the truth that their farm dog or beloved pet had slipped away to join his kind. By that time, however, the problem was well out of hand.

The pack, spotted only later that same night by the hunting patrol, flitted oddly silent ahead of them through the night streets like some amorphous thing. The men agreed the pack was easily twenty in number. They also nodded to one another that the animals seemed like no pack of dogs any of them had known before.

"Of one mind," one said.

Four shots had been fired, all to no avail. If any of the animals were hit, they did not fall.

...

Night had long been settled in when the Sweet brothers and Thompson finally approached the outskirts. The other men of their crew, James, Joseph, and the foreman Goodman, had all departed along the way for their farms, most of which sprawled off over the more fertile land between the town and open water.

The Petry woman had thankfully remained sedated in the back of the wagon, so much so that Wallace couldn't be sure there in the dark if she hadn't passed on. He'd stopped checking; he'd know soon enough. The buildings were almost completely dark, unlit or shuttered tight, or both. The streets were as empty as though it were the wee hours. The brothers rode in the wagon while Thompson followed on his own horse.

No one had spoken of it, but all the men's thoughts had fallen on the dogs. They'd been knocking off work early for the past week if only to ensure they were back safe indoors before nightfall. They were no longer young men after all. And if there wasn't the dogs to be concerned over there were always the residents. Who could say what new madness they might encounter?

Thompson rode up alongside of Wallace where the latter had stopped the wagon. Staring down the dark maw lying ahead that during the daylight hours was Main Street, Thompson said, "Good call on them streetlights, Wallace." He followed up with a mocking snort.

He was referring to the introduction of streetlights that'd been proposed to the town council twice in as many years, but undermined by Wallace as an unnecessary expense on both occasions.

"You got your electric lines," The elder Sweet brother, Wallace, said, nodding to one of the rough-hewn poles that bent near the top like an elbow weary with the weight of the wire.

"What? That weren't none of your doin'. Council seen to that," Thompson argued.

Caleb Sweet snorted. "Council...." He threw out a dismissive wave. "And you're good as blind anyhow, Thompson. A hundred streetlights or nary a one isn't doing you a lick of difference no how."

The introduction of electricity and phone lines had long been a bone of contention between the Sweet brothers and their fellow townspeople. Electricity, the brothers had argued, only meant folks would be about during the odd hours when they should be home. Out drinking. Out whoring. Ironically, it was the Sweet brothers who owned the saloon. The whores. But they were in private agreement; they'd rather make that filthy lucre on the hours they preferred to keep, not on the hours of night owls and drunkards. The phones, likewise, were to be shunned because they brought in the outside world. That offered the possibilities neither brother wanted.

But Thompson was right. Streetlights were in order and long overdue. Caleb knew this and cursed his own cataract-dimmed vision under his breath.

Somewhere ahead on the dusty street they caught the diminishing thump-thump-thump of running footfalls—human, thankfully—followed by the slamming of a door and then perhaps a shutter. The disturbance was enough to silence the old men's bickering before it could get out of hand again.

"I don't live here. This isn't my town," Thompson muttered in complaint.

Caleb was bothered to understand Thompson all too well, and wished he could ignore him. He was sick and tired of agreeing with the man. He turned to Wallace seated beside him. "What happened back there?" he wanted to know. "Back in that house?"

When his brother didn't answer he looked to Thompson. The man only shook his head. Not to say he didn't know, Caleb could see, but that what he did know concerned him deeply.

Caleb lifted his hand to rub his swollen cheek from where he'd briefly fought with Wallace, over just what he couldn't recall either. Pain shivered not from his jaw but down from his mangled hand. He looked again to Wallace and then both looked to the woman in the back of their wagon.

"What happened?" Caleb prodded again.

"Little brother, that's what I wish to God I could tell you," Wallace sighed. "Sorry about that lick to your jaw there."

"Well, I reckon I could be sore and sport a grudge…if only I could recollect what you hit me over."

"Bill Petry dead in his field," Thompson said. "You two was all riled…arguing over what it was you were to do with him. His body."

Caleb grunted acknowledgement even though the memory was still lost. "And this?" he asked, holding up his badly injured thumb and finger.

"Hammer," Thompson said. "Hit yourself."

Looking to the jagged remains of his half a bloody fingernail, that explanation made little sense to Caleb.

Wallace was equally confused, much of the last several hours were vacant spaces to him as well. He'd been keeping his concern to himself, however, and so he was relieved to find he was not alone in the matter. He took Caleb's hand gently in his for a moment and examined the torn fingernail. It made no sense.

"We can jaw this over back at Sweet Wood," he said, releasing Caleb's hand. "Ain't safe out on these streets."

As the words left his mouth, Wallace was disheartened to think that here in this town he and his brother had seen built there had come to be good cause to say such a thing. And not much more than a long Sunday morning stroll from the doorstep of the home the two called Sweet Wood, at that.

"Even the public house gone and went belly-up," Thompson noted sourly with a nod into the darkness where copious lights should have blazed. Even the light over the door was dark.

"So maybe you'll make it home to Maddie tonight after all then, eh?" Caleb said.

Thompson made as though his ears were as bad as his eyes and ignored the younger Sweet brother's acerbic quip. He cracked open the breech of his shotgun to check by touch that it was loaded. His calloused finger circled the single brass casing three times before he was satisfied and clicked the breech back shut. It was the fourth time he'd done so in the past hour. Unfortunately, Thompson's short-term memory was going the way of his eyesight. With that he nudged his horse to push forward into the gloom. It complied with a nervous snort that worried all three men. Perhaps the animal knew something they didn't. Once Thompson thought he was far enough out in front of the brothers in their wagon he stole the last slug from his flask. The deed failed to escape either of the Sweets, however, and Caleb would have told the man so but for the fact he didn't want to raise his voice.

Wallace gingerly lifted the reins and brought them down with just enough of a snap to set the wagon horses following. As if on cue, the woman in the back woke from her silence and let up a lingering moan.

"Dandy," Caleb muttered. "Bad enough she stinks ripe with blood…now she wants to offer up the call of the helpless and dying to boot. Ring the dinner bell, boys."

Wallace frowned at his callous brother. It wasn't that he disagreed, but he didn't feel the need to let the poor woman hear it. As the wagon eased slowly along Wallace leaned around and whispered to soothe her, "You try and hold still now, Mrs. Petry. We're going to get you to a right proper bed and set you on the mend. You're going to be fine. I give you my word. God's truth. Just fine. You just settle yourself and be still now." As he shifted in his seat, turning his attention back to Thompson and the dark road ahead, Wallace added in a sotto voice, "For the love of the Almighty…be still."

The dirt of the street beneath them was hard and compacted. Even in the dark Caleb noted this. He felt it in the rough jarring of his sore backside and aching spine, heard it in the clomp of the horses' shod hooves. Usually the earthen streets were made soft and loose by the busy passage of wagons, horses, mules, townsfolk, and even the occasional automobile. But the streets had been very quiet for a few weeks gone by now, and after hard rains pelted and packed the dirt it'd dried undisturbed into the consistency of baked clay, becoming once more like the arid land that sprawled on for countless miles between the town and the distant high country.

Thompson stared at the darkened windows regretfully as the trio of men passed the saloon. He worried that something horrible had transpired while they'd been away and that those doors would remain locked shut forever. Caleb and Wallace, meanwhile, both strained to pierce the inkiness ahead along the other side of the street where the meager skeletal remains of their original funeral parlor jutted at odd angles up from the charred debris. Not far beyond that was Sweet Wood. The residence's proximity to the burned business was the reason they'd decided to rebuild far outside of town. Had the winds not favored them on the night of the fire, Sweet Wood might well have been lost in addition.

The distracted thoughts of the three men were interrupted when the unmistakable tinkling of the saloon's piano began. Thompson stopped short causing the wagon to halt as well. He looked back to the brothers.

"So?" was all Caleb said.

As his brother spoke, Wallace caught the acrid scent of smoke on the night air. He assumed it was just the remnant odor of the nearby funeral parlor's charred remains, and so dismissed it.

"Kind of odd, wouldn't you say? Playing piano in the dark?" Thompson said. Before the brothers could dissuade him, he'd dismounted.

"What the hell are you doin', old man?" Caleb hissed. "Get back on your horse!"

Wallace bleated, "We don't have time for this." He nodded once to the back of the wagon. "*She* don't have the time."

Thompson waved them off.

"What about the dogs? The damned dogs?" Caleb said with a nervous look about as Thompson ascended the steps up to the bar's entrance, a typical pair of swinging saloon doors followed by a pair of closed double doors. Not even bothering to look back, Thompson lifted his shotgun a bit and shook it as his silent rebuttal.

Caleb whispered to Wallace, "Any sign of them dogs, you get us the hell out of here right quick like, you hear."

"I'm about to do just that, little brother...dogs, or no dogs."

Caleb shook his head in dismay as he watched Thompson nose up to the front window in an attempt to peer into the black beyond. "That man there ain't never met him a watering hole he could let pass by, now has he? Fool."

The tinny emanations, which had begun as musical nonsense before evolving into a few bars of Ragtime, suddenly ceased in mid-tune when Thompson neared. He looked quizzically back to the Sweet brothers. They could barely discern him up under the cover of the saloon's awning, however. Caleb, not altogether sure whether Thompson was even looking to him, nonetheless waved him back and mouthed, "Come on."

Thompson ignored him and turned back just as a knock came from inside the saloon. All three men heard it. It was a knuckle-rap upon the inner doors, the unmistakable first five beats of *Shave and a Haircut*, as if asking permission for—or maybe inviting—the doors to be opened.

Thompson considered it odd, but also a bit whimsical. He was a regular patron of the establishment, and now was certain it was the barkeep, Earl Hodges—or better yet, one of the girls—having some fun with him. Even as he crossed over, one of the inner doors slowly pulled back, unexpectedly creaking ajar.

"All-righty there now.... Who's this having so much fun with ol' Patrick Thompson," he said, and gingerly reached out to ease the door open a little ways more.

Caleb was about to scold Thompson again, and Wallace was impatiently sucking at his teeth, seconds from announcing they were leaving with or without him. Neither would get their chance, however.

Like some gargantuan amphibian's tongue, a ghostly white arm shot out from the mouth of the door, latching its hand around the nape of the man's neck. Before he could react, it was quickly followed by two or three more viciously groping limbs. From their vantage out on the street, the Sweet brothers couldn't be sure what they were witnessing. All Caleb and Wallace knew for certain was that Thompson was snatched through the jaws of the saloon's swinging doors, dropping his shotgun onto the planks of the sidewalk as he went helpless, dragged into the void beyond.

With a muffled and confused cry the old man was gone, the inner doors slamming shut behind him. The loud clack of the deadbolt being thrown on the far side immediately followed. That and then only silence.

...

Evan Evers knew now what other men had meant when they'd told stories of how time had once stood still for them. He'd heard so many of these remarkable stories: dogfights over France, stampedes, gunfights, encounters with grizzly bear. He'd doubted those men in the past. He'd dismissed them out of hand. He'd suspected their tales ran tall, likely nothing more than a poker player's feeble attempt at distraction. The hyperbole of liars and poor bluffs. But that was the past.

As Evan stood in the archway to Colonel Hawkins's dining room, and, as the old man cast down his flaming lantern into the kerosene spilled thick around the feet of his old horse, the flow of time eddied and pooled. To Evan's skewed and faulty perception only the flames appeared capable of moving with life. He and the old man and his horse were all caught up like characters rendered in portrait.

But time had not come to a complete halt. As Evan's mind raced, the inferno overtook him like an unexpected wave rushing up onto the sand. If only his body could have moved as quickly. As he was washed over in fire, Evan had the strange presence of mind to consider how commonplace it must be for a man's last thought to be "I am going to die."

Then, just as Evan felt time had been stalled, it erupted. The old man, a demonic figure set aflame, threw his sword across the room burying its point in the wall near Evan. This even as his damned beast reared twice and then crashed headlong through the front windows. Evan, clothes afire as well, fled the house next, careening back out the hall, dropping first one of his guns and then the other as he went.

Although Dale and Merritt had expected the house might very well go the way of the burning barn, they hadn't been prepared for the mayhem of the Colonel and his horse exploding from the front windows in a fireball. The horse broke one of its forelegs in their mad egress and the two spilled out down from the porch and onto the lawn. The Colonel was thrown and rose briefly only to collapse right off into a burning bundle. The horse—even crippled as the poor creature was—raced off into the night, hindquarters and saddle ablaze, the smell of its burning hide hideous.

It was all the brothers could do to stay in their saddles as Evan's horse got away from Dale and bolted into the night, following in the burning horse's wake.

Before the brothers could fathom what they should do, Evan stumbled out of the burning house and ran down the lawn. He was screaming incoherently as he threw himself to the ground and tore off his shirt. Dale quickly followed Merritt's lead when the older brother had the quick thinking to leap from his horse and rush to Evan with his canteen. Between Evan's hysterical rolling about and the splashing of much water the flames were quickly doused. Even so, Evan had been burned severely. His face and neck were blistered and most of his scalp singed away. Far worse than that, however, his right arm was badly charred from the wrist to the shoulder.

"We got to get him into town," Dale advised. Merritt agreed.

"First…farm…house…we get…to," Evan said through chattering teeth. Shock was setting in.

…

Young Walter Petry stood in his backyard staring off in the direction opposite the construction of the new funeral parlor. The night—and the wind that conspired with it—made the field of tall grasses appear as a rolling sea. And the sea whispered things to the boy, things that were only just now beginning to make sense.

In the distance he could see the flames rising from Colonel Hawkins's ranch. The boy was sure marauding Vikings had made landfall. Burning and pillaging. Raping.

Murdering. Soon they would come to terrorize his home, to make a meal of his small fingers, he thought.

Good. He was hungry, too. And he would be ready.

Chapter Eight

Caleb Sweet couldn't be sure whether the silence they left behind them boded weal or woe for Patrick Thompson. He knew the odds were slim it was the former.

Caleb had long warned his old friend Pat that his love of the bottle and penchant for habiting saloons would bring about his end, but the aged Sweet brother had never fathomed his prophecy would be fulfilled in so dramatic a fashion. *Pat's dead for sure*, a little voice inside him spoke. *No need to go back. No call to feel guilty to not help*, it reassured. Caleb hoped against that little inner voice and the twisting knot growing in the pit of his gut that they were wrong.

Beneath him—and his brother Wallace beside him and the injured Mrs. Petry in the back—the wagon bucked as though with life as it tore down the street at a pace unheard of for anyone save bank robbers. At least, that was the next thought Caleb had as Wallace cracked the reins again and yet again. He was sure Wallace wouldn't have paid heed even if he had protested. He was right.

Wallace was hell-bent. The swollen hinds of the wagon's whipped horses were proof. He *would* see his home. This he promised both to himself and his companions. To make it true, Wallace made the affirmation to them.

"We'll see home!" he shouted. "Almost there. Almost! Hold tight now. Safe soon enough!" he cried over the din of their wild passage.

As Wallace cracked the reins even harder Caleb

realized that the horses weren't pulling the wagon, so much as doing their damnedest to flee from Wallace's abuse. He wondered if they'd be able to stop the poor, mad creatures when the time came.

Abigail Petry lay bound, wrapped tightly in bed sheets, staring up at the host of stars above. Just as she thought they should, they swirled and danced like fireflies. When her journey in the wagon had begun—something more than an hour but what now seemed like days ago to Abigail—she fancied she was being carried by some chariot or barge off to the afterlife she had scoffed at in good health. She had since come around and now she knew better. The fire that'd raged in her abdomen had subsided. It had burned so long and so fierce that she could only conclude it had consumed her life. Out of fuel, the fire was spent. Released of the mortal coil and so released from her agony, Abigail reasoned. Perhaps that, or maybe she was still with life and there was a God. A grand architect of all things as so many men had said. An all-powerful being that had finally seen fit to ease her suffering, her damnation. She couldn't be sure, and knowing her mind was yet vexed and body still ached only compounded the delirious woman's confusion and uncertainty.

What she was sure of only troubled her all the more. The men who bore her body in their rickety wagon like so much baled hay were the Sweet brothers. The town elders. Founders. Undertakers. To be dead was frightening enough. To be caught in-between life and death and soon to be on the mortician's slab was the horrifying stuff of a deranged soul's nightmares.

...

Tucked away in the corner of the saloon, at the foot of the staircase leading up to the apartments of the bar's proprietor, Earl Hodges, and his prostitutes—two perpetually blurry-eyed women who fancied themselves showgirls—the Brazen Head waited in silence to be fed its nightly meal of coins. An amazing construct of ancient and mystic technologies much lost to the ages now—or so its display case advertised—the Brazen Head, an automaton's brass bust encased in glass, was the saloon's prized arcade game. In exchange for a mere two pennies, the machine promised to reveal a glimpse into a man's future. Many a night, destinies were laid bare to peals of laughter or groans of displeasure; the significance of precious days yet to unfold reduced to nothing more than casual, drunken entertainment.

Earl Hodges let slip a second penny and the Brazen Head whirred and clicked with its imitation of life. After several seconds of nodding and blinking, from its mouth a sliver of paper prophecy ticked out, falling into the drawer beneath where it could be retrieved.

Earl Hodges took the fortune up and read. "Your days are numbered." Unimpressed, he shrugged. "Ain't everybody's." He finished reading. "Beware the color yellow."

As Pat Thompson's eyes opened, Earl turned to him and spoke as though the old man had been conscious and engaged in conversation with him all along.

"Told you so. Didn't I tell you so? Don't know why I pester this damned thing. Truth is, sends me the willies something fierce. "Got to say though," he said with a thoughtful pause, "then again, the mighty ol' Brazen Head, he do give the girls and the regulars a good laugh from time to time. Yes, it do, I suppose. And I never did cotton to yellow no-how. Too sickly. That's one thing for sure."

Thompson rubbed his pounding forehead and collected a good deal of blood both dried and fresh for his trouble.

"Where am…what're…?" was all his mouth and clouded brain managed to put together between them.

He was laid out on the floor of the saloon with a frilly purple chair pillow nestled under his head, a filled shot glass of whiskey beside it. The pillow reeked of the women's cheap perfumes and the musk of the men who'd known them. Thompson lifted his head slightly, slowly. They were alone. Relieved, he let his head drop back to the pillow.

"Red. Now there's a man's color. You got some pennies on ya?" Earl asked. "Let's see what ol' Magellan has to fess up about you and your future."

Magellan was the name that'd long ago been handed down to the Brazen Head on the day it first arrived. No one could remember now how the name had come about precisely. Some said it was due to the fact that the Brazen Head had traveled so far to get there. Others disagreed even if they could supply no explanation better. The truth was forever lost, however, as the night the name was bestowed had been one of much imbibing, even more so than most in Earl Hodges's saloon. On that particular night, one pane of the new arcade's case had been shattered, and, much to the crowd's wild amusement, one fool—a young prospector come down from the distant hills—had tried to force his flaccid penis down the brass head's throat. It took Hodge's shotgun and the promise of another whiskey to convince the man better.

The prospector paid for the damages and left town that night never to return. No one thought so much as a gnat's breath of his disappearance, however. He was forgotten before he was gone. In any event—if nothing else from that night of drunken frivolity—the Brass Head's new moniker, Magellan, had stuck.

"Two pennies," Earl pestered. "C'mon, let's see 'em, let's see 'em," he said. He held his hand out like a child, opening and closing it in demand.

Patrick Thompson shook his head and sat up with a pained grunt. "I don't know," he muttered.

"Fine, I'll spot you this time, ol' fella," Earl said and dug the pennies from his pocket. "But even though I'm the one feeding Magellan, this here's still your future, agreed?" Thompson stayed quiet and so Earl answered for him, "Agreed."

Thompson sat dumbly watching the bartender like a dog witnessing things well beyond his ken as Earl Hodges paid the arcade its two pennies and retrieved the fortune when it dropped.

"Let's see here," he said and mumbled a first silent read through to himself. As he did, he began to slowly shake his head in disapproval. "Oh, lordy, lordy. Well, that is…speaking of red. I don't know what to say about this one here."

Earl looked to Thompson with concern while the old man only stared blankly back. Earl thought that the old man might have been rendered addled. The barkeep glanced down at the fortune and then back to Thompson. Still, the old man only looked through him with glazed eyes.

"Maybe we best let this be," Earl said, folding the small piece of paper three times and slipping it into his vest pocket. He patted it in place, drew in a deep breath and scanned the room. His eyes settled on the bar. A meat cleaver, standing on the top corner of its blade, was buried into the expensive mahogany. The blood around it, which Earl had been meaning to clean up, was now good and dried. As he considered the mess, he chewed his inner lip and strained his faculties to turn a weighty matter over in his mind.

But before it seemed Earl could reason his troubles out, something large and made of glass—a mirror perhaps—was shattered in a loud commotion upstairs, accompanied by a pair of women's near hysterical laughter. Earl's face went red and he swelled to yell up to the ceiling, but was cut short when Thompson finally found his voice.

"I need a drink," Patrick said. "Think I...."

The old man was teetering to his feet. Earl rushed to aid him as he did.

"Hey now, there you are! There you are! I was wondering where you'd got yourself off to. Welcome home."

"I ain't home," Patrick Thompson said with a spit of venom.

Earl laughed a disingenuous laugh. "Now there's the amiable cuss I know and love."

"Need a drink," Thompson repeated.

"Yeah, sure," Earl said. He considered the shot of whiskey on the floor next to where the old man had been, but immediately gave up the idea of retrieving it while still keeping Thompson upright on his feet. "Belly up to my bar, my good man," the proprietor said as he led Thompson to a barstool. "If it is a drink you desire, then it is a drink we shall have."

From upstairs, more things shattered. Something quite heavy—furniture, maybe; a body, perhaps—fell over, while escalating laughter proved that the women found it, or perhaps something else, very amusing. Pat Thompson recognized the laughter as that of Earl's two prostitutes. Strangely, even as things were getting more and more out of hand above them, Earl paid the growing disruption not the slightest bit of mind.

Thompson didn't have a chance to mull that over, however, since, as he sat down at the bar he was confronted with the mess of the blood and cleaver.

"What's all this then?" he said, taken aback.

Earl only laughed his all too practiced laugh once more as he rushed to get around behind the bar. "Oh, that?"

"Yes, this. What the blazes?"

Earl smiled. "You don't want to know, Mr. Thompson. Trust me. You do not want to know."

...

The distance to Caleb and Wallace's estate, Sweet Wood, was covered in no time at all as the horses pulled with a fury. Not only did they want to be free from Wallace's whipping, but they smelled what the old men could not; they smelled the dogs.

The horses had yet to see the pack. Blinders and the veil

of night conspired to ensure that much. But, commingled with the smoke of the fire now raging some miles off at Colonel Hawkins's ranch, the horses were made more agitated to know the unmistakable gamey scent of canines. They sensed also that the pack was near at hand, trailing. Hunting.

As the wagon drew near to the gate of Sweet Wood, which was really nothing more than a pole of stripped ash that barred the drive, the old men were surprised to spy a shadowy mass of something lying in their path. If the horses saw it, the pair, William and Charlemagne, gave no sign. They thundered ahead with unchecked determination.

"Dog," Caleb said, even as Wallace realized the same.

If not for the manner in which the collie blocking their way glared at them, the men would have thought the thing oblivious, perhaps deaf and blind with age. But even as the team trampled over it, the dog held its ground and lunged for one horse in a vain attempt to lock its jaws on the sweat-sleek throat. The wagon lurched to one side and the front wheel cracked as they crushed the dog beneath them. Still the horses drove on. The gate proved to be no better deterrence either. Even as Wallace hollered and pulled back on the reins with all he had, the horses hardly buckled to one side. Instead, they tried to jump the ash pole barring the path. They failed—harnessed as they were—and so the team smashed through, Charlemagne nearly losing his footing save for the rig supporting him. Still, that horse would be lost. Neither of the men could see, but a shank of wood had splintered and lodged in the creature's breast, a mortal wound.

As the wagon bounded down the drive, finally

beginning to slow as the dying horse's strength quickly ebbed, Caleb looked back over his shoulder to survey the shattered gate and the trampled collie. To his surprise he discovered the pack of dogs behind them rending their fallen companion apart. Caleb realized in an instant and without a doubt that the dogs had been after them. They had been the prey. Only the convenience of an easier meal had spared the Sweet brothers and Abigail Petry from their attack.

"We had us an escort," he said to Wallace with a nod back to the carnage.

Wallace only glanced behind them long enough to take in the scene. As soon as he turned back to see the wagon safely up the drive and to their house just ahead, he was discomforted to realize the pack was feeding on its trampled brethren in silence.

...

Merritt listened to Evan moan in agony and wondered if his little brother was even worth the trouble. The eldest brother had started out riding behind Dale and Evan, watching closely while the middle brother had struggled something fierce to keep himself and Evan on the horse they shared. The ground had been easy going, but Evan had not. After Evan's third episode of delirium, Merritt couldn't stomach to witness any more. He spurred his horse and rode ahead with a muttered excuse of needing to reconnoiter.

Dale knew better. He didn't protest, however. He was glad to be out from under the elder brother's watchful gaze.

As Evan began acting up again, Dale tightened his arm around the wounded man's waist where he held the reins and gave Evan's charred ear a sharp smack with his free hand. Evan howled and whimpered in protest, but ultimately this settled him from then on.

It still did little to assuage Dale's frustration with Evan, since he was also none too happy at having to abandon his favorite saddle to accommodate riding tandem with his wounded brother. This after discovering Evan was too hurt to hold onto Dale from behind. There was no denying Evan his wounds, but Dale was sure that if it'd been himself or Merritt so badly burned, they could have handled it. Probably could have ridden on their own, for that matter. If there had been another horse, that is. But Evan had always been a little brother, even as a man. All that, and the stink of Evan's burnt hair and clothes irritated Dale. Yeah, Dale thought, maybe they should leave him behind.

Almost as if he finally knew his brother's thinking, Evan whispered hoarsely, "Please don't let me die out here, Dale. Please...."

Like so many countless times in the past, not only did Dale not answer his younger brother, but more so, he didn't even acknowledge he'd heard his pleas.

Evan recessed into the corners of his mind, seeking a place where the pain would not know him. He held his burnt arm to his chest, protecting it as best he could and suckling the back of his thumb knuckle like a small child. Dale ignored the infantile behavior. He was satisfied to have his brother remain quiet and still.

With only the great luminous ghost of the Milky Way haunting the heavens to light the way, the Evers brothers rode in silence through the tall, whispering grass of the recently deceased Colonel's long-neglected land. They were agreed to seek out the nearest farmhouse—not the nightly patrol of the local sheriff—and so kept the distant dirt road just that way, distant. They'd thought there might be a volunteer fire crew to come along at some point. But, even after the Colonel's engulfed home and barn were well off behind them—and beginning to collapse by the sound of it—the brothers had yet to see any sign of help rushing to extinguish the blaze. Maybe the Colonel's ranch was without a phone, Merritt had considered. It wouldn't be that unlikely given the locale. If Evan had had his faculties about him he would have pointed out what it took Merritt a bit longer to put together; since the fire was deliberate, telephone or no telephone, there would be no call for help. And so then, isolated as it was, there would be no help coming.

"Maybe…if it ain't too far more," Merritt said, following that sudden realization, "I'll ride back. Track Gale's horse down. Gather up Evan's saddlebags and catch up rightly."

Dale nodded. "Evan had him Gale's share on him too, you know."

They rode for a ways before Merritt responded, "Figures."

They came to an old split rail fence, meant only to mark the property line and worthless to contain livestock. The field beyond had been mowed and the fallen hay gathered in long windrows. Merritt dismounted long enough to pull down a section of fence to allow them passage. Even in the dark he couldn't help but notice that the hay was rotting.

He could smell it. It'd been cut and forgotten, it seemed. He wondered if there'd been something discovered wrong with it—such as parasites or such—or if there was some other intention behind what otherwise appeared to be simple neglect. He knew nothing of farming, however, and didn't care to know anything of farming, and so let the matter go.

The land was flat, so the Petry farmhouse did not appear then unexpectedly. Instead it was perceived in increments. At first as merely a darker mass in the near distance, and then it stood out as something clearly manmade. There'd been no need as such to announce its discovery, and so when they stopped, Evan—who'd not been so alert—became concerned and all but erupted from his stupor.

"No! Don't leave me!" he screamed. "Please, Dale, I'll be good."

"Ah, for the love of God, Evan. Shut the hell up," Merritt said.

Dale called out to the darkened house. "Hey there! Anybody home? Got a hurt man out here. Hurt bad."

Silence.

"We only need us some water. Bed maybe. Phone to a doctor if you got one," Dale added.

Evan turned his pleas to the home he'd not noticed before. "Please. For the love of…please. I need help…."

"We're Christian folk here," Dale called. That was a ploy he'd seen Evan use to great success in the past.

Merritt couldn't suppress a grunt of amusement.

"What?" Dale whispered.

A light in one of the upstairs windows came on. "See," he said.

"Thank God," Evan sighed.

They waited, but nothing more happened. No one appeared, nor was there any other sign of life.

"What the hell…?" Merritt said and spat.

He dismounted in a flourish and marched to the front door. He drew his gun and kicked in the door all in the same movement without bothering even to check the lock. Dale had seen this all before. He drew his own sidearm in preparation of the inevitable gunfire. He would've normally swung his horse about so that he only offered his smaller profile as a target. But, realizing he had Evan seated in front of him allowing for even better cover, Dale remained facing the house.

After two minutes crawled by with no sign of Merritt, or anyone else for that matter, Dale holstered his gun and roused Evan into holding onto the horse's neck while he dismounted. Evan groaned and seemed to be set against it, but did as he was told. The horse—which had no name even after three years—was made nervous by Evan's fumbling grasp, but the relief of its burden being lightened allowed Dale to keep his mount calm.

"C'mon," Dale directed his brother. "Climb on down here and we'll lay you down in the grass."

Evan couldn't hear him. In his agony and shock he'd become convinced his brain was exposed to the elements. That delusion had evolved into the certainty that fire ants were now crawling over it, swarming, burrowing into the folds and ridges, stinging and snipping away miniscule bits to carry back to their nest. Evan was sure he was being lobotomized by insects. He could feel their trail down along his burnt shoulder and arm. He sensed every tiny footfall, thousands marching to and fro. Worst of all, he'd become immobilized. He could neither swat them away nor even cry for help. A tear ran down his cheek and he wondered if it might fall to Dale's arm and attract his brother's attention. Maybe then Dale would notice the ants and wash them away with his canteen, saving what little was left of Evan's mind. God, but how his head burned. It was a pain of hellfire. Damnation.

Evan realized Dale was moving him. He was being taken off the horse, laid down in the grass damp with dew. It was little relief. The ants tore on. His body was racked. No doubt next he would know that Dale had left him. No matter. It only meant the ants would be done with him all the sooner. If not the ants, then the coyotes and other predators of the night. All of the natural world would have at him. He would be scattered to the four corners. And then would come the other side's turn. Now Evan knew; this torment was merely a taste of his eternal reward to come.

A voice boomed down from the heavens. It rumbled around Evan's skull like the thunder of Zeus. He recognized the voice. In fact, he knew it well. Strange, he thought, to find God's voice so familiar. But then he realized it was his brother speaking. Not Dale, but Merritt. And while Dale was just above him, kneeling at his side, Merritt was someplace even farther above them both. Had Merritt perished as well, Evan wondered. All was confusion and pain.

Evan chose to close his eyes and do his best to die.

"Get around to the back porch," Merritt called down from the upstairs window where the light had originated. "Tell Evan, watch the front."

Dale started to reply that Evan was in no shape to watch, much less do anything if he did see something. Then he thought better of it. "Kill anybody what comes out," he barked loudly to the supine and barely conscious Evan, if only for the benefit of whoever else might hear. Then he ran for the back as Merritt had ordered.

The back of the house was dark and quiet. Dale nearly ran into the water-well hand pump at the corner in his rush to get the drop on anyone who might be in wait there hoping to get the better of him. But there was no such ambush coming. He paused just briefly to listen and survey the windows but all was still. He slowly stepped up to the screen door. The inner door was wide open and through the screen door the tantalizing smell of roasting chicken wafted. Dale's mouth watered and there was no silencing the rumble that rose up from the pit of his hollow stomach. Leading with his pistol he swung open the screen door and stepped into the darkened kitchen.

He was still expecting a confrontation, and so Dale took two quick steps to the side where he ducked down and waited. His eyes adjusted slowly as best they would to the pitch, but there was nothing that could be seen save for the glow from a small red light on the nearby stove; the cackle and hiss of the chicken roasting inside the oven, the only sound.

Dale was on the verge of standing and stepping forward when the sounds of gunfire rang out from somewhere upstairs. Judging by the incredible rapidity and cadence of the shots, Dale was confident it both began and ended with Merritt's colts. He knew his brother—when surprised or called upon to act quickly—tended to let go two quick shots from his right-hand gun, followed by a third single shot from his left, and then finished off with two more quick shots from his lead right again for good measure. A dot, dot, dash, dot, dot of Morse code that translated into death.

Dale cursed the darkness and charged ahead only to crash into one the chairs of the kitchen table he'd also not seen. The chair splintered under Dale and he tumbled headlong into the table, splitting his septum before rolling off to the floor. He wasted no time in getting to his feet, however, moving all in one motion even as he ignored the searing pain of his nose as well as the deep gouge he'd received to the shin of his left leg. Blood gushing down his face, he limped forward and found his way from the kitchen to the living room and the foot of the stairway ascending to the second floor. In that short span he'd heard nothing more. Either Merritt was dead or Merritt's intended target was. Dale had no doubt the latter was the case and so, not looking to become his brother's next victim, he called up.

"Merritt!" Thick blood spluttered in his mouth, sprayed off his lips.

For a response, Merritt switched on the light where he stood at the top of the stairs. Any other man besides his brother Dale might have been startled by this. Dale only shook his head and holstered his pistols.

"What happened to you?" Merritt asked, looking down with a quizzical cock of his head.

Dale cupped his hands and tried to wipe the blood from his face, but it remained in the craggy lines giving him the appearance of a haggard, if not demonic, rodeo clown.

"Tripped," he said.

"Uh-huh."

"What about you?" Dale asked. "Who got killed up there?"

Merritt weighed Dale's question for a moment before looking back over his shoulder into the hallway disappearing behind him. When he turned back to face his brother it was with an expression Dale had rarely known from Merritt. He looked worried.

"Well?" Dale pressed.

"Nothing."

"Nothing?"

Merritt only made a shallow nod before beginning to descend the stairs.

"What were you shooting for then, you don't mind my askin'?"

"I told you," Merritt said as he needlessly shoved his way past Dale, "nothing."

It was the kind of evasion he expected from his little brother Evan, not Merritt. Determined to better know what was going on, Dale mounted the stairs as Merritt went into the kitchen and began, of all things, looking to see if he could fix the chair Dale had broken in his fall.

Dale made his way through the upstairs. After a time he became confused, and, entering one of the bedrooms the man couldn't be sure where he was. He thought perhaps he was back home…his boyhood home. He called out for his mother that she might be there, and waited patiently for her reply. All the while, Merritt meticulously fussed about the kitchen doing nothing at all. He opened and closed drawers, folded and unfolded linens, moved spoons and forks from one side of the counter and back again. All the while he chose to ignore the awful mess that had come from the dressing of the chicken still roasting in the oven. Feathers were strewn everywhere and the old rooster's head was propped upright on the counter almost purposely, it seemed. The innards had been discarded in the sink and had begun to cake and dry there, the stink thankfully concealed by the wafting goodness of the roasting bird. Only the feet were not to be found.

Outside the house, Evan crept closer and closer to death. The ants the dying Evers brother had imagined before had been just that, hallucinations. But now, such was no longer the case. In the interim since Dale had deposited his brother in the grass and abandoned him there, Evan had become the living banquet for a host of bulbous-headed fire ants as well as an assortment of other foraging nocturnal insects.

Chapter Nine

It wasn't the first time Patrick Thompson had lost himself to liquor in the saloon. In fact, that was where he usually accomplished his most spectacular feats of intoxication since he did little drinking at home and did his best to hide his habit on the job. His wife referred to spirits as the Devil's elixir. Madeline Thompson had, against her better judgment, partaken in two glasses of port and one glass of champagne on their wedding night and that was the sum total she'd imbibed in the forty-one years gone by since. But she wasn't intolerant. Given Patrick Thompson's ways the couple would not have gone so far if she had been. At least, not happily. "Maddie" Thompson merely preferred to turn a blind eye to her dear old Pat's love of the bottle. *Better the bottle than some object of affection that might love him back*, she'd deluded herself long ago.

Patrick was half-drowned, two fifths into a fifth of bourbon, and had almost forgotten the day's troubles and the sour knot on his head, when the commotion upstairs broke out again.

"What the blazes is going on up there? Where is everybody anyways?"

The bartender, Earl Hodges, only twisted up his thin lips and shrugged. He'd cleaned up the bloody mess at the bar and moved on to the busywork of polishing highball glasses that needed no polishing.

"Well, that's that then. I got to get me home," Patrick Thompson announced with a slap on the bar. "Dead men in fields. Public house gone jiminy-jumpy. Got no time for all this tomfoolery. Ya ask me, Earl, this whole town is done shot to hell with madness."

Patrick stumbled in freeing his backside from the barstool. But he was a practiced drunkard and found his feet readily. He dug about his pockets while Earl waited as patiently as the clearly nervous man could.

Finding nothing but roofing nails and a balled and knotted arm's length of twine, Thompson waved the bartender off. "Tab," he said, and turned to find the door.

"I can't let you do that, Patrick," Earl said.

"Do what? Why, son, I could buy this place if...if...if I had me more money," Pat said, cackling at his own joke.

"No sir, that's not the matter here. Money's not...."

"Damn right. So put it on my tab."

"Say, why don't we put on the player piano?" Earl said.

Patrick waved him off.

"Or maybe ask Magellan some questions?" Earl pressed, referring to the Brazen Head fortune-telling machine.

Thompson waved him off again and this time threw in a grunt of derision.

Suddenly a scream, this time not issued in merriment, erupted from a woman upstairs.

"What the...? What kind of sick...?" Pat began, but didn't finish.

Earl tried to ignore it. "Them dogs is about out there, Mr. Thompson. It ain't safe. You best sleep things off right here. Go home come dawn. Yeah, that'd be the smart thing. Dawn. I can set you in a room upstairs."

"Up there? Up there with them crazy banshees you got curdling milk? No thank you. I'd rather take my chances with the dogs."

Patrick Thompson was nearly to the door and Earl was searching for the words to stop him when Claudette and Mariel called down from the top of the stairs.

"Now where do you think you're going?" Claudette said. "It's about time you woke up."

"The party's right here, Mr. Patrick," Mariel giggled with her overly girlish laugh. "You can't leave the party."

Their jovial banter deeply contrasted their gruesome disposition. Mariel—a pretty girl who probably could have done much better than she'd made for herself—stood with one hand jauntily on her hip while the other arm, a bloody stump, lopped off inches below the elbow, hung limp.

Patrick's mouth fell open and he turned back to Earl in his befuddlement. That was when the old man recalled the bloody bar and cleaver. Earl grinned sheepishly and kept at his polishing.

Claudette smiled the practiced smile of an accomplished whore. "We was beginning to think you went an' died on us. Now that, that would've been rude."

"Aw, he's fit as a fiddle! C'mon now, let's have us some fun!" Mariel squealed as she bounded down the stairs.

"I'm sorry," Earl Hodges whispered from behind the bar.

...

Abigail Petry woke from a sleep that had been as deep as death, a place of emptiness, nothingness. It was as though she had simply ceased to be for some time gone by that she now could not fathom.

She didn't know where she was. A bed in a room, but not hers. She couldn't say whether it was a Sunday or Thursday, whether she was thirty-nine or forty-two. She looked to her hands for answers and upon seeing the ugly wounds about her wrists she suddenly became aware of her pain, there in her wrists and in her back, her head, her neck, her stomach. Her stomach now the worst of all. Knives in her stomach. She cried out.

"Bill!"

Her husband did not answer, of course. Wallace Sweet, seated in the corner of the room where he'd only just dozed off while watching over her, did, however.

"Here now, Mrs. Petry. Be still. Be calm," he soothed as he hurried to her side.

Her eyes still showed a glimmer of wildness, but her expression was no longer that of a crazed woman. There was no spitting and baring of teeth as she'd done before. Even as Wallace reached her, she subsided and sank back down on the mattress. The old man was glad that he'd gone against his brother Caleb's advice to bind the woman to the bed as they'd found her in her own home. No doubt that would have only served to stoke her fear and feed her frenzy once more.

Wallace wondered whether it wasn't that very wildness that'd kept her amongst the living. He brought a damp washcloth to her forehead. She closed her eyes and her heaving bosom slowly settled to shallow, even breaths. Wallace was surprised she'd come around and still suspected she wouldn't last the night. The woman had lost so much blood that she was as pallid as a warm body could be. Indeed, she had the look of the dead about her. And, as an undertaker, Wallace knew the appearance of the dead all too well.

"Wallace Sweet," Abigail said to let the man know she recognized him.

"Yes, Mrs. Petry. That's right, it's Wallace. I'm here. Right here looking over you."

She was quiet and then asked, "Am I dead? Don't feel like death. Hurts too much."

"No ma'am, you're right here with us," he assured her. He even attempted a smile.

"Thought you Sweet brothers—" she began, but was cut short by a spasm of pain digging into her abdomen. When it subsided she asked, "My son? Where's my son?"

Wallace shook his head. "I don't know. We didn't see him."

"Bill, where's Bill? Where am I?" She tried to sit up again. The pain and Wallace's gentle hand eased her back down.

"You're here at me and my brother's place, Sweet Wood."

"Where's Bill?"

"I'm sorry," Wallace said.

"You're sorry? Sorry for what? Where is he?" she demanded.

"I'm afraid he's gone on to his reward."

It came as a blow and she sank back under it. She lay quiet then for a long time. Long enough that Wallace wasn't sure if she'd fully understood. But then she asked, "And my son? He dead, too?"

"I don't know, Mrs. Petry. We didn't cross paths with

your boy. Didn't see any sign of him. You were alone when we found you. You'd been hurt very bad. You need to rest and we'll talk some more after."

"My Bill's dead?"

"Yes, I'm afraid so. I am so very sorry."

"Bill…he didn't do this," she defended, referring to her injuries. "Where's Walter? You must have seen my boy. You must have looked!"

From a small kit at his side, Wallace slowly retrieved and methodically prepared a syringe. He was used to his charges being unaware of his intentions. Only when he finally looked did he see how she had twisted back from him like a rabbit in a snare.

"This will be for the pain…and to help you rest. But not too much. Just a very small dose. I know it won't be enough…can't give you too much. You're very weak, you know. You must rest," he said as he brought the needle to her arm.

He was relieved she didn't resist. Soon enough the bed linens loosed from her fingers. As the morphine washed over her and she began to drift back into the darkness, she fought back one last time just long enough to speak.

"You have to go back. Promise. Find my son. He didn't mean to do no harm. It's this sickness. But it will pass. I had it. It's passed. Look at me…I'm fine…all better. Find my boy." He was smiling and nodding as she grabbed his arm with an unexpected fury. "Please."

"Fine, then. Yes, we'll find the boy. But you must rest." Wallace tried to remain calm as Abigail's fingernails dug into his arm. "I promise. We'll find him."

And with that she relaxed. Her hand slipped away and

so did she. Wallace checked her pulse. Satisfied, he folded her arms and tucked the thin blanket snuggly about her.

He'd noticed before, many times over the past few years in fact, but now standing at what was likely her deathbed, Wallace was struck by how much this woman reminded him of a girl from long back in his past, his youth. Her small and delicate nose. The line of her lips. The woman before him was older, but then so too would the girl he remembered have aged. It wasn't her of course, only a striking resemblance.

In his twenty-second year he'd met and fallen in love with a newspaper man's daughter. That had been back in San Francisco, shortly before he and Caleb thought to make their fortunes where other men had yet to forge the way before them.

The newspaper man hadn't approved of Wallace's intentions for his daughter. She was still but a girl, only sixteen. That, however, was not the root of his disapproval. He simply couldn't see them as a good fit. His daughter was beautiful while Wallace was rather plain. His daughter longed for finer things. Wallace had no prospects, was light in his wallet, and had yet to find his path. In the end then, nothing was to come of Wallace's attention.

Wallace Sweet would spend the rest of his years pining over his unrequited love and cursing the newspaper man for denying him his happiness. The truth of the matter was that the girl cared even less for Wallace than her father had. Also, she fancied at least two other suitors over him and would never for a moment have entertained the notion of spending her life with Wallace Sweet. In his heart of heart Wallace knew all this, too. It was easier, however, to blame his sorrow on another man as opposed to the girl he loved.

As the years sailed by Wallace would drift, first from bitterness to reminiscent melancholy and then slowly back to bitterness again. His heart was a bottle on a circuitous current far out to sea never to near the shore. But, always being carried on by Caleb and sharing in his brother's obsession with carving out their place above those who they'd gathered around them, Wallace had long ago accepted that he would never marry. As it seemed with all wounds, with time's passage he wasted less and less of his days taking stock of his loss. The love of a woman, he'd finally concluded in his old age, was simply the foolish business of other men.

The door behind Wallace squeaked as it opened. Caleb stood there in the door jamb blinking. It appeared he'd fallen asleep fully dressed as well. Wallace held a slender finger over his lips and Caleb acknowledged with a nod. Once they were both in the hall with the bedroom door pulled closed behind them, Caleb spoke in a hushed voice.

"Mr. Platt…he never came back in," he said.

He was speaking of their assistant, Moses Platt, who tended to their house and horses and drove the Model T that came out of their garage maybe once a month. He'd gone out to put down the wounded horse and get the other safely to the barn. That was the last they'd seen of him.

"How long's it been?"

"Little more than two hours."

"God have mercy. Either he's trapped, holed up out there, or…." Wallace couldn't finish the thought.

"Or….yes. *Or*."

Wallace shook his head. "Shouldn't have let him go."

"I tried to stop him. You know how he gets over them horses. Like they were his children."

"Well, there's no sense going out after him now."

"Agreed," Caleb said without hesitation. He'd had enough for one day for a man aged half his years, he'd decided. "It's about time for this town to get the telephone. Catch up with the rest of the world. Keep pace. "

"Listen to you now. Sound like your old buddy, Patrick."

"Might be there's a vacancy opened up in that department," Caleb said.

Wallace slumped against the wall with exhaustion. "Might be. Might be," he said.

"What does it matter, phone or no?" Caleb shot back. "Who would we call, the sheriff?"

Wallace nodded with a grimace. "We could call the saloon. Check on Patrick…likely get the sheriff…two birds, one stone."

"Hiring that lush didn't turn out to be our best idea ever, eh?" Caleb said.

"Worked well enough for the past dozen years. Did as he was told. Stayed in his place."

"True enough, I suppose." Caleb chewed his lip a moment then said, "Come dawn, if he ain't back in here, I'll be going out to look for Mr. Platt. And, depending on how that pans out, I'll be heading over to the saloon next for Patrick. You're welcome to come along for the ride if you'd like."

Wallace shook his head. "Don't suspect you'll be riding anywhere unless Mr. Platt turns up fine and dandy."

Caleb saw his point. Moses Platt cared for the horses

and was the only one of the three who knew how to drive the Model T.

"True enough, but I'll be going one way or the other, I reckon."

Wallace was quiet for a long moment and then said, "You do that. I'd best stay on to look after Mrs. Petry."

Caleb produced a small penknife and began cleaning under his nails. "Suit yourself."

"When you're done rounding up all our strays," Wallace said, "I'll need you to spell me watching over her. I'm going to need to head back out to the Petry spread."

Caleb raised an eyebrow. "What, for Bill Petry's remains? Might be our business, but sure as blazes doesn't seem worth dying over."

"No. Business has nothing to do with it. I promised Mrs. Petry. Promised I'd go fetch her boy."

There'd not been too much spare time for weighing the day's events and so Caleb was slow to piece together his argument. For the time being he could only offer some delaying tactics.

"It's late and so we shouldn't go downstairs and have some hot tea," Caleb said.

Wallace smiled. "No, that wouldn't be the thing to do. Not at all," he agreed. And, patting his brother on the back, they eased their way quietly downstairs to do just that.

As Caleb alternated between sipping and rippling the steaming tea in his mug with cooling blows of breath, he did his best to see things clearly. *Reading the tea leaves might have been more enlightening*, he teased his tired mind.

There was no doubting that Bill Petry had bound his

wife to their bed. She certainly didn't truss herself up so. And the boy could never have pulled off such, even if the woman hadn't been as mad as a rabid dog. But then there was the boy's bloody footprint there at the bedside. *Did that mean the boy had been there to witness the stabbing, or worse, did the boy do the unthinkable deed himself?* If Caleb had considered the question a scant few weeks earlier he would have surmised Bill Petry had been to blame. In his many years he'd twice known the sorrow of men committing downright heinous acts to their loved ones. These days were different, however; with this madness, anything was possible. The boy might well have been the culprit. And so then, *what would Wallace be walking into to go back out there?*

No doubt some of the men would be at the construction site come the morning. He wondered if Patrick might not be there as well. It was a foolish hope he admitted. But still, his brother wouldn't be alone. That thought settled his troubles a bit. He'd forgotten once more that the morrow was their day off.

Wallace had been quiet across the room. Despite the heat the windows had been kept shut what with things being the way they were. So when Caleb's thoughts were disturbed by a rustling noise he was distracted to know the cause.

A rat—not a mouse, but a rat—stood on its hinds and surveyed him as if to wonder why the old man was trespassing here in its domain. Normally Caleb would have leapt to action at such a sight. This night he only mused silently over the fact that he was surprised his hearing was still so well with him as he watched and listened to the creature clean itself in their cold fireplace.

"I imagine I should take one or two of the boys over there when I go," Wallace said.

Caleb was shaken from his reverie and was even more surprised to see that Wallace was watching the rat as well.

"What's that," Caleb said.

"When I go over to the Petry place tomorrow. Was saying I'll take Goodman or maybe Miller over from the site when I go. That boy might not be right in the head, you know. Dangerous."

Caleb nodded as the rat departed, scurrying back up into the recess of the chimney. "Was thinking the same. Good idea."

"What's happening here, Caleb?"

"If only you could tell me, brother."

"Something in the water maybe?" Wallace offered.

"No."

"Plague of some sorts?"

"Even you know that's not what we have here," Caleb said.

"Well, what then? What's got into these folks?" Frustration crept into Wallace's words and he sounded afraid.

"I don't know. But I do know we need to figure it out before there's nothing left. This town is teetering on tearing itself apart."

"And I know another thing. I'm going to see those dogs are put down once and for all."

"That'd be a good start," Caleb said. "But you and I both know that's naught but a symptom, not the root. We need to cut the root. Weed it out. Carve it down to the core.

Kill it. That's what we need to do."

Wallace scoffed. "Can't kill what you don't know. Least, not intentionally."

They said nothing for a few minutes.

"It's been quiet," Caleb said, and Wallace's silence only added credence to the observation. "You think that bodes well for Mr. Platt, or no?" Caleb wondered aloud.

"With all this madness, I'd be mad myself to say either way," Wallace said. He put his tea, only half-finished, on the table near him and got up from his chair.

Watching him, Caleb said, "Time to call it a day, yes?"

"No, little brother. I'm going to the kitchen to fetch some salami and then I'm getting me my pistol. I don't abide rats."

…

Dale and Merritt finished the last of the chicken. All that remained was the lingering smell of the roasted bird that had drawn them back to the kitchen to begin with. Around them, on the floor, the table, the counters, feathers were strewn. Whoever had cooked the bird hadn't bothered to pluck it outside, or in a bag as one should do indoors. Nor had the unknown cook bothered to dispose of the old rooster's head. Its dried mucus and milky, pus-filled eyes stared at them from the bloody counter. They ignored it.

As Dale tossed the last bone into the pan beside the rest of the carcass he felt his mind gathering coherence once more as though he were coming around from a daydream.

"Where's Evan?" Dale asked.

Merritt looked at him as though he'd spoken in a foreign tongue. "What?"

"Evan? Where's Evan? Did we bring him in?"

Merritt had yet to return from his own befuddled state. "I don't...no...I didn't...."

"Jesus Christ." Dale kicked his chair back sending up a small flurry of feathers. More feathers took to the air as he rushed out the back door. Merritt wasn't sure what the fuss was all about, but still he thought it best to follow.

They found Evan where they'd left him. Merritt didn't doubt their little brother was dead. But as Dale touched him to brush the ants from his face, Evan's eyes fluttered open and he moaned. It was low and slow like the death rattle of gas escaping a corpse.

Dale cursed some more and barked at Merritt—something he never did—to help him get the man inside.

They carried their brother upstairs and would have chosen the first room they came to but for Dale's suggestion to put him at the end of the hall, far from the room and bed he had his eye on. He felt a tinge poorly for how they'd abandoned Evan, but not so much that he planned to lose sleep over it.

A cloud of yellow dust puffed into the air when they hefted Evan onto the bed. Dale had never seen so much pollen. Especially not indoors. He began to say as much when the bloody window sill distracted him.

Upon a field of warped wood a fingernail did battle with a fly's corpse. They wrangled and twisted, neither managing to get the better of the other. Still their dance amused Dale and so he clapped to egg them on and show his appreciation. A tiny yellow mushroom strolled up along the sill's edge and Dale became disturbed to think it meant to leap off and end its days.

"Don't do it," he whispered.

It bowed in thanks and called up in its tiny voice that only Dale could hear. "*Truly my God is most merciful and forgiving,*" it shrilled.

It crouched then to join in watching the battle royal between the fly and nail.

Dale turned to Merritt to get his take on the strange little scene and that's when he realized his brother was no longer in the room. He looked to Evan. He would get no response from him either, as his younger brother had lost consciousness once more.

Evan had slipped back into his dream world, but not before undergoing a great transformation. Where pain had racked him a new sensation took hold. This had taken place when his brothers put him onto the bed. He'd descended into a thick golden cloud and it washed away the fire. He felt as though he was submerged in a mother's soothing bath. The strength to draw in a deep breath returned to him and so he did, taking in the cloud's vapors to make it part of him. One with him. Giving him life. Its life. Evan Evers was reborn deep within the golden cloud's healing womb.

His vision shifted and the room was lit seemingly from nowhere and everywhere as all about him glowed, each object with its own particular aura of radiance. He'd been delivered from Hell and ascended to Heaven. Just as a priest had once said just moments before Evan was to snuff out his life, and so he whispered it now, "Truly my God is most merciful and forgiving." And so he slept.

...

Patrick Thompson didn't need another drink, he needed his shotgun. The drink was right there in front of him, however, while his shotgun had gotten off to who could say where; so he tossed another whiskey back. The women on either side of the old man shrieked and hooted with delight. Their madness had been easier for Pat to ignore when it had been confined to the upstairs, behind closed doors. Pat couldn't say if it was the booze or the women's boisterousness that'd brought on the ringing in his ears. He wondered if he could still walk. And, if he could, whether or not they'd kill him before he might reach the door.

Mariel pounded her bloody stump on the bar, creating wet, sickening smacks in the bloody fluid that seeped from between her haphazardly sewn and gaping sutures. They'd used twine. The wound was swollen and red with an infection more healthy than its host. Still, the woman appeared not in the least bothered by it. The meat cleaver had reappeared as Claudette used it now to hatchet the bar. This, to express her delight. Earl didn't protest, remarkably, instead only smiling dumbly as though this were just another night.

"I want to go home," Patrick said. It felt to him—and sounded every bit like—a schoolboy asking to be excused.

"Home?" Claudette scoffed. "Whatever for? Wanna get back to your ol' harpy wife?"

"Maddie's...no harpy. She a good...decent woman," Patrick defended, gulping hard with each pause as if his protest was making him ill.

"Oh, that bitch is a harpy alright! Always quick with the stink eye, that one," Mariel said. She scrunched her nose up in thought. "What's a harpy?"

She'd begun to slump, Patrick had noticed. It gave him pause to question the hour again. He couldn't be sure though since the cuckoo clock normally found behind the bar had gone missing. He suspected they had to be on the cusp of daybreak.

"Look, fun is fun and all, but I need to get home. Get some sleep." He looked to Mariel. "You appear pretty tuckered yourself, missy. And you need to have that looked at," he said with a nod to her truncated limb.

"Sleep? Bah!" Mariel waved what would have been her hand at him. "Sleep is a lie. Big-old fib, Mister Patrick. Don't need no sleep. Why I ain't so much as winked in three days."

Claudette agreed as somberly as if the girl was testifying the gospel in church. "Truth," she said with a nod.

"Uh-huh. That so?" Patrick said.

"I swear on Lucifer's shiny red ass!" Mariel shouted, finding her belligerent voice again.

"Just the same," Patrick said as he pushed his stool back and steadied his weak and whiskey-addled legs with a hand on the bar, "I'm going home."

The hatchet bit into the bar close enough to his pinky finger that there was no telling whether Claudette had missed her intended mark or not.

"Before you go runnin' off, we got something upstairs to show you," she said.

Mariel began laughing hysterically at this proposition. So much so that she fell onto the floor onto her backside. The fall did nothing to subdue her crazed glee. Patrick looked desperately to Earl, but the bartender refused to meet his beseeching gaze.

...

Caleb woke to Moses Platt's gentle touch. He opened his eyes and mumbled something nonsensical before he found his mind. Moses was patient. The morning air was already heavy with heat, but also inviting with the promise of coffee and sausages and fried eggs.

"What time is it?" Caleb asked as the back of his fingers searched out the sleep pestering the deep folds of his eyelids.

"Near going on ten," Moses reported. When Caleb looked surprised to get the news that the morning was all but gone, their old hand offered, "They thought it best to let you sleep on a bit."

"They?"

"Mr. Sweet and Abigail."

Even after just over twenty years in their service, Moses Platt still referred to both brothers as "Mr. Sweet." Some confusion had arisen from the formality, but Moses retained the habit just the same. The brothers had enjoyed Moses's courtesy at first. Then, after six or seven years, they looked to find more familiar ground as the novelty had worn thin and confusions proved bothersome. Moses preferred his way best, however, and so the matter was resolved. As a result, and as a matter of mutual respect, the brothers never took to calling Moses by any name other than Mr. Platt. Around town, on the other hand, Moses's friends—who numbered all he encountered—affectionately called him by his boyhood nickname, Mop.

Moses 'Mop' Platt was as diminutive as a man could be before some fool might take him for a child. Not quite a hand over four feet in height, he was in fact at first mistaken for a child when he wandered into town, appearing out of the heat mirage one June morning like some sort of magical dwarf from a fairy tale. He'd naught but the clothes on his back and a smile. When asked his name he replied, "Water." They brought it to him and when asked where he'd come from he replied, "Beer."

It was thought that his incredibly pink complexion was a result of his traversing the hard country. But as the weeks passed, and folks became accustomed to him, it became clear Moses's rosy hue was the small man's natural disposition.

Both Caleb and Wallace had met Moses in the saloon on that morning of his first appearance. They wanted to see who was causing such a fuss among the gossips and assure themselves he was not of the 'unsavory ilk,' as Wallace phrased it. By the end of the second round of drinks Moses had been hired by the Sweets and had remained in their employ ever since.

Moses explained, "She…Abigail…Mrs. Petry…she couldn't make them stairs just yet. So we're having us our breakfast up in her room." As he spoke, he reached to help Caleb to his feet. That was when the old man realized he'd slept the night on the downstairs sofa.

They were making their way across the room and

heading for the stairs when Caleb blurted out, "Mr. Platt, you're alive!"

"So's they tell me, yes."

"No, I just…you went to see after the horses…."

"Horse," Moses corrected. "Charlemagne, he was expired by the time I got out there."

"Oh, I…I'm so very sorry, Mr. Platt. He was a fine animal."

"Only the finest. Never be another."

Caleb nodded. "But you? How are you? What happened? You didn't come back," he said.

"No, and ain't nobody came out after me, neither," Moses said rather flatly.

"I planned to. I was waiting for dawn," Caleb said. When Moses gave no reply Caleb confessed. "I was frightened. I'm sorry, Moses." He hadn't called the man by his first name in two decades.

They were at the foot of the stairs and paused there at Moses Platt's direction.

"Never you no mind. I was plenty scared, too."

Caleb nodded. "So what happened?"

"Them terrible dogs. Them goddamned, terrible dogs is what happened. I had to sit up in the hayloft all night. They sat and sat up under me, watching like school children studying on their teacher. Damnedest thing. Then, come daybreak, they split out."

"Thank God."

"No, sir, I won't. God didn't save William," he said of the horse he'd gone out to care for.

"They got William, too?"

Moses Platt would have spit if he hadn't been indoors. "Tore him to pieces right there in the barn. My poor old William, he stomped two of the mangy things but good 'fore the rest took him down."

Caleb was distracted from his pretense to be grieved over the horses when he suddenly remembered his friend Patrick.

"We need to get to the saloon!"

Normally such a remark would have been curious to Moses, but not with the madness of the last few weeks.

"Already? On an empty stomach?" It was Moses's little joke. He didn't want the real reason for going there. It could only be for more trouble.

...

"You ate that?" Evan chided.

Dale and Merritt had been dumbstruck when their little brother Evan walked into the kitchen and crossed to the sink. Somehow, he gave no sign that he was so mortally injured as they'd thought. It was there at the sink that he'd aired his disgust for the chicken the two had just finished.

Dale raised a greasy hand to rub his brow as if the gesture would help him find an answer. That was as far as either brother had gotten towards responding. Evan used a wooden ladle from the counter to flick the decapitated rooster head at them. "Diseased," he said. "Look at the eyes. And what's all that around the beak? Disgusting." They remained quiet. "That crust all dried up there…that's not post mortem. Thing was diseased. Who knows with what. Probably died from it. I swear, you two would probably sustain yourselves on the spring thaw carcasses if the buzzards and wolves weren't so nimble."

Dale smirked. "You sure are doin' better. Still look a sight. Like you done went through hell and back, but, hey, just as mouthy as ever."

Merritt wasn't so jovial. "You dead, Evan?" he asked. It was almost a threat. Dale's smirk faded away as he realized his brother was serious. As if Merritt's tone hadn't been enough, the eldest brother drew a pistol and laid it on the table pointed in Evan's direction.

Evan only stared them down.

Merritt pressed, "You answer me, little brother. You dead?"

Merritt Evers was not a superstitious man. At least, he never had been under normal circumstances. His mind had become quite addled since they'd made the Petry farm, however, and more so, no body such as Evan's should have been on its feet, much less making glib remarks in casual conversation.

Evan's good hand rose up, and even though he wasn't armed—he'd dropped his Colts back inside the inferno of the Colonel's home—Merritt matched the movement by bringing his own hand to hover above his revolver. Evan's eyes stayed locked on Merritt while his hand continued slowly up to the side of his head. Evan scratched there and a small portion of his scalp sloughed off and fell to the floor.

"You'd be amazed at how much that hurts," he said with a grimace. "You really would."

"Go," Merritt said. He nodded to the stairs.

"Go where?" Evan demanded. He noticed for the first time that the sky was pale, the sun on the verge of rising.

For an answer, Merritt lifted the gun from the table. He pointed it to the spot between Evan's eyes.

Evan knew his brother. He didn't waste words or threats. He rarely missed even difficult shots. Evan held his hands out in defense, to bide for time. "What if I just go back upstairs, nice and quiet? That bed, it was real nice." He realized as he spoke the words, that, indeed, the bed had been the nicest he'd ever known. It had soothed his wounds. He remembered his rebirth. A transformation.

"You do that. You get back up there where we put ya," Merritt said and cocked the gun in case his words weren't enough.

The unmistakable sound shook Evan from his momentary reverie. Looking down into the cylindrical abyss of Merritt's piece only made Evan's head swim, the pain in his body surge to the surface. Sucking hard for air—as if breathing through wet cloth—he stumbled to the stairs. As he went, he beseeched Dale, but it appeared that he'd gone the way of madness as well. As Evan climbed the stairs to return to his room he easily overheard Merritt now giving Dale direction. He paused to listen.

"And you go out to the barn and get a shovel," the eldest brother ordered.

Dale had never taken to Merritt's bossy side. "What for?"

"For to dig your little brother's grave, that's what for. Might be he's a pain in the ass, but he is your brother, after all. We got to do right by him."

"Evan? You want to bury Evan?"

Merritt searched through the discarded chicken bones on the table for any tidbit of overlooked meat or even some gristle to suck. "He's dead," he answered without pausing his search. "You bury your dead." When Dale offered no sign that he'd so much as heard him, Merritt bared his teeth like a dog. "I got to threaten to shoot you too?"

Evan listened as Dale got up from the table and left out the back door. Not wanting to test Merritt any further he crept away up the stairs as quickly as he could go. He wondered how long it would take them to dig his grave. No matter, Evan settled with himself before he finished the stairs. Long before that would come to pass he would find the means. He'd kill them both.

...

Young Walter Petry overheard all this too. From his secret hiding space he could even watch some of what transpired.

At first he was so very excited by the prospect of witnessing these men kill their brother. One less for him to fuss over. He was glad they enjoyed their last meal. The space was cruelly hot and cramped. He was hungry. No, not hungry, thirsty. Yes, both. "Both," he whispered. Hungry and thirsty and his father was right. "Not both. All three." Yes, his father was right. Always right. All three. Do not let another man finish the work God puts before you.

He would kill them. Kill them all.

"Three blind mice," Walter whispered and choked

down his giggles when Merritt cocked his head and looked to the place where the boy was hidden.

Chapter Ten

The morning sun shone through the blue sky filled window, promising to make for a beautiful new day. Patrick Thompson opened his eyes, awaking to that welcome discovery, only to find he was unable to move.

He was bound—nearly mummified, in fact—wrapped from his ankles to his neck in torn strips of bed linens, seated in a chair within what he was sure was one of the saloon girl's gaudy boudoirs. His mind was alert, but his body remained numb, caught up as it was in his incredibly tight cocoon. Patrick's head throbbed with the previous night's over-indulgence, and no doubt he would've had trouble recollecting the last events of the late evening but for the gruesome reminder facing him from a mere four feet away.

Seated and trussed-up in the same manner as Thompson, was the town miller, Curtis Toole. His face was bloated and it took Patrick a moment to recognize him. A thick colony of golden-yellow mushrooms sprouted over his entirety, from the top of his head to the tips of his otherwise bare feet. Curtis was stone dead.

The fungi were clearly all of the same species, although varying slightly in size and color. The majority were thin, wispy and bright yellow, while a few—one sprouting from the deceased miller's knee in particular—were squat, thick, and more brownish gold in hue. A coating of the same colored spores covered the floor surrounding the cadaverous garden. Patrick noticed then that a set of bare footprints—small, those of a woman—coursed through the carpet of spores. He was sure they'd been made when he was brought there sometime in the past few hours. Since that passing, more spores had fallen—he also noted—not too much unlike the morning dew on otherwise fresh tracks.

Patrick guessed by appearances that the miller had expired at some point in time at least a week or two gone by, and the retch-inducing smell assured Patrick that Curtis Toole's remains were still lingering with the earliest and most vile stages of decomposition. Patrick complimented the foul odor by vomiting. The old man, swaddled snug as a loved babe like he was, could do nothing to escape the upheaval. It gurgled forth, even as he tried to hold it down, spilling down his chest and gathering in his lap.

Desperate and disgusted, Patrick fought to push his chair away or even over, anything to be away from Curtis. It was impossible. After he failed without gaining so much as a teeter, he realized why. The chair, an ornately carved wooden design painted in gold, had lion paws for feet. And through those paws, nails had been driven into the floor. He looked to Curtis to confirm the same had been done to his chair only to find that was not the case. The chair legs had not been nailed; Curtis's feet had.

"Small mercies," Thompson said, mindfully under his breath.

He scanned the room desperate for some means to free himself. Nothing. Velvet pillows swimming in a great, rumpled, matching velvet bedspread, all smothering an overstuffed king bed, and opposite that, a claw foot tub—something of a motif, he noticed—was all he was afforded from his awkwardly-bound position.

Patrick Thompson had long been fond of saying he may not have been born to the town, but he would certainly be buried there. He wasn't prepared to fulfill that vow in the same manner as Curtis Toole, however. Still, the prospect was beginning to appear all too likely.

...

Caleb knew it was his friend Patrick's horse long before they reached it. He also knew the dogs were to blame. He moved his hand to Moses's knee and the man pushed up the hand throttle to slow the Model T to a coasting stop.

"God a'mighty," Moses said, "They killin' just for the sport of it. I swear, if I hadn't seen what they did to William, why I'd never believe no dogs could take a horse like that."

Caleb only grunted. He looked around to assure himself again that he and Moses were alone in the street. It was a ghost town.

Moses noticed his boss's concern. "Most folks lit out yesterday not too long after y'all was off out to the new funeral parlor, like I said. Guess they didn't want the fuss. Looked like Moses had parted the Red Sea."

"What, did they think we'd shoot 'em?" He shifted the double-barreled shotgun in his lap. "What do I care? Go if you want to go," Caleb said. He turned to the quiet businesses and shouted over the low rumble of the idling engine, "Go! Go and go to hell, the lot of you! Cowards! I don't need you! This town don't need you!" He slapped the dash. "Go and don't think of comin' back! Ya hear? Don't come back!" He was trembling by the time he'd finished.

Moses was relieved that Caleb had stopped yelling and wondered nervously if the dogs ever slept. "Let's just get us to the saloon," he said. "Whatdaya say?"

Caleb was still riled, however, and barked back, "Well, yeah, that's what we're doing. We're going to the saloon, aren't we?" When Moses only stared at him, Caleb deflated. "I'm sorry, Mr. Platt. It's just...I just...."

"No need. I'm right here with you to suffer witness to all this madness."

Caleb sighed. "Well, okay then." He rubbed his eyes and considered something more. "Maybe we should go out to the job site...collect up the boys from there. A little more manpower certainly couldn't hurt our cause."

"Today's Saturday, Mr. Sweet. Ain't gonna be nobody on the job."

"Oh, right. Saturday. So it is," he agreed. He still would have sworn it was Friday. He trusted Moses's mind better, all things considered, however. "Well then, to the saloon it is, as we've intended all along. Drive on, Mr. Platt. Drive on."

They hadn't too far to go, and hadn't gone too far of that, when unexpectedly Moses Platt cut back the throttle again and eased onto the brake with the cane he kept for just that purpose. He'd stopped them in the middle of an intersection. Before Caleb could question why, he had followed the driver's gaze down the intersecting street and discovered the reason for himself.

Two long blocks down, almost to the edge of town, like sentinels in the noonday sun, a pair of huge dogs stood shoulder to shoulder watching them from the middle of the road.

"I know them two," Moses said. "No mistaking, not even from here. Them two there are Paul Butterfield's mastiffs. Name of Black and Britches."

"They're near about out in front of Patrick's place. That might not be a good sign," Caleb said.

"Good sign or no, I wouldn't tangle with them two even if they was right in the head. An' I know from firsthand that they ain't."

"That's where you're wrong, my friend," Caleb said.

"What's that now?"

"Tangle with them is precisely what we're going to do."

Moses drew back in a huff. "You'll pardon my making sense, but have you lost your mind?"

"Hardly. We're armed for bear and this is no horse beneath us for those two scoundrels to spook. We take it to them. Full tilt. You run the one on your side down and I'm going to give the other a taste of both barrels," Caleb said as he reached up with his good hand to unclasp his side of the Model T's soft-top.

Moses gave the dogs a second consideration. "Near big as bears," he muttered.

The pair remained as statues.

Caleb was adamant. "Look, we can do this here and now, on our terms, or maybe you'd prefer to wait and see those two again some night alone…on theirs. Likely it'll not be just the two come that time around, either," he said.

Moses saw the point. Without further argument he unclasped his side of the soft-top as well and they pushed it back. Caleb rose in his seat onto one knee and steadied the shotgun over the top of the windscreen, struggling a bit with it as his injured hand was now bandaged.

"You see any others?" Caleb asked. Moses shook his head. "Good," Caleb said, "To quote the great architect of war, Sun Tzu, 'If my enemy leaves a door open, I must rush in.' Let's give 'em hell, Mr. Platt."

Moses had never heard of this "Son Sue" fellow Caleb quoted, and he certainly had no time to weigh the man's wisdom. Just the same, Moses got an ache in the pit of his gut that it was a dubious bit of philosophy. Maybe it was Mr. Sue, or maybe Caleb's misunderstanding of the man—Moses couldn't know for certain—but something, somehow felt off the mark.

The engine made what sounded like a nervous cough as Moses turned the wheel hard and pulled down the hand throttle. He took his foot from the brake and with a sharp jolt the auto bounded forward as they turned onto the clay street and quickly gained speed. The dogs were not in the least moved by their charge.

"Steady…steady," Caleb repeated.

Moses yelled, "Hold tight…may need to swerve iffin' he scrambles." A few seconds more, just as they were almost upon the dogs—who'd still hadn't so much as flinched—and Moses cried with foam flecking from the corners of his mouth, "This is for William!"

There was no need for Moses to swerve. The dog he was determined to run down, the mastiff bitch called Britches, leapt at the last second. Not away from the speeding auto, but at it. Into it. Britches effortlessly cleared the hood and smashed headlong through the windscreen. The unexpected maneuver startled Caleb and the old man shifted his target at the last second and fired at the dog just as it collided with them.

Had Moses Platt been the size of most men, he would likely not have been able to avoid Britches's lashing jowls. Being that he already sat barely a hand above the steering wheel, however, he was able to duck and all but disappear. Somehow the dog still managed to get hold of the little man by his ear and take a sizable chunk of it even as Britches lost the better half of her left hind—to include the leg—to Caleb's buckshot. The air became a mist of blood and the mayhem sent the Model T careening off the road and into one of the town's few decent-sized trees. On impact, the mastiff was thrown clear and Moses cracked his nose on the steering wheel. Battered against the dashboard, Caleb was sorely bruised, but otherwise, by some grace, unscathed. That is, until the other mastiff, Black, set upon him.

Black desperately tried for the old man's neck. Caleb sacrificed his arm, throwing it up to shield his face. The dog took him by the triceps and tore deep. Black shook his massive head with a relentless fury and the damage to Caleb's arm was horrible. Caleb dropped his shotgun—which was spent of both barrels in any case—and feebly struck at the dog with his free hand. The blows were less than futile.

Moses was too stunned to help. As a result of the blow to his face his vision had gone dark for a few seconds, allowing the other dogs—the rest of the pack that had been secretly waiting off the street in ambush—to make good their assault. Before Moses could gather his wits, two dogs—sheep dogs by the look of them—were vying for his neck as well. He made an effort to fend them off, blindly throwing his arms about. It would only be a matter of time—seconds, likely—before his pathetic defense would no doubt fail.

Two factors came into play to save Caleb and Moses. The first was that several of the pack turned on the mortally wounded Britches instead of the easier and intended prey of the two men. It was not the normal way of dogs—be they domesticated or feral—but this, the animals did just the same. The second, and most deciding turn, was Maddie Thompson. As luck—if it could be called that—would have it, the Model T had smashed into the dogwood tree in front of the Thompson home. It was a tree Maddie had planted so many years before as a sapling when she and Patrick first moved to the town in their youth.

She knew of the dogs in the street. She'd been watching them, worried for her missing Patrick. So then, there was no delay in her arrival. She'd already been waiting, ready.

Maddie wasted no shots with the .30-30 Winchester she carried at her hip. She ignored the dogs nearest to her, the ones on Britches. Instead, she rushed to the auto. Steps from it, she brought the rifle to her shoulder and fired two shots at the dogs on Moses. She did this as quickly as she could work the gun action, hitting her mark both times with deadly accuracy. What she did next would later even surprise her. Cocking the lever action and chambering another round, she leaned across the dying dogs and the stunned Moses. Extending the rifle with one hand she stuck the barrel to Black's forehead and dispatched the giant animal in a point blank eruption of blood, brains, and scalp.

She spun about, ready to face the dogs she'd left in her wake. They were gone. Where they'd been, on the wooden deck that led to the porch of her home, what remained of

Britches was dragging itself toward her, hackles raised, one remaining eye wide, teeth bared. Maddie couldn't help but pity the thing even as she saw it meant her harm. She raised her rifle to end its misery, but, before she could fire a loud pop sounded from behind her. Britches fell, shot in the head. Maddie jerked around to discover Moses holding out his smoking pistol. His other hand cupped the stump of his ragged ear.

"Sorry, but I owed Britches that one," Moses said.

...

The rhythm of Dale's shovel work was as steady as the thrum of the locusts in the tall grass. Walter had returned to the crawl space in the attic above his room. From there he could hear Dale hard at work digging the grave in—of all places—the front yard.

Walter didn't remember the night just passed. He'd forgotten how he'd become excited and then frightened to know these men were on their way. The boy had forgotten how he'd took flight, racing off into the night—no destination in mind—only to run in circles and find himself back home. The men had arrived by then and young Walter could see their shadows moving about inside.

At first he thought they were his mother and father. He almost called out. He almost ran inside with tear-filled eyes desperate to embrace them, to be sorry for running away. Something held him back though. Something said to him, this is not right. He even heard the voice. It startled him and sent him dashing for the barn.

The old dead rooster was there. He lifted its limp corpse and began tossing it about the inky black of the barn between the wispy skins of light cast from the cracks in the walls, making a game of throwing the bird and finding it. He should tell his father the cock is dead, he thought. The old man wouldn't be so amused. He wondered where his father was. He thought he knew. It seemed on the tip of his tongue. With his mother, no doubt. But where was she? Walter couldn't answer that question either. A feeling of dread came over him. An image of his mother caked in blood suddenly invaded his mind. And then she was upon him there in the barn, a revenant, a creature, clawing at him.

The boy woke a few hours later in the hayloft. He didn't remember falling asleep. In fact, he awoke and lamented that he couldn't sleep. Hadn't slept in days. Weeks. In his arms, like some perverse stuffed animal, he'd been consoling himself with the old dead rooster. He held the old bird and wept again. He cried for the dead rooster, for himself, for his lost parents.

He would find them. He would take the bird to his father. Father would know what to do. Father would make the world right again.

Crossing the yard in the dark of night, the boy was stopped cold to see Merritt staring down at him from his own bedroom window, a scarecrow that didn't put young Walter off in the least, because then Walter Petry knew again some of what he'd lost. He remembered the men who had come to call. *These ravagers from across the sea.* They must have killed his parents. They killed everyone. He remembered what he must do. His heart filled with rage.

And so he set off into the night to be about it.

He was almost found out. Spying on them and giggling at their expense as they hungrily devoured the rotten and sick bird.

The scarecrow man alone after the others had left the room, pointing his big, shiny gun to the secret space in the wall between the cupboards where Walter hid. But then, after an eternity, the scarecrow put his gun back in the holster and went to the window to stare off into nothingness. *Maybe,* Walter thought, *he was watching him out in the yard again.* The boy wondered, *could he be both places at once?*

And now Walter was back up in the attic. Hot.

Unbearable heat. Hotter than he'd ever been in his life. He was so thirsty. Maybe his mother would bring him some water. He cried and called for her, but she did not come. *Would she never come?* Outside the digging continued. The man dug and dug, and the sound of it grew louder and louder. Walter knew it was this man with his digging that was keeping Mother from hearing his desperate cries.

Walter would shut this ravager up. He would bring peace to the farm again.

...

Patrick Thompson had been a young man when he first came to the town. He and his fresh-faced bride, Maddie, had arrived at the urging telegraphs of Caleb Sweet, the two men having met as they were both headed out west to seek their fortunes. The trail was months in traversing and along it they made fast friends. They'd parted ways upon reaching California, however, each seeking his own direction but vowing to keep in touch. It'd been several years gone by when Caleb was the first to make good on that promise when he unexpectedly tracked down and contacted his old friend, Pat, to send him news of the "paradise" he and his brother Wallace had carved out for themselves. Caleb was adamant that Patrick and Maddie should join them. Three months of what Maddie called "pester-grams" ensued and culminated with Patrick packing-up what little the young couple had and taking on the long journey to reunite with his old friend.

They would travel most of the way by train, until the track ran out, and then by stagecoach. When it was clear that the final leg, still a good week's travel shy of their destination, could only be completed by horseback and mule train, Patrick should have trusted Maddie's misgivings. Stubborn to a fault, however, he would not be deterred, and even after harrowing encounters with both bear and Indians—and the loss of their mules and much of their belongings—he saw his bride safely to their destination.

From the moment of their arrival it was sadly clear; there was no paradise. Dusty roads met at a crossroads converging on a struggling creek where a handful of clapboard ramshackle businesses huddled together as if holding one another up. The place was nothing more than a hardship's respite, offering the handful of local farmers and prospectors a place to meet and make exchanges out of the harsh sun and dry winds. The paradise Caleb had spoken of was nowhere to be seen and never to be found, but its promised arrival was ever-near and forever on Caleb

Sweet's lips.

The first several years were more than hard. But the same streak of Patrick's stubbornness that'd brought them, kept them. And now, so many seasons later, after the town had finally grown to see some hopes of true prosperity, it had come to this. Bound and battered, it looked to the old man as though he would perish in a hellish nightmare bloomed from the paradise promised.

Patrick pretended he was still unconscious when Mariel, the prostitute with the infected stump for an arm, came back to the room. Trussed up as he was with the door at his back, Patrick wasn't sure which of the women had entered, but whichever one, she was whispering. It was naught but nonsense the old man could barely make out, just catching a word here or there, but enough to know it wasn't Earl puttering around behind him.

"You must be thirsty," she said.

Patrick couldn't see her, but was sure she wasn't talking to him. He was thirsty, however, more so than he thought he'd ever been in his life.

"I wouldn't drink this, but I'll bet you will." She crossed the room to him. "Quit pretending you ain't awake or I'll poke out your eyes and put some pennies in there," she threatened.

It was enough. Patrick looked up at the woman to find her holding a chamber pot. It was white enamel with a twisting grape vine motif for a handle. His mother had one very similar to it when he was but a boy.

Mariel balanced it in her only hand, intentionally sloshing the contents. "Thirsty?" she asked in mock innocence.

Patrick closed his eyes and shook his head.

"Suit yourself," she said with a shrug and put the pot on the floor beside his foot. A good deal of stale and foul smelling urine spilled onto the floorboards as she did. It pooled momentarily into a dark yellow sphere, growing and gathering where the warp of the wood brought it together, until it reached its breaking point and ran off into a trickle that found its way to the carpet of golden spores surrounding the corpse of Patrick's companion, the town's miller, Curtis Toole.

Patrick watched the rivulet go. Within a few seconds it had dissipated, dispersed and sucked into the dry wood and seams of the untreated floor. After it was gone he looked to Mariel who he discovered had been similarly fixated on it. She matched his gaze, and for the briefest instant he thought he caught something of her old self. Across her face a slight and mischievous smile evolved into a frown. But then, as if acknowledging her transgression, she shook her head violently and the deranged Mariel reemerged.

"What did you do you naughty boy? You smell as bad as Curtis. You puke yerself?"

Patrick looked like a tail-tucked dog. He said nothing.

Mariel stroked the stubble of his cheek. "There, there. Don't you worry your pretty little noggin none. It'll all be over soon."

She grinned at him madly once more and he noticed two of her teeth, an upper canine and the incisor next to it, were now missing. Two bloody gaps ruined her once beautiful smile.

"Oh...you like that?" she asked and ran her tongue through the space.

Patrick closed his eyes and turned his face away. He waited for her to punish him. He was sure she meant to end him here and now. He held his breath. He prayed. When his lungs ran out of patience with him and his weary mind could no longer formulate coherent prayer, he took a breath and opened his eyes.

Mariel was seated cross-legged on the floor tracing a finger from the carpet of spores to the damp stain of the spilt urine.

"Mary, Mary, quite contrary, maybe that'll help my garden grow," she said and patted her hand gently. She rose in one quick motion that clearly left her dizzy. But for the grotesquely red and swollen trunk of her arm, she was ghostly pale and beaded with sweat. She turned back to Patrick once her spell had passed. "You sit tight, Mr. Fertilizer." She patted his vomit-stained knee, "And I'll bet you ol' stogies never thought some worthless, sinful, dirty little whore could become a farmer like you *proper* folk. Ha!" She ran out then as a child might leave a room, slamming the door behind her. She didn't go away entirely, however, as Patrick could hear her cackling just beyond the door long after she'd left.

"I never thought low of you, Mariel," Patrick said, certain she could hear him.

...

A fist-sized sphere of grey smashed through the bedroom window pane startling both Abigail Petry and Wallace Sweet out of their much needed rest. Glass sprayed across the room and Wallace accidentally threw himself into its path when he leapt to his feet from his chair with a speed belying his age. His was not the body of a young man, however, and for testing his worn joints so he paid with a spasm of pain. Abigail was similarly wracked, although her torment came from aggravating the wound to her stomach and was far worse. She cried out and Wallace feared she'd been struck. He hurried to the window to confront who'd assaulted them only to come to a loss. He stood at the window, a grave and perplexed expression overtaking him, and muttered something the woman could not make out.

"What is it? What's wrong?" she called.

Wallace shook his head and drew the curtain. "Nothing. Nothing at all." He turned back to collect the broken body of a mourning dove amongst the shards of glass scattered across the floor.

Even in her condition, Abigail would not be dismissed. "Nothing?"

"A bird," he said softly. "Just a mourning dove."

He dusted the glass from its feathers and lifted the lifeless creature to present the answer to their fright to Abigail. Wallace smiled to offer a bit of relief as he did so. Abigail was not so easily assuaged.

"An omen. An omen of death," she said, and cast a grim eye to the shattered window pane.

"No, Mrs. Petry. Now don't you vex yourself so. Bird striking a window is nearly about as natural and commonplace as lightning. Alarming, yes, to be sure, but plain natural."

He stooped slowly to take a knee and laid the dove down on the rug with a solemn nod of his head. Then he began collecting up the larger shards of glass.

Abigail turned back to him. "Careful. Mind yourself there," she said. "You'd do better with a whisk broom. Surely you have one."

"Aye, for certain you're right, Mrs. Petry."

It was far harder for Wallace to stand, especially following the flare-up his joints had just given him, and now with one hand filled with jagged pieces of glass.

"You forgot the bird," Abigail noted after he'd finally gotten back on his feet.

Wallace sighed heavily. "Right once more." He started for the door. "Do you need anything from the pantry, Mrs. Petry?"

"Some cool water would be nice." Without missing a beat she directed, "Wash your hands thoroughly if you don't mind. Use soap."

"Now of course I will, Mrs. Petry."

"Please," she said, "you know my name. Call me Abigail."

He nodded. "Abigail. That I do. A lovely name, I've always felt. That is, if you don't mind my saying."

She smiled politely. He thought that was that, but then she blurted out, "When are you going to keep your word?"

"I beg your pardon, Abi—"

"And I yours. But I can't stand on niceties. My boy, Mr. Sweet. You said you'd go for him. You gave me your word."

"I did. Yes, I did…and I will."

"Well then, go. I'll be fine until you get back."

Wallace shook his head. "I would prefer it to wait for my brother's return."

"And when will that be?" The impatience grew in her voice.

"Why, shortly. Any minute now, I'd suppose. He just went—"

"What if my Walter doesn't have minutes to spare, Mr. Sweet? What if—"

"Please...call me Wallace, Abigail."

The impatience begat anger. "Fine. Wallace. But what if—"

"If Caleb and Mr. Platt aren't back within the hour, then I'll go on ahead."

"Why wait then? Why—"

"Mrs. Petry!" Wallace finally snapped and then just as quickly caught himself. "Abigail...." He corrected himself and continued in a soothing tone, "You might have not noticed, but I am no spring chicken." He waited for her to interrupt again, but she held her tongue. "So then," he went on, "all things considered, I'd prefer to wait until my brother and Mr. Platt have returned and then one of them might accompany me." He could see this wasn't going to satisfy her. Before she could chide him again he added, "However, if the next hour comes to pass and they've not made it back by then, then I shall keep my promise and go look for your son Walter on my own."

"Thank you," she whispered.

"Right. Good and agreed then. You rest. I'll fetch the whisk broom and dustpan and I've not forgotten your cool water." He started again for the door adding with a wagging index finger pointed heavenward, "And I will cleanse my hands thoroughly first and foremost."

"Wallace," Abigail called after him. He stopped and turned back. "Honestly," she said, "Thank you. Thank you and the Lord bless and keep you."

His wet eyes twinkled as he nodded appreciation and offered a gentle wave to rebuff her gratitude as unnecessary. Without another word he headed off to attend to things.

Abigail settled back into her pillow. She breathed deep and concentrated to fill her mind with positive thoughts. She would not entertain her fears. The old man was right. She would brook no superstition. Walter was fine. Her son would be with her before the day was done, she told herself.

Just then—likely coming in through the broken window—the most horrendous fly, coarse black hairs jutting from between iridescent chitin plates of metallic green and blue, lit on her bandages and scurried across her stomach searching for any purchase to get at the wound beneath.

...

"Another whiskey, Mr. Sweet?" Earl asked with more than a sliver of eagerness tainting his query.

"I guess things been slow," Moses said. He slid his own glass closer to Caleb's to ensure he wasn't left out when Earl brought the bottle around.

They'd rushed in from the streets—Caleb, Maddie, and Moses—where they'd left the wrecked Model T hissing and ticking off the last of its heat in the growing midday sun. The three had only paused long enough to wrap

Caleb's arm in the torn-off hem of Maddie's dress before storming into the saloon with Maddie all but screaming for Patrick. She'd quickly grown quiet following Earl's claim that he'd not seen Patrick in three, maybe four, days. It was a poor lie and not one among the three believed the bartender, with Maddie doing an even poorer job of concealing her skepticism. Caleb was too injured to care—his head light and his arm searing—while Moses was merely content to be alive. The diminutive man had called for a drink and settled at the bar with the weary air of a man whose long day was done.

With Maddie befuddled, they'd lingered long enough for a third round while Caleb fretted over what to do next now that the woman's leadership had run out of steam. In the interim, Claudette had sashayed down the stairs. If Maddie had not favored the woman before, she loathed her now.

More whiskey was poured.

"Is it tender?" Claudette asked as she fussed over the makeshift bandage on Caleb's mangled arm. He winced in acknowledgement and took another long pull on his drink.

From behind the bar and over Caleb's shoulder, Earl called across the room to Maddie where she'd found herself absentmindedly scrutinizing the Brazen Head. "That's a grand idea, Mrs. Thompson. Good ol' Magellan, he might can tell you where it is Patrick's got himself off to. You need you some change?"

Claudette leaned closer to Caleb and licked a spattering of his blood from his forearm. When this shook the old man from his growing stupor she smiled innocently and he let her youth and beauty help him dismiss her bizarre act.

If only Moses and Maddie had not themselves become distracted. Moses drank deep and Maddie slipped further into her despair.

"Some folks say this be the end of days," Earl said, picking up again on the chatty banter he'd been bombarding them with since they'd entered. "Me, I says no such thing. There ain't nothing new under the sun. It's like the weather. Some days it's rain, most other days it's shine. But, by and by, when you're tired of the one, sure enough you'll be getting the other. And no sooner have you got your wish for this kind of weather or that, then you'll want your druthers and be wishing for the other to roll back around. Am I right?"

No one answered. Not one of them had heard a word he'd said.

The Brazen Head whirred to life.

"I didn't touch it," Maddie Thompson said defensively. She stepped away from the case and held out her palms as if doing so proved her honest.

"No, no. It does this from time to time these days. Seems like everything about this town has gotten a little screwy," Earl said. "Just read the slip there," he went on, stepping around from behind the bar. "That'll be your future. Go on, then. It's fun."

As promised, a slip of paper fell from the head's mouth as it returned to its inanimate state. Gingerly, and with the goading gestures from Earl, Maddie retrieved the slip out of the chute. She read it over silently and as she did her face twisted up. By this point all eyes were upon her and Earl was rapt with impatience.

"Well, are ya going to tell us what it says, or do we got

to—" Earl started, but then cut himself short. Moses turned a raised eyebrow to the man. Earl pretended not to notice. "So...go on then," he persisted.

"Stop pestering the woman, would you!" Caleb barked.

"It says," she said with a dramatic pause, "Your days are numbered. Beware the color yellow."

"What's that?" Earl asked and crossed to her. "Here now, lemme see that."

She handed it to him. "See for yourself." She was glad to be rid of it.

"Don't that beat all," Earl said.

"What?" Moses asked.

The bartender held the slip out before him. "This here is the exact same fortune I got the other day. The exact same."

"So?" Moses said.

"So? So? See here, you know how much money I paid for this contraption?"

"No," Moses said and poured himself another shot.

"A pretty penny, that's how much. A very pretty penny!"

"I still say *so*. Looks like it's working to me."

"No, sir. No, it is not," Earl argued. "That man promised me this here...this...*Brazen Head*...that it would never give the same fortune twice. Each one an original. He gave his word. And they're supposed to be entertaining. Cheerful. Not this...this...."

"I don't see the big deal," Moses said.

"You don't, do you?" Earl had worked himself up into a good lather. He rushed back behind the bar where he snatched the whiskey bottle and shot glass away from

Moses.

Hey now...." the small man protested.

"You want a drink?"

"Yes, I would, if you don't mind."

"Well here you are," Earl said, dumping out the half shot of whiskey and refilling the glass from a pitcher he quickly produced from beneath the bar.

He slapped the amber drink down in front of Moses.

Moses eyed it with suspicion. "What's that?"

"That? Why that'd be your drink, Mop," Earl said with a cocky air about him.

Moses sniffed it. It told him nothing. Nonplussed but undaunted, he tasted a sip. "That's tea," he said with a disgusted spat.

"And so now you know," Earl said.

"Know what?"

"The outrage of not getting what you've asked for. What you were promised. What you paid for!"

Claudette snorted a laugh that she couldn't keep down. Her amusement did nothing for Moses's disposition.

"Say, where's the other whore?" Moses asked casually. The drink had loosened his spirits and his tongue.

"Beg your pardon?" Claudette hissed, her own demeanor turning about.

"I don't employ no such here, *Mister Platt*," Earl said.

"My mistake...dance hall girl. Where's the other dance hall girl?" He slid the shot glass of tea back to the bartender and gestured for him to refill it from the bottle.

Earl was vexed momentarily, but then, when Moses laid a bill out on the bar, he came around and obliged him. He produced a fresh glass, and, as he was pouring, he answered Moses.

"Mariel, my other *dancehall* girl, is sick. Upstairs."

Maddie perked up at this. "Sick?"

"How so?" Caleb asked.

"No, no...nothing like that," Earl fumbled. "She's...just..." He looked to Claudette, but the woman was no help. "We were fooling around. Bored, before you all got here. It's been real slow the last week or so." He paused there. He had their attention. He'd rather he didn't.

Finally Caleb grew impatient. "So, how's that got anything to do with her being sick?"

"Oh, nothing at all, really. We were bored and she was blabbing her jaw going on and on about how hungry she was." Sweat was dripping down the man's face. "She just...ate something she shouldn't. You know after we dared her...like a game." No one said anything and suddenly Earl was compelled to blurt out. "Was her fault," he said, pointing an accusing finger at Claudette.

"Was not!" she argued back.

"Yes it was. It...it was your idea," he stammered. "I ain't afraid of you, woman."

Caleb wasn't sure if it was the whiskey, his blood loss, all their nonsense, or all of the three combined, but he suddenly realized he didn't know what they were all talking about. So he made that much clear. "What the blue blazes are you two talking about?" he demanded.

Earl tossed his bar towel over his shoulder and threw up his hands. "Nothing. We aren't talking about nothing," he said, directing the last of his reply to Claudette. She shrugged.

Moses finished his new drink in one slug and spoke up.

"These two here," he pointed to Earl then Claudette and then back to Earl again. "They dared that other little gal to eat something stupid. She did. It didn't agree with her," he said as matter-of-factly as a drinking man might.

Claudette suddenly burst into hysterical laughter as though she'd just been witness to the funniest joke of her life. She laughed and laughed some more, finding even more hilarity for being the only one in on the joke. It was a boisterous fit that was too loud, and went on too long, and she cackled and cried all while seeming to want to stop but not being capable. Maddie thought it was as though she were the victim of the relentless tickling of invisible hands. As her fit continued, it made the men uncomfortable and Maddie irritated.

"It ain't that damned funny, Claudette," Earl eventually shouted over her. But his admonishment only served to make her fits worse.

...

Patrick was awakened by the ruckus downstairs. Apparently he'd slipped into unconsciousness again and when Claudette's hysterics finally roused him, he did so to find Mariel sitting cross-legged at his feet between him and the mushroom colony that had been Curtis. Mariel was chewing on one of the larger mushrooms and she held the stalk to her yellow-stained lips and whispered, "Shh…don't you give us away now. Don't you let Claudette hear us. Don't you call her."

The woman's pupils were so dilated that her eyes looked to be nothing but black marbles. Doll's eyes.

Whether Patrick would have called for Claudette, even without Mariel's warning, was something he doubted. Having been warned, however, made him think otherwise. He assumed it meant there were folks downstairs other than the deranged Claudette and her conspirator Earl. Not that figuring this out mattered. The cleaver lay across Mariel's lap. Patrick curled his toes and strained to pull his feet as far back away from her as he could. Mere inches.

Mariel began to recite a nursery rhyme. "This little piggy went to market. This little piggy stayed home…."

"Please…."

Downstairs, the woman's horrible laughter continued.

Chapter Eleven

The stallion reared high above Dale and its massive bulk blotted out the sun. Fore hooves pawed the sky wildly, the mad beast all but climbing into the clouds. It finally made some sound then—having come upon him without warning—an angry snort followed by something that reminded Dale of frightened sheep. If the horse was afraid, however, it apparently had decided to face its fears head on. It meant to trample the man to death.

Dale had been hard at work—preoccupied to a fault—digging Evan's grave. In fact, he was past waist deep into his work and nearly finished. He'd not taken any breaks save for pausing every ten minutes or so of the past few hours to vomit and retch. The dinner of chicken had not settled well and nearly every bit of it had come back up, not that this had relieved Dale of the sickness.

The sun was thankfully no longer directly overhead, but casting long shadows across the yard. When the horse reared, the sun was suddenly eclipsed and the unsuspecting man turned to find the source, his own horse, rearing over him. It was only because Dale had the hole to crouch in that the stallion failed to crush his skull with its iron shod hooves.

Still, the hole was quite narrow—no casket was planned—and it afforded little retreat. Dale turned away and ducked, best he could, as the horse brought its fury down on him. As Dale cowered, he stabbed upward with the shovel back over his shoulder. Only one hoof landed successfully, striking Dale's shoulder blade with the resounding crack of bone. Dale was knocked senseless to the bottom of the hole, but not before he managed to inflict his retaliation.

The force of Dale's defensive stab with the shovel was only half-hearted, but the horse's hoof crashing down was not so feeble. Unfortunately for the animal its flailing forelimb connected with the blade of the shovel, near-severing away the foot at a point just between the hoof and ankle. So, as the first hoof knocked Dale into the earth, the crippled animal came down on its other severed leg. Wide-eyed, lips drawn taught and nostrils flaring, the stallion pitched headlong into the grave on top of Dale, the sound of more bones failing as it went.

Merritt was in the house. He was pacing from room to room. He needed to find something…to do something…he couldn't say what or which or why. Confusion battered his senses. Light seemed too bright one moment and in the very next he found himself groping as if plunged in shadows. Odd smells came and went and these taunted his mind, dredging up memories he'd rather forget. Blood. He kept smelling blood. He became angry. Recollections from his childhood invaded his mind, one on top of the other. Waves upon the sand. Eroding his mind.

Just like his brother, Merritt had been battling the sickness brought on by the meal of rancid, diseased and undercooked chicken. He'd long emptied his stomach's contents and been reduced to dry heaves which no longer required he find a sink or toilet. Now he wandered the house like its resident specter. In fact, he wondered if perhaps that was what had become of him.

At one point, as he stood lost at the foot of the stairs, he thought he saw a child, a boy, watching him through the rails on the second floor. Merritt called up to him. He swore to the youth that he wouldn't hurt him. A lie. No response. Sweat filled Merritt's eyes. Stung like salt and vinegar pickling the orbs. He rubbed with the back of his hand and dug the knuckles of his greasy fingers into the sockets. The boy was gone by the time he'd finished. Had the boy even been there? Maybe he was the boy. This was a dream.

Odd screaming erupted from a commotion outside. Good. Something to shoot. Someone to kill.

Merritt burst from the house and down off the porch to find the earth swallowing a horse, Dale's horse, saddled, but rider-less. Hind legs desperately kicked at the heavens, seeking purchase where none was to be found. Merritt wasn't sure of what to do. Merritt was sure of what to do. He charged.

Two quick shots from his right-hand gun, followed by a third single shot from his left, and then finishing off with two more quick shots from his lead. The last two just for good measure. The horse was dead after the second shot had finished dancing around inside its ribcage.

He'd pressed his charge on the horse even as he fired his last, superfluous shots.

And then the world was quiet once more. Still wary of the animal, he stood several feet away, rigid but for eyes darting, fingers undulating over his gun triggers like worms drawn up by rain and drowning in it. The earth seemed no longer interested in a meal of dead flesh, however, and so the horse remained half-consumed, still as a stone, still as Merritt. Would the ground open up and devour him now? It was only the briefest of concerns. He'd gladly go down to hell. See what all the fuss was about.

Nothing of the sort happened.

Merritt began methodically reloading his guns from his belt. Cartridges were dwindling, he noted. Only some dozen or so remained. He took his time. Reloaded, he holstered the guns and, hands to his hips, admired the remains of the day. He sucked in a double barrel dose of air and held it for several long seconds before exhaling with an overly-dramatic, "Ahh!"

Merritt thought—but would never say out loud for fear of a jinx—that it was good to be alive.

He turned and was startled to find he'd been being watched. Startled mostly to realize he'd been caught unawares, off-guard. He usually had a sixth sense for those sorts of things.

From a window upstairs there was the boy again, an apparition hard to discern through the grime and glare of the panes. Evan, meanwhile, stood on the porch, no such shroud to conceal him and twice as troubling for it. His appearance of scalded, sloughing flesh—which was also bruised, battered, and ravaged by insects—made him a far more disturbing figure.

Merritt went for his gun but didn't draw. It'd be plenty easy to kill Evan if need be. That is, if the dead could be killed.

Evan blinked and cleared his throat. "I watched," he said. He nodded up to one of the windows above him. "From upstairs. I watched. It was the damnedest thing. That horse...it snuck up on him like a cat taking a bird."

"What's that now?" was all Merritt could muster. He

stole a glance back up to the boy in the window. He was gone. A play of light?

"Dale's stallion," Evan said. "I said I saw it crept up on him, head hung low until the last second. Attacked him. His own horse. No reason. I think it might have killed him." Evan pointed out past Merritt to the horse in the hole.

Then, confirming all but Evan's last statement, a moan rose up from the earth, from beneath the dead horse. Dale had regained consciousness. No sooner had he come around from the double blow of the hoof to his back coupled with the animal thrashing down upon him, then he howled in pain from the dead weight of it crushing into his shattered scapula.

...

The boy had watched it all from his bedroom window. He'd come down from his secret place in the attic. He'd tired of playing cat and mouse. He didn't even bother to see if anyone was in his room before he opened the hatch. He was going to yell at the man to go away, to stop digging. The noise of it keeping him awake. The shovel scraping his ears. But then, once Walter had gotten to his bedroom window—still undiscovered—he was curious to see the horse. Not a horse he knew. It must have been the man's horse. How odd, it played a little game and snuck up on the man as he dug. The man didn't see. His back was turned all while he dug on and on, never satisfied, never tired. He was chipping away at the end of the trough he'd dug, ignorant to his horse and the game it played with him.

It made the boy cry. Not much, but just a bit. He wasn't

a little girl, after all. But still he cried. He envied the man to have such a keen horse. *A horse that would play games. Even better than a dog. Old Paint, his horse, had never known any games.*

The man's horse was right there at the edge of the hole now. Wouldn't the man get the surprise of his life? Walter reached out a sweaty hand for the window to open it, thinking to spoil the horse's fun. He would be in on the game as well. The winner.

But too late. As Walter took hold of the sash, the horse rose up. He rose up and all hell broke loose. *Not such a neat horse after all.* Walter thought maybe he screamed. Or maybe the man screamed. He wasn't sure. Gunshots drowned out everything. Walter ran. Like a mouse once more, he scurried back to his secret hiding place.

His father had never cared for visitors, and now Walter understood why.

He missed his father. He missed how they would spend their Sunday mornings at the breakfast table. Sunday mornings were his favorite. The only Sunday chores were to feed the chickens and collect any eggs. That was it. No school. No other chores. Certainly no church. And then they would have their breakfast. Sunday breakfast was always the best. The biggest. Sausages and flapjacks. Father had eggs over easy and sipped down four gallons of coffee while Walter read the weekly paper to him. He didn't sit on his knee anymore like he used to, but still he read. They'd pull their chairs close together and Walter would run his finger beneath the lines of newsprint as he went, Father following along and making the hard words easy. "Sound it out," he'd say. "Sound it out." Mother would smile her approval and nod. The world was right then.

He missed them and wished for all his life that he could remember where they'd gone. He wasn't angry anymore for them leaving. Had been, but not anymore. He swore he wasn't. He swore with cusses and swears, too. The kind that used to make his mother take his supper away.

Walter had sworn quietly to himself at first, and then later he swore like his father out in the barn on bad days when the old man thought no one could hear. And then, thinking his swears might have been the cause for his troubles, the boy begged God to forgive him his transgressions. He wished he knew a Bible prayer. If he had he swore he would have prayed from his heart as he'd once heard you should. None of it came to anything, however. Not the swears, nor the offer of prayers. Mother and Father never came home.

Outside, the strange men fussed over the man in the hole. Alive after all. His howls proved that. Walter knew them by their voices. He'd heard them. Spied on them close. The two scarecrow twins and their fat friend. The fat one had wet Walter's bed. Walter hadn't done that in years, and now here this fat burnt man had peed Walter's bed. If Mother ever did come home she'd be mad. She'd be mad and no doubt she'd blame Walter. How he wished they'd go away. They wouldn't. Howling and howling. Walter plugged his ears. The man was hurt bad—must be—and so the howling wedged its way past his fingers.

All around Walter his secret hiding place was in bloom. The golden mushrooms that the boy had originally collected and brought there were now dried, dead, and shriveled, but their children thrived, spreading not only along much of the floor, but now a few silly caps even hung upside down from the slant of the roof. Walter wondered if his mother would ever see. She loved to garden. How proud she would be of his crop.

He tip-toed along the attic beams, relieved to realize the strangers had finally grown quiet. Maybe his father had come home and run them off. Maybe his mother. Or both! He doubted that, however. If only he could remember where they'd gotten off to. Walter plucked one slender mushroom from the ceiling and snuck it into his mouth. And then the boy remembered too much.

...

Wallace Sweet needlessly crept around the downstairs of his home. There was no real chance that Abigail Petry could hear the old man from her convalescence bed in the last room of the long hall upstairs. No matter. He winced at every inadvertent noise he made, a dropped tea spoon here, an accidentally slammed cupboard there, shuddering plumbing, and each squeaking floorboard, hinge and doorknob. He would freeze and cock his head to better discern whether she might have heard him.

He'd given the woman his word that he would go back out to her farm. He'd said he'd go whether his brother and Moses Platt returned or not. It'd been an easy promise to make when he thought they'd be coming back, when he thought he would not need to go alone. Hours had passed. It was late afternoon and still there'd been no sign of the two men. Wallace had broken his promise. As the hours had slipped by, Wallace at first had been greatly concerned for their passing. That had eventually changed, however, as a plan sprung to his mind. It was a plan requiring even more time to pass. His hope now was for the woman to sleep long enough to make his scheme feasible. And all the while there was the hope that Caleb and Mr. Platt might yet return.

Wallace wasn't proud of what he'd made up his mind to do. But his pride and integrity were easily trumped by his instinct to survive. He had no intention of making the trek to the Petry farm alone. He'd seen the dogs firsthand. He fretted over his brother and Moses Platt's absence. He knew that some townsfolk had gone mad. "Mad dogs and madmen," he said several times. He was afraid.

"Better a liar than a fool. A dead fool," he muttered to himself.

He'd retreated to the kitchen where he thought his little movement was best concealed from Abigail. He took turns sitting in the corner with his trusty shotgun and absentmindedly watching out the window where nothing changed except for the length of the shadows.

It was during one of these wistful breaks at the window that Wallace thought about the first time he'd seen Abigail Petry some twenty years gone by now. He and his brother Caleb had braved the fierceness of the dry season to go in search of the hopeful migrants passing through and headed west, or the failed westerners giving up and hightailing back east. The brothers would make their best case to convince them to halt their journey and join their small town instead.

The brothers would make the circuit of the distant

pockets of civilization—such as they were—and also the regularly trafficked trails, spending a few days at each stop making their pitch and promises to any and all who would listen. They'd done this three times before, and on each occasion they'd brought several more members to their community. They were half-through their most recent recruitment expedition when they crossed paths with the Petrys. They'd already wrangled six good folk to their fold, two young couples—one with a daughter of eight or nine— and a single gentleman who had designs on opening a barbershop, and the brothers agreed the success bolstered their chances to gather in more.

The Petrys were met on the open trail. They were a lone wagon, a man and a woman, a risky endeavor. Two pitted against a bewildering and unforgiving terrain of flash floods and drought, predators and the dangerously unpredictable, snakes and mountain lions and wolves and man. The last being by far the worst of the lot. Even a broken bone could bury a body along the trail. Ignorance of so harsh an environment could prove fatal, and all too often did.

Abigail Petry was beautiful. So much so that Wallace had let Caleb do all the talking. She remained quiet. Wallace found himself wondering what voice was hidden behind her perfectly shaped doll-like pursed lips. Her skin was fair, porcelain like a china doll as well. Too fair for the sun and hellish air of the region, even with the great bonnet she wore, Wallace thought.

Abigail Petry remained stoic with a small box in her lap, seated next to the man whose name she'd taken just eight months prior. Wallace incorrectly assumed her reticence derived from subservience to her husband, as most religions bade she be. Abigail made no sign of hearing the men's conversation, not even allowing her eyes to consider them as they spoke. Instead, she kept her focus on the trail ahead.

The exchange was unbelievably short. Caleb explaining himself, talking as fast as his tongue could wag. He painted a floral portrait of their town and how he hoped the couple might come see it at the very least. The isolation of the place was pitched as a boon. The ways of the "outside" world were shunned. It was a place where folks could be to themselves. To live and breathe with no laws but their own laws. Theirs was a paradise not unlike Eden, Caleb extolled.

Bill Petry asked for a moment to consider Caleb's offer and confer with his bride. He whispered a few words to Abigail. She nodded and stroked the box in her lap. It was agreed.

As the small party took turns shaking hands mightily, wiping the sweat from their brows, and otherwise exchanging all manner of introductions, only Wallace noticed the beautiful woman's grief.

...

"What are you doing?" Abigail asked.

They were not on the trail. It was not twenty years ago when they'd first met. It was the here and now, the kitchen of Sweet Wood, the brother's home, and Abigail Petry leaned against the doorjamb with one hand to hold her steady and the other pressed across her stomach as if to hold herself together. The gouges along her arm where she'd clawed herself were swollen and red against the pale skin Wallace had so admired once upon a time. Now, she looked like a ghost. Or worse. The transformation did nothing to diminish the man's desire.

"Mrs. Petry," Wallace startled, jolted back to the present. "Here, here, Abigail, how did you...? You shouldn't be on your feet."

"You said you'd go for my boy, Mr. Sweet. What are you doing? Why are you still here? You said you'd go. You promised."

She looked on the verge of fainting and so Wallace rushed to bring her a chair over with him as he hurried to her aid.

"Sit, sit," he urged. His mind was racing for an answer to her barrage of questions.

"No. I will not sit. You promised."

He could see she would not be swayed. How she'd managed to get from bed all the way downstairs and right up on him without his hearing was a mystery that he'd no time to solve. As he fumbled to explain himself, he almost let slip the lie he'd been toying with. But then he looked into her eyes. A mistake. Wallace could not deceive her. Not to her face at least, and not in her fragile state. He held her by the arm and whispered emphatically, "Please, Abigail. You must trust me. You must let me take you back to bed."

She refused to move or speak. Wallace bowed his head. "I'm going. Just as soon as I have you to bed. That's why I had the shotgun. See here? I'm going."

She gave him a hard look. She clearly had her doubts.

But she was too tired to fight. With no more words she let him lead her away.

As they crossed the parlor she stopped them to consider the stairs. "I can't," she said.

He judged the ascent and agreed. "You can take Mr. Platt's room, just down the hall here. And this way he's sure to look in on you right away when he and Caleb get back in." He smiled, but it was lost on her fatigue.

"Your brother…and Mop…they've not returned?" A bit of despair found its way into her voice, a cat creeping in shadows.

"Not just yet, no."

There was nothing left for either of them to say. Wallace made Abigail comfortable once more, this time in Moses Platt's bed, and then in quick order brought her a large thermos of hot soup, two apples, a pitcher of slightly sweet tea, utensils, and a tray of cornbread. He fetched a clean bedpan from upstairs and placed it without comment along with a quarter-filled wash basin and clean washcloths and a towel on the nightstand opposite. Lastly, he tucked one of his brother's .32 caliber pistols under her pillow with a knowing nod shared between them.

"I'd be relieved to know you'll be sure to announce your intentions and know your target before that sees any use. Remember, Mr. Platt and Caleb will expect you to be upstairs," he said before announcing he'd best be off.

He paused at the door. "I may need to stay the night out to your place…so…well…so if I don't get back directly, don't you fret none," he said.

"We," she corrected.

"Pardon?"

"You said *I*. You mean *we*. You and my son, Walter."

"Of course. We. Walter and I. The two of us will be back by morning. Sure as the sun." He left her with another smile.

From the kitchen he quickly collected a half-loaf of bread, a link of salami, and cold thermos of tea. He almost forgot the torchlight from the front hall table and had to go back for it. He tested the light and shook it to see whether it would stay lit. It did. *Yes, it works for now*, he thought wryly. He added four more shotgun shells to the four already stuffing his front pant pockets. As he locked the back door behind him, he wondered for the hundredth time what had become of his brother and Mr. Platt. The thought of the wraith-like arms clawing out of the saloon doors to snatch Patrick Thompson made Wallace shiver and he couldn't bear to entertain the image further.

He adjusted his wire-rimmed spectacles and pulled the brim of his prized Stetson cowboy hat down low and snug over his eyes. It was the last Stetson his father had owned, the most expensive brown felt, long worn-out past its prime, but his now. Too many times he'd teased his brother Caleb that he'd leave it to him when he passed. "That-a-way you can wear it for at least a week or two," he'd add with a mischievous twinkle.

Tightening his grip on the shotgun, Wallace rushed off across the lawn stealing nervous glances over his shoulders as he went. His mind, meanwhile, went to strange places.

Of the folks the Sweet brothers had recruited along with the Petrys on that trip so many years gone by now, the childless couple did not stay, but moved on to no one could say where. This after the woman's second pregnancy failed in just as many years. The other couple, the Giles, they'd remained, however, and were blessed with three more children along with the daughter they already had. Presently, some of those children were having children of their own.

The would-be barber never married, but he had remained and even opened his shop as intended. In fact, Wallace and Caleb had helped build it, just as they'd promised when they'd sought to convince him to join them. Over the years to follow, the barber did well enough for himself, trimming and shaving beards, cutting hair, pulling teeth. To this day, he was still the town's only barber, although his business had grown leaner in the seven years since the arrival of an accredited and certified dentist deprived him of the five dollars he usually extracted from his client's wallet for each tooth yanked from their jaws. Just the same, the barber refused to take down the enormous, weathered and paint-flaked molar that hung suspended above his barber pole, fruitlessly advertising his obsolete services.

As Wallace reached the barn—the garage and stable really, where Moses kept the automobile and horses—he was reminded that someone had burned the Milton's barn down just recently. It's not barns they're burning, he told himself as he slipped inside. There was also the dentist's home and office that'd been set fire to, just as the Sweet brothers' own funeral parlor had been likewise destroyed the same night as the Giles's barn.

But he'd be safe here, Wallace assured himself. After all, Mr. Platt had fared well enough the night prior. His reasoning was specious and he knew it. He chose to ignore the voice that said so.

Wallace opened the barn side door and flicked on the torch to inspect the shadows. A blurred scurry of something, maybe the size of a human head—all fur or feathers—flitted across the torch's searching beam, this but for an instant, before the thing found concealment in the barn's cluttered and cavernous gloom once more. He cast the light about after it, but all to no avail. Sporadic images of tractors and tools, benches covered in machine parts, saddles, coils of rope, spools of cable, lengths of chain, jars and cans, barrels and hay bales. The place was quiet. On any other day Wallace would have ordered Mr. Platt to seek out and exterminate whatever the thing had been, and the old man would not have entered the barn until the reliable Moses had seen to it. This was no ordinary day, however.

Wallace peeked back out across the lawn one last time and once satisfied, ducked in, closing the door to secure himself inside.

He'd be fine for the night, he repeated to himself as he became one with the dark place. The odor of manure and petrol saturated the air, clung to him. "Dung and diesel," he complained. He wondered how Moses stood it. Wallace Sweet rubbed his nose with his kerchief as he waited for his eyes to take to the pitch.

His plan was to hole up in the loft as Moses had the night prior. Come dawn, he'd go back to the house and tell Abigail he'd been out to her farm and found it abandoned. He would argue that those who'd fled the town had likely taken-in the boy as part of their exodus. Then, if his brother and Moses had still not yet returned—and with more daylight at his disposal—he'd go in search of horses and a wagon or buggy to get himself and Abigail very far, far away from this accursed place. San Francisco, perhaps.

"Balderdash. I'm not afraid of any child," he argued out-loud with his guilty conscience as he settled down for the night. He laid his bundle of supplies out before him and began slicing the hard salami. "Probably dead or run off on any account. Loco as the rest of them."

He chewed on wedges of salami despite having no appetite and was getting groggy even as he wondered if he'd be troubled to find sleep. His jaw was sore yet from his fistfight with Caleb. The blood from Caleb's injured hand that sweat hadn't washed away had caked along with dust and dirt to fill the folds and creases of the old man's neck and face. His clothes were similarly stained, although in that regard it was mostly Abigail's blood and it was much more copious.

He sat in the shadows of the loft, flummoxed and put off that he'd not thought to change clothes. The stains were long dried and so he picked them, plucking away the cracking bits where he could.

He knew he must reek of it. "A fine time to stink of the slaughterhouse," he bemoaned. With no remedy available, however, he eventually decided to let the worry go. He was safe, he reminded himself. Mr. Platt had been fine here. The dogs had been right below and couldn't get at Moses Platt for all their bedeviled wiles.

His mind turned to his missing brother. "Oh, Caleb," he sighed. "Caleb, Caleb, Caleb."

Wallace had failed to consider how the dogs had gotten into the barn to corner Moses in the first place. He'd assumed—without giving it even an iota more of consideration—that Moses had left the stable doors open behind him. Moses Platt had not.

...

Mariel dreamed. Like the slumber of an infant in the womb, hers was a sleep untainted by any knowledge or understanding of the world as mankind knew it. She dreamt a place of sensation. Colors produced responses of pain and pleasure, numbness and cold, fire and warmth, hunger and satiation, each overwhelming and all of them equally welcome.

She lay in a thick pool of blood at Patrick's bare feet, curled up like a faithful dog. The stump of her severed and swollen arm kept her cleaver tucked into her bosom as if it were her beloved.

Patrick's face was turned down upon her, but his eyes were glazed and unblinking. From his mouth a froth of dirty yellow—like ocean detritus, storm-whipped up onto the shore—heaved and rolled out of his slack-jawed mouth with each breath. It was the only real sign that life still lingered within him. The mushrooms Mariel had decided to force down his throat had been for the most part spat up, but their wonder had still bound the man's faculties in a grip tighter than any physical ties Mariel could have applied to his limbs.

Hidden in the grip of Mariel's remaining hand, the pinky toe that she'd lopped off Patrick's right foot had finally been forgotten by both. Thankfully for Patrick, she'd fed him the mushrooms before the cleaver fell, and so he'd even giggled along with her as she'd swung.

...

Merritt stood over the messy tangle of the dead horse trapping Dale at the bottom of what was to have been Evan's grave. Dale moaned and Merritt did nothing. Evan remained on the porch. His concern for Dale and the bizarre behavior of the horse had elapsed. Now Evan was fighting to suppress his mirth.

"The sun is setting, eh, big brother?" Evan said.

After the pause of a slow-witted man, Merritt looked to the horizon. There was still an hour of good light. That, and at least another half-hour of dusk.

"No," Merritt disagreed.

"That's not what I meant," Evan purred. "Probably wasn't best to shoot him while he was all gummed up on top of Dale like that. Don't see how we're moving twelve hundred pounds of horse flesh from out of there."

Merritt turned to face Evan. Dale had grown quiet once more. "Why don't you take your stinkin' corpse out to the barn," he said. It wasn't a request. "See about a tractor or such to get this sorry animal up off your brother."

Evan raised the charred flesh where an eyebrow used to reside and cocked his head with an amused and quizzical expression. "Or such?" he questioned.

Merritt wasn't going to abide much more. His voice went flat, his expression indifferent. "A winch, pulleys, a come along, maybe some sort of rig to set up over this here hole. You're the smart one. I trust you'll figure something out."

"*Trust*. What a wonderful word."

When his comment failed to elicit even a hint of reaction from Merritt, Evan knew to leave well enough alone. As Evan ambled off to do his brother's bidding, Merritt turned his eyes on the horizon again. He called after Evan just before he turned the corner of the house. "If you can't find nothin' better…bring an axe."

Evan screwed his face up in disgust at the notion. He knew who would be on the handle end of that back-breaking, grisly task.

The Petry's barn was well kept. A string of bare bulbs hung from a wire that was strung along the center beam, but either all the bulbs were bad or the electricity had failed.

Evan found a light switch and flicked it several times. Nothing. He wondered if perhaps there might be another. He shrugged and let it go. Satisfied with the light from the open barn doors he began his search. He took his time. He was in no hurry. Dale was dead or dying and he hoped it was the latter. As far as Evan was concerned, a purgatory of pain would serve Dale right.

"My brother, my grave-digger," he muttered.

He had to chuckle when he realized the stench of the place wasn't the place at all; it was him. Burnt flesh and body odor.

I should shit my pants and complete my masterpiece, he thought. It made him grin.

He spent some minutes searching the empty chicken coop. He realized he was hungry. *Fiercely hungry*. He hoped for an egg and likely would have sucked it, not bothering with whether it was bad or not.

From there he moved on to the stable. Empty as well. And clean enough to make him wonder if any horse had ever resided there.

"What the hell happened to our horses?" he asked himself as he toyed with the pitch fork hanging near the stall. "My horse...." He said, trailing off as he recalled the snippets of his recollection. Shooting his horse and taking Gale's. And then he nodded as he recalled the old Colonel. The horrible fire. Gale's horse ablaze and tearing off into the night.

"And Dale's horse," he said, stabbing a finger in the direction of his dead or dying brother.

"The haul!" he all but shouted as he suddenly realized he'd no idea where it was.

Almost comically he covered his mouth to hush himself. He quickly found a stool to sit on. It was just outside the stable door, kept there for tending the horse's hooves. Evan sat quietly for a long while, at turns nodding his head and then shaking it. Clearly he was at odds.

When he settled on the truth that he was getting nowhere—and fearing his mind would fail him again—he started up a chant. "The haul. The haul. The haul." Eventually his fear came to fruition. He rose from his stool and began his search for what he could not say. His mnemonic chant melted away to silence.

There indeed was a tractor. It perched on thick wooden blocks with the two front tires removed, rims and all, and lying nearby. Evan paused briefly in thought before checking back to the open doors to see that Merritt wasn't coming along. Then he rushed back to the tractor and propped open the hood. He plucked out the distributor along with a few other wires and hid them behind a stack of crates in the corner.

"Get them tires on," he said, hiking up his shoulders and throwing out his chest, imitating Merritt. "I would Merritt," he then feigned his own supposed and innocent reply, "But look here, the engine is all busted to blazes."

Evan was wiping his hands on his pants—oh so proud of his quick thinking—when he realized the keys dangled in the tractor's ignition. All he had needed to do was toss them.

Suddenly, like the surprise of a bee sting, his hands erupted in fire. Thankfully it was naught but a brief flash of pain. Just the same, it knocked him to his knees, stealing his breath and choking his throat. As it passed, washing out from him like a receding wave on the shore, he held out his hands and saw that the palms had peeled away a bit when he'd rubbed them on his pants. He ran his fingers gently along the horrible terrain of his charred arm. Evan was waking from something. This he realized. That he wasn't in constant agony was a remarkable fact he finally had the sense to appreciate. He considered his arm again and then feared for what had become of his face. He wept.

Evan Evers was drowning in his self-pity when the axe landed almost at his feet. With the thud of impact, dust kicked up around it capturing the feeble light. The surprise of it shook Evan, and rightly so, and he looked up to the rafters and loft to see who had thrown it down. Hay bales and shadows.

"Who's there?"

There was no reply.

He repeated his demand and was met with the same

quiet.

Evan would have no doubt searched out his unseen companion. Would have, had Merritt not screamed his name from the front yard.

"Evan! God damn all, man, move yer hide!"

The axe at Evan's feet spoke as well. *"Yes, move your hide."*

Or did he say it? Evan Evers couldn't be certain. The pain was returning. The dust motes were settling from their golden dance around the axe. His mind's-eye flickered like the choppy images of a silent movie. Ants and birds and shovels of earth....of blood.

They had dug his grave. Dale and Merritt. His brothers.

"*Brothers?*" the axe was there questioning...answering.

Ants were feeding on his heart, his intestines...his brain. Birds at his eyes. His brothers wouldn't save him. His brothers had dug his grave.

The sun, although now soft and teasing with the promise to tuck behind the line of distant trees, still seared Evan's tender flesh. It was hurting him more and more to move, but thankfully he didn't need to hurry. Evan's older brother was still too preoccupied keeping vigil over Dale and the horse. His back was to Evan. He didn't see him coming. His back was always to Evan. Evan approached.

If Merritt had bothered to look, he would have been struck by the way Evan carried the axe in both hands; how he gripped it with purpose. He would have seen his eyes.

But Merritt didn't see his brother coming. Without even bothering to regard him, Merritt scolded the man when he heard his footfalls approaching from behind. "About damned time. What the hell kept you?"

As the last words slipped from his mouth, Merritt did notice, however, the thin shadow that rose above his own head.

...

When it became clear that Claudette would continue to rave and cackle, Moses pushed himself back from the bar, and, getting a nod of agreement from Caleb, announced they'd be leaving.

"If you see Patrick Thompson or get any word of his whereabouts, we'd appreciate it if you let us know over to Sweet Wood," Caleb said to Earl. He'd tried to include Claudette in as well but she was a lost cause.

"Sweet Wood?" Maddie questioned. "But I need to be home…in case Patrick gets back there."

Caleb shook his head. "Sweet Wood will be safer. Wallace and Mrs. Petry are back there and we best be joining them before nightfall keeps us here."

Claudette howled at this.

"Good point," Moses said.

Maddie started to protest. "But—"

Caleb stopped her with a raised finger. "We'll swing by your place on the way. Maybe he's there. If he's not, we'll leave a note. He'll be along directly."

"Caleb," Maddie pleaded, "I still think—"

But this time it wasn't Caleb who cut her off.

The reverberating stomp of fast-moving booted feet came from outside along the saloon's wood plank sidewalk. The small group exchanged nervous glances, but before any could think to say or do more, a man, half-dressed in only jeans and cowboy boots, and as bloody as if he'd bathed in it, crashed through the doors. He was not alone. In his throttling grip was a bulging-eyed sheep dog. The two exploded into the room and were quickly down on the floor rolling about in a knotted fit of fur and bloody flesh.

Earl dropped the glass he'd been cleaning, letting it shatter on the floor as he snatched up his shotgun. Moses drew a pistol and stepped back while Caleb fumbled to take up his own shotgun. In her panic, Maddie worked the lever action of her rifle to chamber a new round, needlessly ejecting the perfectly good cartridge already there. Claudette only laughed and pointed in glee.

"More fun!" she whooped.

The shirtless man and the dog tangled on the floor as the men and Maddie all vied for a shot to dispatch the animal. And then, just as quickly as he'd burst in upon them, they began to realize one by one that the situation was not what it first appeared to be.

"What the hell?" Caleb muttered, slowly lowering his shotgun from his shoulder.

Moses immediately understood his employer's bewilderment and lowered his pistol as well. Maddie and Earl would need a moment more. Claudette called out what the men were just realizing.

"Fight that dead doggie! Fight 'em! Go, dead doggie, go!" she cheered.

It was true. The dog the man was so violently thrashing around with was dead, its body as limp as a worn raggedy doll.

Claudette clapped and cheered.

"Deputy Pine?" Moses asked incredulously. He wasn't

sure he recognized the bloody man, but his query was acknowledged.

Deputy Pine ceased his struggles and looked up at them from the floor. This revealed another chilling aspect. It was indeed Deputy Pine. Or, had been. Of his face he was missing both an eye and the entirety of his lower lip. The latter having been torn away down to the mandible, exposing the teeth and gums. His left hand was all but gone as well. Somehow it had been severed away such that only his thumb and forefinger remained.

"You ain't pretty no more!" Claudette cackled and let loose her girlish squeal.

The deputy cocked his head and shifted his jaw with a disturbing grinding of teeth that almost sounded like a growl. Then he lunged. If Claudette was afraid, her laughter belied it. She did throw her hands up in defense, at least. Although that kept the deputy from her throat, Pine was satisfied to bury his teeth into her arm instead. He wasn't satisfied with biting down. The chunk he came away with was significant and Claudette was no longer amused. Her peals of laughter twisted and disfigured into shrieks of pain.

Six shots were fired. The first five overlapped. They were three rapid firecracker shots from Moses Platt's pistol, the loud report of Maddie's carbine rifle, and the ear-splitting boom of Caleb's shotgun. Two of Moses's shots struck the deputy in the same thigh where he'd aimed to bring the man down but not kill him. Maddie's shot struck Pine in the ribs and was more than enough to be lethal. It didn't matter. Caleb's shotgun blast followed on top of Maddie's and ripped the man open wide even as it knocked him across the room.

And then—something of half a heartbeat after the initial volley—came Earl's shotgun blast.

As the acrid plumes of gunfire slowly cleared the air, the small group was silent. There was no need to see if aid could save Claudette. Finally, as their eyes fell upon him, one by one, Earl spoke to defend himself.

"I was aiming for Deputy Pine. I swear…I was. But, well, you all saw. He got…he was…. It was an accident, dammit. Why would I shoot Claudette? Stupid whore. I didn't…." He turned away from them and began cleaning the shards of glass up from around his feet. From behind the bar his quivering voice rose up. "Terrible…terrible…."

The room was quiet once more as the Brazen Head inexplicably whirred to life.

Chapter Twelve

Evan was famished. He dropped the gore-caked axe on the porch and wiped the mess of splatter from his face with the back of his scorched shirt sleeves.

"Who's hungry," he called out as he threw open the front door and marched back inside the house. The thing in his hand dripped a crimson trail as he went.

Out on the front lawn, a murder of crows, nine in all, lit on the butchered remains of Merritt, splayed out face-up across the hinds of Dale's dead horse. As they hopped about with raucous cries vying over the fresh meal, occasionally their curiosity was piqued by the low moans of Dale emanating from where he still lay trapped at the bottom of what was to have been Evan's grave.

With his would-be treacherous brothers now dispatched, Evan thought he had the run of the house. He was startled then as he walked into the kitchen to find the eyeless, bloated corpse of Bill Petry seated at the small dining table. The man's hands were folded in his lap where he held a small bouquet of long, slender golden mushrooms. Small animals had nibbled away much of his extremities such as his fingers, ears, and nose.

Evan was startled enough to drop Merritt's heart to the floor where it landed with a wet thud. He instinctively went for his gun. The holster was empty. He'd meant to take Merritt's guns, but he'd forgotten. Left with little other recourse, Evan stood dumbfounded. Only then did he realize the man was long dead.

The initial shock of the unexpected discovery quickly

dissipated, and, as it did, Evan found the scare quite ludicrous and entertaining.

"Hey now, mister. You should not ought to sneak up on a feller like that," he said and then snickered and spat.

Evan ambled across the kitchen casting a suspicious look around. "So...what do we have here?" he said, once he was satisfied they were alone. "A corpse come a courtin'? Don't that beat all?"

He retrieved Merritt's heart off the floor. "Pretty sure I don't have enough here for company. Then again, like I said, it is a bit rude of you to drop in unexpected like."

Evan kept a wary eye on the corpse as if he expected at any moment it might spring to life. He pulled down an iron skillet from a rack above the stove and lit a burner.

"It's an old Injun thing," he explained as he buttered the skillet. "The heart of my enemy."

The heart hissed and spat back at him when he dropped it in the skillet. He paused briefly in quiet amusement. "Oh, Merritt, you always had to have the last word," he said before going about his business, turning the heart over as it sizzled, adding salt and pepper and keeping close watch on the fire. After a few minutes of cooking he had an epiphany.

"Say, do you mind?" he said to the corpse and relieved it of the bouquet of mushrooms. Tossing them into the skillet as well, he nodded a polite thank you. "I take it back. *You* are a most welcome dinner guest. I would be remiss if I failed to educate you, however, that in the future you should always know to arrive with a bottle. Common courtesy, my friend. We are little more than savages with nice houses without such pleasantries."

He lowered his nose to the skillet and savored the aroma. "Mmm-mm. Now that there is smelling spectacular! Wouldn't you agree?"

...

Patrick Thompson's consciousness grated and gamboled about in circles like a rusted windmill, lopsided in disrepair and near collapse. He had no concept of the space and time his body occupied. His only perception was that pain sloshed about him, but not in him. It was the environment he occupied, the breeze between his blades, nothing more. There were sounds, but other than the steady whooshing of the windmill, slow then fast, slow then fast, nothing penetrated his senses. Perhaps it was his heart he perceived.

For a while he watched his body decompose, moisture fleeing molecule by molecule as the flesh shriveled and receded making teeth and nails appear longer, grey rot seeping deeper and deeper, foulness taking over. His body was wrapped like a Pharaoh he'd once seen in his wife's encyclopedia, carefully prepared for the afterlife. Patrick's vision could peel away those wraps, however, revealing the decay beneath.

But no, that was not his body, he realized. He was looking at the man seated across from him, the man who ran the gristmill; a failed man in so many ways, now culminating those shortcomings in this final sad state.

Patrick was momentarily aware of the woman curled at his feet. She was licking the stump where his little toe had been. In-between licks she sang disjointed verses of nursery rhymes. Her voice was poor, lilting and child-like, and grew more and more tainted with each breath of her mounting agitation. Despite her best efforts, she simply could not make Patrick's small, severed pinky toe take hold again. She began running the bare needle back and forth sewing the flesh, but without thread it was fruitless work.

She whispered, "Little Miss Moffitt sat in the corner…with all the king's horses…all the king's men…whore…."

Patrick hadn't made an effort to speak, but a noise rose from his breast just the same. It was something Mariel imagined would issue up from the bowels of a cave in winter or some other such dark place that only a fool might explore in one of the dark fairy tales her Nana May had read to her so many years lost now.

She abandoned her thread-less sewing. Ever so slowly she rose—the cleaver clenched in white knuckles, ready to strike—and brought her ear to Patrick's mouth.

"What was that, my sweet?"

From downstairs a series of loud, troubled voices broke out, mostly indistinguishable except for Claudette's repeated shouts for someone, or something, to fight. Gunshots followed and then silence. None of this made any impression on Patrick or Mariel. The cleaver quivered as she waited for a word or a sign. Any sign. Any word.

...

Walter had watched from his kitchen hiding space as Evan ate his slain brother's heart. The man had plopped himself down at the table right beside Walter's father and made the smallest of talk—weather good and poor, saddle sores, bad beats at poker, the toil of a farmer's life he could never bear—all this he prattled on about as he cut and chewed. For his part, Bill Petry was a seemingly polite and attentive companion.

It was not how Walter had imagined the ravager, this marauder from across the far-away land, would react to finding the deceased seated there. Then again, given the pudgy bad man's appearance, he and the corpse made quite a matching pair. *Salt and pepper, knife and fork*, Walter thought.

Apparently, while Walter puzzled, his father's corpse had told a joke. Walter didn't hear it, but the jest brought tears to the plump marauder's eyes. He pounded the table and choked on his blood-drool guffaw. Catching his breath, the bandit slapped Bill Petry's back in approval and sent him spilling across the floor, a pratfall finishing touch which only entertained the bad man even more.

That settled things. The boy decided right then and there that just as soon as the man gave him the chance, he would steal out to the front yard in search of one of the other dead men's guns. The time for pranks and foolishness was over. Walter would fetch himself one of those horse pistols and there'd be two corpses in the Petry kitchen come the next sunrise.

...

Wallace Sweet dug into the warped boards of the loft as a tick might, mindless but for his drive to not be cast off as he was certain he would be at any moment. Hours passed.

Every finger and toe stayed clenched white and aching in his precarious hold on the world. He felt like a parasite, siphoning life in exchange for nothing. He was a starving babe at the dry teat of a dying woman. So went the tormenting visions of Wallace's shallow sleep, and so this was how the old man awoke from his stupor, cold as a winter penny despite the heat. He had purged something from his body. He was himself again.

"What am I doing here?" he asked himself aloud.

He knew where he was. He knew the decision he'd made to come to the barn to hide. Just the same he was perplexed by it all.

"Like a child," he said. He rubbed his eyes and ran his thin fingers through even thinner hair.

His actions were replayed like a man might recall the hazy events of a long, drawn-out bender. His mind had not been his own. Shame welled. He wondered if Abigail was aware of his misdeeds, his cowardice. How could he have failed her like this? He had no answers. *Others had done far, far worse*, a voice inside him defended.

"Stop it," he said and collected himself. He would not compound his failings by attempting to rationalize them.

Spending a moment to make sure he wasn't forgetting anything, he considered going back to the house to confess matters with Abigail. *No*, he nipped the notion in an instant. *What's done is done. Now was the time to set things right, not proffer apologies.*

All was still outside the barn. The soft light of dusk was a blessing to the old man. He'd feared it was much later. At least the first leg of his journey, the dash through town, wouldn't need to be made in the dark.

"Please, Lord, help me save the boy," he said.

He hadn't prayed in more than forty years. He wondered if that would count against him. He started off down the gravel drive at the briskest trot he could hope to maintain until at least reaching the far side of town. The crunching passage of his footfalls seemed so loud that they echoed. They did not. It was only Wallace's nervous imagination. For the sake of stealth he quickly moved off the gravel into the grass. Ahead of him lay the unmistakable remains of the dog that had meant to block their path. The animal was in pieces now, scattered like so much wind-strewn litter along the drive. A small bird—a brown finch that Wallace would think would rather fancy feeding on seed—teased at a portion of meaty bone. Even as Wallace passed near, the miniscule bird kept at it, pecking and pulling at the bit of carcass undeterred.

The streets were quiet. Wallace couldn't settle his mind as to whether that boded well or not. Little voices wrestled about in his head arguing each side. Clearly some, if not many, townsfolk had fled. No doubt others had gathered in refuge, perhaps at the town hall or among the outlying farms. That was his hope at least. Others still, he was sadly certain, were dead. Even as he wondered who might remain and what horrors might be hidden behind their drawn curtains, he was stopped in his tracks to spy a face in a window. It was the Burroughs' residence, the druggist and his worthless gossip of a wife. Far worse, a petty woman. Wallace only caught the briefest glimpse before the figure drew back into the shadows. He couldn't even be sure which of the couple he'd seen. Wallace Sweet didn't linger to see if the apparition would return. If the old man had only looked back over his shoulder he would have known that in fact both the druggist and his wife returned to the window to watch him go.

The street was hard and dry. Rain had fallen not long ago but it took no time for the sun of that harsh season to make it as though perhaps it never had. A wind picked up at Wallace's back and began to carry away the loose sand. Pressing on, Wallace felt as though blinders, or the proverbial rose colored glasses, had been taken away. The town no longer appeared vibrant as he would have described it any day before. It was a place of decay, and clearly had been lost to that state for some time. Buildings pitched and sagged at their roof beams and too many leaned into one another like limping soldiers weary to find their way from the battlefield. Paint peeled in the few places where anyone had bothered with a coat in the first place, while windows, porch rails and picket fences were gapped and broken as if the ghost of those places had shuffled off their confinement and broken free. Or so went Wallace's imagination.

As Wallace approached the center of town, and his concerns became concentrated on the saloon ahead, he was surprised by the sight of his wrecked Model T in front of the Thompson house down the street opposite. He cursed under his breath. Indecisive, he turned about where he stood in the middle of the intersection to survey each direction. Nothing. Before he could think better of it he did something he immediately knew was foolish.

"Ca-leb!" he shouted.

He waited—doubled over heaving and out of breath from his pace and his panic—and after a few long seconds, when he thought he would receive no reply, a voice boomed from somewhere near, but otherwise unknown.

"You go to hell, Wallace Sweet!"

Wallace bolted upright and turned about twice in quick succession trying in vain to get a bearing on the voice taunting him. It'd been a man, he was certain of that, but who precisely, he couldn't say.

"Who's that? Who's there?" he called out. When he received no response he realized he would have preferred more threats to the silence. "Show yourself, you want to damn me! Show yourself!" he screamed, with his voice breaking as he did. "Coward!"

Wallace tightened his grip on his shotgun, but kept it low at his side. He'd no foe at which to direct it. He weighed how close the voice might have been. Distant, he decided. Distant, but still well within an easy rifle shot.

...

The Brazen Head was just spitting out another unrequested fortune when its interruption was followed by yet another; a chorus of men shouting back and forth floated in from the streets. With the front doors smashed in, the voices were more clearly audible, but still indiscernible. Before any of the saloon's group could comment on them or question if anyone had made out the exchange, three sharp shots, a second or two between them, echoed through the streets. Quickly following these, there came a rapid barrage of gunfire, numbering seven maybe eight shots in all. Then things outside went quiet once more.

"Thought you said you all were in a hurry to be getting

along on your way," Earl said. He'd directed the comment to Caleb, but then shifted to Moses Platt when Caleb proved none-too-tickled by the comment. Moses only shrugged.

"Somebody emptied their Winchester. Maybe we'd best go upstairs and see whether we can spy what's going on out there before we go stickin' our necks out," the small man suggested to his employer. "That might start up again after they get reloaded."

Caleb made no sign that he'd heard Moses. Instead, he stared down Earl. Caleb couldn't say whether the barkeep was taunting them to go or stay.

"Well, makes no matter to me," Earl said, and then stammered, "Though I guess I feel a bit better to have your company, Caleb, Moses. What with Claudette dead…and the other girl, Mariel…well…you know." He began snatching glasses from beneath the bar and lining them up for cleaning even though there was no need for it.

A short series of pounding thumps came from upstairs—just over their heads—ending as abruptly as they began.

"Mariel's ears must be burning," Moses said with a grin.

"Would one of you gentlemen mind?" Maddie called over. She'd collected some table cloths and was looking to move and cover the remains of Deputy Pine and Claudette. "It's the least we can do. For now," she added, folding Claudette's arms.

"Here now, let me attend to that, Mrs. Thompson," Moses said, rushing to her aid. "But somebody might ought to watch the door. Maybe fashion up a barricade," he suggested to Caleb over his shoulder.

Earl finished with a glass and smacked it down on the counter. "I don't know what's going on here, but I can't help but think it's you and your brother that should be held accountable," the barkeep said to Caleb.

The room went still for several long seconds.

"Accountable for what, precisely?" Caleb finally replied just when it seemed he'd no intention to.

"For this town's demise. The suffering."

"*Demise*? Being a tad dramatic there, wouldn't you say?" Caleb shot back.

"Hardly."

Caleb sighed. "Now buck up, Earl. We might have hit a rough bit of road here, but—"

"Rough bit of road? Are you deaf, dumb, and blind, mister? Ain't you seen what's been going on around you?" No one spoke and Earl suddenly realized he had their attention. "Houses...hell, *businesses* burned to the ground. And by God only knows who. Packs of dogs roaming the streets come a night, killing right and left like wild animals. Men and women tearing at each other's throats over nothing. Hell, in the past two weeks near about everybody what come in here has been cut, or burned, or, or downright mutilated," he stabbed a finger at the corpse of the deputy to make his point. "You yourself, Caleb Sweet, just look at you," he said. "Fingers all smashed up. Arm tore to pieces by them dogs. I think we need, we need, well uh—"

Caleb had begun examining his hand when he interrupted. "Thinking never was your strong suit, Hodges. That's why we had to get rid of the faro table. Remember?" He crossed to the doors to survey the damage there and steal a look outside.

"Careful. Watch yourself, Mr. Sweet," Moses cautioned.

"That so, Caleb?" Earl kept at the old man.

"Yes, that's so. Why don't you drop the female histrionics and be a man. Put your head to thinking about solutions, not problems," Caleb said. In an afterthought he turned to Maddie. "Apologies, Maddie...but...well, you understand my meaning."

Maddie nodded in such a way that none of the men could say whether she saw past the slight or not.

Earl was far from being finished with his venting, however.

"You want solutions, Sweet? How about you tell me what the problem is first? You know what's going on here? Because I'd love to be enlightened. Solutions. I have a solution...we shouldn't be here. There's your solution. Should have done like those others yesterday and hightailed out of here. There's your solution!"

Moses spoke up, his voice quiet, sardonic. "So, why didn't you?"

Earl knitted his brow and sucked in his cheeks. He was wrestling with his response to the small man, but quickly lost that bout and so chose to change tack. He turned back to Caleb. "Well then, Caleb, how about you try this on for size," he said. "Who among us...who of just about anybody in this *town* would be here but for you and that brother of yours, Wallace?"

Caleb hung his head. He felt like an old hound with a pesky mockingbird worrying his hinds. He could just catch the wheeze of the breath moving through his lungs.

"Nobody made you come here, Hodges. And nobody damn sure never said you couldn't leave," he said as he leaned his shotgun against the wall and began to manhandle what remained of the doors to get them back in their frame.

"I don't know about you all," Earl said to Moses and Maddie, "but I was told this place was like a Garden of Eden." Then he turned back to Caleb, "We didn't need no God on account of you already found Paradise on Earth, ain't that what Wallace told us?"

"You've done well enough. Especially considering the laws of the land," Caleb growled. He began upending a table to block the damaged doors.

"Well enough? Well enough? Shoot fire, ain't that just dandy? Well enough."

"Yes, well enough. Maybe too well," Caleb said.

"You think you're so damn smart," Earl hissed. "You and that brother of yours, you two ever stop to ask yourselves why there wasn't nobody else laying claim to this godforsaken country?"

Caleb paused to consider the man's point. He lolled his tongue about momentarily but gave no reply before getting back to the doors.

Earl kept at him. "Maybe all this insanity goin' on here might be why. You think on that, will you? All this…this place is cursed. Maybe it's some old injin curses, or maybe you and your brother brought all of us folks into damnation with the two of you and your false praises. Maybe God didn't like you laying your claims to have yourself Eden. Maybe he wasn't partial to you leadin' his lambs astray. 'Cause I can tell you, this here is not paradise. It's hell. Ya drug us down to hell with you."

Moses had finished moving the bodies to the far end of the foot of the bar where he covered them. Wiping his hands on his trousers he said, "Nobody convinced me to come here." Then he scoffed, "Lambs...heh."

Earl ignored him. "*Well enough*," he fumed. "You think I own this place?" he demanded of Moses and then Maddie. "Well, do you?" They were at a loss. "I don't own this place. Never did. He does!" Earl's finger trembled as he pointed to Caleb. "Him and his brother!"

Caleb spoke softly. "And your point?"

"I'll tell you my point. My point is that this whole place is your fault. You brought the people here to this godforsaken land with your promises, brought us all here to the dead end of the God's good Earth, and here we are...lost. All the while you and your brother sit up there in Sweet Wood, a pair of feudal lords siphoning off everything...everybody. Hell, you even make a pretty penny when it comes time to tuck us peasants in the dirt." Earl turned to Moses where he stood at the end of the bar looking to pour himself another drink. "Don't bury those two yet. Your Mr. Sweet here, he might want to check their teeth for gold fillings."

Caleb had had enough. "We came in here looking for Patrick Thompson," he said. "Yes. Now, I admit...my mind, it's been a little off kilter. A little. Maybe I seen me too much sun...working out on that construction. Or maybe those dogs...this damned throbbing arm. Probably much more likely, though, it's been too much whiskey plied by you this afternoon since we found ourselves in here. But no matter. I've full handle of my faculties now. We were coming here, Mr. Platt and myself, because this was the last place I saw my friend. I saw what looked like those two whores snatched him in here last evening."

Maddie was taken aback. "I beg your pardon! What was that?"

She was ignored by all.

Despite Caleb's declaration to the contrary—that he was recovering his mind and his health—his face had gone pale, his jaw hung slack and he'd begun to waver. He took hold of the table with his good hand and with the other he reached out to retrieve his shotgun where it was propped against the wall, well beyond his grasp. Moses was the first to realize the old man was blacking out and so began to rush to him. Too late, however. Moses had barely moved two feet before Caleb stumbled forward and pitched to the ground.

...

Wallace had no more than realized that he was within range of being fired upon by his unseen heckler, when a sharp crack resounded and the dirt at his feet was kicked up by a shot.

He bellowed. "To blazes now! There's no call to be "

Either there would be no more warning shots or the first hadn't meant to be one to begin with. The next shot whizzed by before Wallace had finished saying his peace and it took a thumbnail-sized portion of his ear with it. His spectacles, jolted by both the shot and the jerk of his neck, flew away as well, skittering across the hard earth like a stone on water.

He'd often wondered, throughout the course of his long

life, what it felt like to be shot. For much of his youth he'd figured it was simply a matter of time before he'd need not speculate on it any longer. As a mortician he'd seen his share of bullet wounds. As the years fell away, however, Wallace began to suspect that he might never know. When he finally got his answer it was really just a nick, but it settled his curiosity more than enough. *Like a branding iron*, was the thought that exploded among the myriad others in that instant. This, even though he knew nothing of the branding iron's touch either. *Hot lead indeed*, was another flash of his mind.

Wallace raised his shotgun to his shoulder and almost began firing with abandon. He had no target. He was fairly certain he knew where the shots were coming from—the second floor of the feed and grain just down the street—but he wasn't about to stand there to confirm his suspicions. Besides, the target would be out of his shotgun's range as he'd already considered, and he suddenly felt like a hay bale with a paper bulls-eye tacked to it. Belying his age, Wallace dove off towards the side of the street and landed with an impressive roll. It proved a life-saving course of action as a third shot split the air waist-high where he'd been standing.

Someone yelled then. Not his would-be assassin, but a new player to the deadly cat and mouse. "Best get outta the street!" the man hollered to Wallace.

Wallace, scrambling on all fours to do just that, couldn't have agreed more with the patently obvious advice. Pot-shots began harassing the old man in rapid succession like pelting hail thumping into the earth all around him as he went. Thankfully, none found their mark.

"It's Avery Stolks," Wallace's advisor reported as Wallace ducked into a narrow alley between houses.

The man who'd spoke up sat in a rocking chair on the porch of the house Wallace had found refuge behind. The man hadn't been readily visible from the street since he was tucked-in beside a large protrusion of bay windows. Wallace knew him well—Neville Hastings, the town's long-retired school teacher—and was struck by the fact that old Neville was out in the open, apparently ambivalent to Avery Stolks and his rifle.

"Mr. Hastings, don't you think you best get from off that porch?" Wallace called around the corner, peeking out as far and as briefly as he dared.

"No. No, I don't suppose I plan on it," Neville replied.

From his assassin's nest, Avery shouted something that Wallace couldn't make out.

"And why's that?" Wallace asked the old retired school teacher.

Neville rocked gently, pursing his lips in contemplation. "Well…he hasn't shot me yet. Hasn't even tried."

"Pardon my saying, Mr. Hastings, but I don't see that as a very good reason to keep testing such murky waters, wouldn't you agree?" Wallace said.

Avery continued his shouting. His ranting was still mostly incoherent except for the occasional slightly louder swears he cast down to echo along the street.

The retired school teacher calmly explained himself to Wallace. "My wife went out to the Volger's spread yesterday evening. Hasn't made it back yet. I want to be out here to warn her when she comes along."

"Avery wouldn't shoot a woman," Wallace said.

Neville Hastings only pointed across the street in reply. In all of the excitement Wallace hadn't noticed the bodies, a woman and a man lying several feet apart, both face-down on the plank sidewalk.

Wallace felt sick to his stomach, the acid boiling up in his throat. "Good Lord...." He thought he recognized the woman, but the man's face was turned from him and so Wallace couldn't say with any confidence who the fellow might be.

"Yes, sir. It'd be Betty Peters and her young brother, Tim," Neville Hastings said as if reading Wallace's mind. "Avery shot them dead...." he paused, checking his pocket watch, "three and a half hours gone by now. Don't risk your neck...they don't need saving. They're in His hands now." His long finger went from pointing to the bodies to the heavens. "I've been trying to keep folks clear. He's fired on a few others, but, like yourself, those folks got away lucky. It is fortunate...for the most part Avery Stolks is about as keen a marksman as he was a mathematician," the old retired school teacher said.

"And you?"

Neville shook his head. "For some peculiar reason he doesn't seem to mind me. Wouldn't even acknowledge me when I tried to talk sense to him after he shot the Peters. She wouldn't leave young Tim. I begged her off. She wouldn't listen. Of course, I've stayed down here on my end of the street. Just called out to Avery after it was over. No good. But he doesn't seem to mind me. Plus, I have my porch roof over me. I'm stubborn, but not too stupid."

"Madness," Wallace muttered.

"*Sic transit mundus*," Neville concurred with a knowing nod.

It was only then that Wallace realized the old school teacher was without his dentures. Wallace had never known the man wore false teeth, but given the situation he accepted that he'd not thought too hard on such matters. Also, it was then that Wallace took notice of the old man's bare feet with toenails amber brown and yellow and long enough to climb telegraph poles. Wallace leaned with his back to the corner of Neville Hastings's home. "What's that?" He asked of the old retired school teacher as he broke open the breech of his shotgun to double-check it was loaded.

Neville craned his neck so that the loose folds of it went taut. "Wouldn't that be your Model T down the street? You had yourself a smash-up? I didn't see the accident. I don't recall...." Neville said and his voice wandered off as he became lost in thought.

Wallace peeked out to look, as if there might be another such automobile in question. "Yes, but it—"

Their conversation was interrupted as another round of shots careened by, not at them, but in their direction. Neville ceased his rocking and craned about once more for anyone who might have wandered up unnoticed. The streets were clear, however.

"What the blazes is that fool shooting at now?" Wallace demanded.

Three more shots were fired. Neville Hastings settled back in his rocker and moaned in despair. His knotted finger pointed back again across the street. As the next two shots came, Wallace was disgusted to discover Avery's latest target was his first. Although the tremors of Betty Peters' corpse were all but imperceptible with each impact, the sound of the heavy lead rounds sinking into her was not.

Then, as inexplicably as he'd begun, Avery Stolks ceased his ranting and his shooting and the world was naught but the slight and pulsing wind kicking sand against the wooden frames and down along the plank walk. Only that and the creaking of the old man in his rocker. Wallace slunk down against the wall and prayed yet again his first true plea to His Father in so many years. He did this as the creeping shadows of dusk worked across the street, slowly consuming the bodies of Betty and Tim Peters.

God didn't answer. But Wallace's clipped ear sang to him its pain. He'd kept a thumb pressed into the gouge managing to suppress a good deal of the bleeding. Still, his head felt as airy as a dandelion clock.

As he waited—for what, he could not have said—Wallace was moved to notice that near the Peters siblings a flourish of wildflowers sprouted out from beneath the planks of the sidewalk. A pastel cluster of yellow, pink and sky blue blooms that suggested life, beautiful life, could find root and thrive even in the hardest and ugliest of places.

These two were not meant for this, Wallace lamented. Young folks such as the Peters were the new growth of the town. They were the future. The town's chance to go on after those such as himself and this old school teacher near his side had gone the way of things. That was supposed to be the course of life. Not this.

"Could he be out of cartridges?" Wallace speculated

first silently to himself and then out loud.

"No good way to know. One thing's for certain," Neville said, "He'll be out of daylight in very short order. Why don't you come up around the back and I'll meet you inside. Get the missus to fix us something nice." The old retired school teacher got up slowly from his rocker. As he did, a small clutch of yellow mushrooms fell from his lap, scattering in a pitter-patter across the porch, some rolling away with the wind. "Ah…no," he exclaimed and stooped forward as best he could in a feeble attempt to retrieve them.

"I thought you said the missus was out to the Volger's place?" Wallace questioned.

But Neville didn't answer. In reaching for the errant mushroom caps, Neville Hastings stepped out too far. Avery was not out of rounds. His shot—if it were for him to say—was lucky. Wallace stood at the corner of the house and looked on in horror as the old retired school teacher's neck exploded in a mix of thick splatter and mist followed in a blink by the distant rifle's single report. Neville Hastings pitched forward across his porch and with a violent jerk of one leg went still.

Wallace lost control.

"Damn you to hell, Avery Stolks!" Wallace screamed as he rushed into the street.

He'd not given his action a moment of thought and now that he did Wallace Sweet braced to accept the inevitable. He would take Avery Stolks with him; that was all that mattered. He threw the shotgun to his shoulder, ready to exchange his rage for Avery's. When no such exchange ensued, Wallace began his rush on the building where he knew Avery was holed up. Where no doubt Avery was carefully drawing him into his sights. In his mind's eye Wallace saw him: *Held breath…sweating grip…squinted eye…the slow squeezing trigger finger.*

There were four windows to the loft of the feed and grain where Avery might have fired from. Although by now the cagey sniper might be at any one of the building's other vantages. With each step forward Wallace knew his odds of survival were diminishing. His would be the second shot…after Avery gave away his position taking his. As each stride met the earth Wallace began a cadence under his breath of "now…now…now…." Forty yards from the feed and grain he stopped again, shotgun once more at the ready…waiting…only to become lost in the fleeting seconds' ebb when nothing happened. The shotgun began to waver in his trembling hands and the sweat of his brow gathered into small rivulets that stung his eyes, blurred his vision. Still nothing. More uneventful seconds collected and yet there came neither sight nor sound to give away Avery Stolks. Wallace's long shadow grew unsteady and he became aware of the warm trickle of blood running down his neck from his clipped ear.

The sensation brought the image of Neville Hastings's gruesome end to his mind's eye. The illness in his gut rose once more. Wallace fought back a dry heave.

"I'll be back for you, Stolks. Count on it! Your murderous hide will hang!" He began to back-pedal away down the street, clenched-teeth certain that at any moment he would know the branding of a bullet once more. As he made the far block he called out one last time. "This town still has justice!"

With that, Wallace Sweet rounded the corner and ran as far and as fast as his tired body would carry him.

In the upstairs bedroom of the Hastings's residence a phonograph turned while the needle scratched and ticked on and on at the end of the record.

Neville Hastings's wife had never gone to the Volger's farm. Not a few nights earlier, not ever in her life. She barely knew the Volger clan as it were, and what little she did know of them she found distasteful; men who were slothful malingerers, waking only to drink and gamble when not fighting or fornicating with the loose women who obliged them. So then, it would remain a mystery where Neville Hastings had gotten the idea that his wife had gone to visit there in the first place.

The truth was that three nights prior, Neville's wife retired to their room upstairs and that was where she'd stayed. Then, as her husband died on the front porch below her, the mayhem surrounding his death finally roused Norma Hastings from her near-comatose vigil at their bedroom window. She stumbled back out of her malaise that evening in the same moments her husband of sixty-one years went still, her senses becoming alert just in time to see the shotgun-toting Wallace Sweet charging off down the street, casting nonsense and vulgarities in his wake as he went.

"What a bedeviled man. I wonder what he's up to."

She hefted the antique .44 caliber Joslyn Army revolver from the folds of her floral nightgown and gently placed it on the windowsill where it joined a small brass plant mister and three clay flower pots, each of the latter containing hardy bouquets of golden yellow mushrooms. She paused to take pride in her green thumb before getting up from her favorite satin upholstered chair—now damp and spoiled by her urine—to go downstairs to ask her Neville what he preferred for dinner. She couldn't recall ever being so famished.

She stopped at the door and went back to retrieve her husband's old cavalry revolver from the sill. What with people like that mad Wallace Sweet running the streets, brandishing shotguns and ululating like wolves on and on about only the Lord knows what, it was best to be safe rather than sorry, she told herself.

The phonograph in the corner, yet unattended, continued its endless revolutions.

Chapter Thirteen

The axe was in the dry grass at the boy's feet. It whispered to him. Begged him. When the begging failed, it taunted. He ignored it. It would be too heavy, too unwieldy, to do the trick. In the kitchen his mother had many long knives. Sharp knives that could butcher a hog, carve a turkey. Out back in the barn there was the scythe, another axe, a hatchet, a machete, crowbars and cat's-paw, hammers both small and large, sledge and claw. Next to the henhouse, the corner of their blades buried in the old killing stump, another hatchet and a cleaver were to be found. But all of those would do Walter no good. No good at all unless he could catch the burned man asleep.

But the man wouldn't sleep. The man—this marauder who dined with the dead and on the dead, eating his brother's heart—he would not sleep. He might pretend to sleep. Oh yes, for *pretend-sies* he might close his eyes and fake a snore and grumble. But Walter was not so foolish as to believe it. Not even for a second.

Walter stole a glance back to the house. All was still and quiet. The night, which used to trouble the boy, had settled over the farm like a comfort. It hid him, gave him freedom. He considered retracing his steps and looking a little longer for the gun, but knew in his heart it wasn't there. It *had* been there. He knew where he'd seen it, tucked in the grass not an arm's reach from the dead horse, hindquarters jutting out of the earth. At some point the man must have come back outside and taken it for himself though.

Maybe he was wise to Walter. Maybe he meant to kill him next. *Maybe he—*

But Walter's rabbit-fast mind was cut short, snared as the front door was flung open wide and the light from within fell out upon the yard, all but tickling his toes.

"Who's there?" the burned man screamed. And it was a scream. It was a voice sick with terror.

There was no place for Walter to run. The boy threw himself behind the dead horse and squeezed tight his eyes. His fingers dug into its short coat as though he feared the dead thing might buck him away.

Young Walter Petry wasn't sure if the lullaby that began to echo about in his head was his own voice or his mother's, whether the song was on the night air or merely in his mind. The only other sound was the unmistakable click, click, click of a revolver's cylinder turning as its hammer was cocked back.

...

As Caleb's vision returned, the first sight he caught was that of Mariel, the saloon's comely showgirl, standing atop the stairs.

"Thank God," the old man muttered.

Those gathered around the table they'd laid Caleb out on—Moses, Maddie, and Earl—were all relieved that he'd come back around. Even more so that he'd spoke, even if they were confused by his words.

"I had me a terrible dream," Caleb said to Moses upon seeing the man's bewilderment. He whispered, "They'd butchered...chopped off her arm."

Moses followed Caleb's eyes up to Mariel where she stood smiling atop the stairs. His first thought was to wonder how long she'd been there, whether she'd witnessed Claudette's death at Earl's hand. That concern was quickly pushed aside when he noticed the woman had both arms once more. The explanation was just as obvious. There was no mistaking the twine stitches, or that it was not her original arm. Even from where Moses stood he could see that she'd replaced her missing limb with that of a much larger man's.

At his side, Maddie gasped and Earl said something Moses's overwhelmed mind failed to process.

Someplace off down the streets outside, more gunfire echoed among angry voices.

"We need to barricade the door," Maddie said. She went to the table Caleb had upended before his collapse. She was alone in her efforts.

"Is it suppertime?" Mariel asked as she descended the stairs.

Moses pinched his face up and stepped back even though she was still distant. "Woman, what've you done there?"

"Earl, I'm starving," Mariel said, ignoring the small man. "Ain't we gonna eat?" she asked and slumped to the old faro table.

The group surveyed one another. No one moved to the girl. She was quiet and that was enough. After a little more of Mariel's goading, Earl fell back to the kitchen to scrounge up "sandwiches or such" while Moses and Maddie worked at stacking tables and chairs in the maw of the ruined doors.

The town was still and without trouble save for a new sharp bite of smoke wafting on the night air.

...

Since he'd been driven out of town and off-course from the Petry farm, Wallace was forced to find his way across several fields which lay well out of his way. These were mostly barley or corn. The majority of lots were ill-tended and faring poorly to prove it. Sparse corn stalks stood as beleaguered ranks of soldiers after having received several volleys. Still, the going was slower than he'd hoped. Both the terrain and his exhausted body conspired against him. The ground was tilled uneven and his feet and knees ached mightily. The failing light, now but a vault of dying lavender, only promised that his progress was about to become even more hindered.

Pausing briefly to take off his Stetson to better cool down while catching his breath, he made a vow to himself not to dwell on Avery Stolks further until the need was upon him again.

He spat cotton and got on his way again. Darkness soon settled. More than a few times along his way he was startled—especially amid the blind passage through corn rows—by fleeting movements haunting his periphery. He stopped the first time it happened. But after holding his ground for several minutes, and seeing and hearing nothing more than the rustling of the corn on an ever so slight breeze, he pressed on. No time to waste as time wasted, Caleb had told them as they'd toiled rebuilding the funeral parlor. That was true then and it was true now. Every so often, Wallace thought, his younger brother Caleb could get things right. Besides, if the dogs were on his trail, stalking him, his forcing a confrontation out in the open as he were would only be to their benefit. He needed to make the Petry farm. Find the boy. Hole up for the night and get back to Sweet Wood with the dawn.

He rooted absentmindedly about in his front pocket for his wire-rimmed spectacles before remembering for the fourth time that he'd lost them back on the street along with a good bit of his ear. Each of those recurring realizations, in turn, had precipitated a resurgence of the throbbing all along the side of his head that he would have preferred remained repressed.

He saw them before he ever would have heard them. He'd been almost stumbling along and their appearance roused his flagging strength. They were children, thankfully, not dogs. Like a myth of fairies playing hiding games in the corn, they scurried along ahead of him without so much as a rustle or whisper, holding hands in a line that began and ended with the biggest, and likely eldest, children on the ends and the little wee ones kept safe in-between. They were seven or maybe eight in number, and moved parallel to Wallace just far enough away that he'd missed them before now. He only spied them as they broke out from the corn ahead and began scrambling one by one over the split-rail fence that marked the crop's boundary.

Wallace held up. He didn't want to startle them and see them scatter off into the four corners of the night. The first two were already on the far side of the fence and the larger children were now conveying the small ones over between them. Little feet pedaled the air madly to find firm footing again. Wallace wished theirs could be a carefree, after-dark adventure such as childhood behooved. Instead he knew they were fleeing from this nightmare. Wallace waited until they were split in numbers, half on each side, and then he called out.

"Children, please, don't be frightened." He began to walk slowly towards them through the corn.

There was only the briefest pause before one little girl whimpered. Soft as it was, still her fright acted as a clarion sounding for their retreat. They scattered in a tizzy, like leaves caught up in a gust, with Wallace waving and pleading in a futile bid to stay them even as they dispersed.

"No…no…please…no…."

But in a blink they were lost to the old man, just as he'd feared.

Of those children nearest to Wallace, some darted back into the corn while one made to skitter away through the fence. Those on the far side, taking advantage of the fence between themselves and this scarecrow come up from the corn, all dashed off into the new field of what they knew from sight and smell to be clover. Only one of the lot, the elder boy on the same side of the fence and nearest to Wallace, didn't flee. Locking on the shotgun the old man held, the boy's eyes swelled so wide their whites penetrated the gloom. Just the same, either out of terror or despite it, the boy held his ground. His mouth fell open but no sound followed. Stumbling back to the fence, he raised a pocketknife in his hand and thrust it forward, broadside facing out and tip to the heavens, like a crucifix meant to ward off the damned.

Behind the boy, the child who'd sought to scramble between the rough-hewn rails, the small girl who'd first whimpered, had instead become caught fast. A thick sliver of splintering wood protruding from the top rail had cruelly snagged her by her long, curly hair and, in her twisting and struggling to back away in the direction she'd been headed, she'd only managed to worsen the matter, allowing the jagged wooden finger to worm itself up into her locks ever so tightly. Finally, at pain's mercy and broken, the poor child clung to the fence and began to wail in earnest. For all the pity of it, her trouble gave Wallace the means to save the disastrous encounter.

"Here now, I'm Wallace Sweet. You know me," he said, and quickly added, "We must help her."

The girl heard this and finally let off her wailing. No mere words were going to settle her completely, however, and so she sobbed. The boy tamed his wild eyes and found his voice.

"Yes, sir. I know you. Hullo, Mr. Sweet," he said.

It was a good start, but for the knife still raised between them.

"You're Richard Worth's son, am I right?" Wallace said.

The night was quiet and still but for the snuffling of the girl. The other children had run far enough that going any further posed more trepidation than what they'd left behind.

The boy swallowed hard, his thick Adam's apple working like a hen's egg in a snake. He nodded first and then answered, "Yes, sir. I'm Richard Junior. Folks, they just call me Junior."

"That's right," Wallace said, "Junior. But I'd have my

druthers to call you by your given name, Richard. *Junior*, it's no name for a man. Wouldn't you agree?"

Richard nodded again.

Wallace slowly raised his hand to acknowledge the knife. "Now, I don't suppose she'll be wanting you to cut her free. Such pretty hair. No need to get so drastic. Let's just see how we might untangle her first, yes?" Wallace took a tentative step forward and the boy swelled a bit. Knuckles whitened on the knife that remained fixed between them.

This boy has seen some bad things, Wallace realized. "Tell you what," Wallace said. "Your eyes, I'd wager, they're probably a good sight better than mine. I lost my—" he waved a thumb back over his shoulder and the sudden motion caused the boy to startle. Wallace eased back a step. "I lost my glasses," he said. He slowly brought the butt of the shotgun forward. "So why don't you, Richard, why don't you just hold onto this and keep an eye out while I get our young lady friend here out of her predicament."

Wallace presented the gun stock first. After it looked as though Richard might not take him up on the offer, the boy lunged forward and snatched it away. Much to Wallace's chagrin the boy dropped the knife and swung the shotgun around to his hip, pointing it at the old man.

"Drop the pistol, Mr. Sweet," Richard Worth, Jr. demanded. He seemed to have grown three inches.

Wallace let his anger preside. "Here now, boy—"

Richard snapped the butt to his shoulder. Wallace saw the whites of Richard's eyes once more, but this time they were preceded by the black hole of the shotgun barrel.

The boy's voice quavered, "You're the cause of all this.

You and your brother. It's your fault. My folks...they's dead on account of you."

As if staring down the barrel of the shotgun wasn't enough, Wallace caught the sound of the children moving closer in the corn behind him. He wondered if any of them might be armed. *A tightening noose.*

He kept his focus on the shotgun, near enough to cut him down like a scythe. "How could this ever be my fault, Richard? I'm not even sure what's really going on...do you?"

"That don't matter none." The boy shook his head and the barrel floated about ever so slightly. "You brought my folks here with your lies. I know. My daddy used to talk about it. About how you'd lied."

"No one was forced to stay. They were welcome to leave if they weren't happy here."

A girl's voice came from just behind Wallace. He made a half-turn to face her. "Daddy said you kept them indentured. You owned everything we had. He said it was like slavery."

Wallace chewed on the truth and could make nothing from it. Time was running short. He could see that the boy was getting more agitated as things wore on.

"Junior, you can shoot me if that's what you think you need to do," Wallace said. "You can blast me straight to hell right here in front of these children...before God. But I am going to help this little miss, and I'm hoping you'll see that I mean you children no harm. I'm trusting you got better sense."

Wallace stepped forward to the girl hair-tangled with the fence rail. Richard flinched as Wallace came close, but thankfully did not fire. Once Wallace was sure of this, and as he made as though to step by the boy, the old man cuffed him hard in the jaw and knocked the shotgun from his hands. The boy went to his knees. Wallace snatched up the shotgun and the little girl began wailing once more.

"Damn it all to hell, be quiet now," Wallace scolded. She did as told. "That's better." He turned his back on Richard and leaned the shotgun against the fence as he knelt to the girl's side. With the deft fingers of a man of his trade he quickly had her free. She scuttled a few feet away into the clover but didn't bolt as he thought she might.

"All better?" Wallace asked.

She kept her face low and nodded. Rubbing her scalp she whispered, "Yes, sir."

With a huff of satisfaction he looked back over and saw that Richard, although still on his knees, had retrieved his pocketknife. The blade remained open.

"Oh, for the love of…. Son, don't you go courtin' some foolish notion. You had that coming to you. You know you did. Boy your age ought should know better than to put a gun on a man. Now I said I was here to help and I meant it." Wallace extended a hand to Richard. Initially the boy refused it. Wallace reasserted it and the boy doggedly tried to pass the old man his knife.

"I don't want your damned pocket knife, son. Gimme your hand. I want your hand." With that Wallace grabbed Richard's wrist and brought him to his feet. He patted his back and took the boy's jaw in his palm. "You're fine," he said, turning the boy's face first to one side and then the other. "Just fine."

"What're you children doing out of a night? Don't you

know things aren't safe of late?"

Richard suddenly found his backbone again. "We know, Mr. Sweet. Trust me, we know."

"So, if you know so damn well then why's it I find you all out here chasing lightning bugs in the corn?"

"We weren't chasing bugs," the little girl behind him spoke up. "We're running away."

Wallace was surprised to discover two other little ones had gathered themselves back up to her while he wasn't looking. The little girl who'd spoke carried a hatchet.

"Everybody get back here!" Richard shouted unexpectedly.

"Lord, son, hold it down," Wallace hissed. "You trying to call them dogs down on us?"

"Sorry, Mr. Sweet." Richard hung his head.

His call worked, however. One by one, the children all gathered back together around them. Wallace recognized each one. Eight in all, they were the children of not only the Worth family, but also the three Baker girls. When Wallace asked the girls whether their daddy knew where they were he had to bite his lip at Richard's reply on their behalf.

"You don't want to know about the Bakers, Mr. Sweet," the boy said.

Wallace looked to the girls and he could see enough in their eyes to know what the boy said was true.

"And your folks, Richard?"

"We buried Mama before we left," he said.

"And your pa?"

Richard looked away. After a long pause he said, "Look here, Mr. Sweet, we best be goin'."

"Is that so?"

The boy snapped back, "Yes, sir."

Wallace hated to admit it, but the boy was right.

"I don't suppose any of you've seen the Petry boy. Walter Petry, have you?" Wallace asked. A few shook their heads. None of the others replied in any fashion at all. "No, I didn't figure you did." He glanced around wishing there were something more he could do. "So, Richard," Wallace said with a long pull on his jaw where the white whiskers had grown long enough that they'd begun to relax, "Where you taking these youngins?"

"Not sure," Richard admitted. "Pellville maybe. Might be Misty and her sisters here got family over that-a-way," Richard said with a nod back to the girls. "They ain't sure, though," he confessed as an afterthought.

Wallace considered this briefly. "Pellville? Now that's a good ways. Clear across the state."

"Yes, sir."

"Can't walk that stretch."

"No, sir. But we'll make the train in a couple of days. I know where the track runs. My daddy used to meet up at the junction in Priestly to deliver moonshine. He took me and my brother once."

Wallace laughed. "Moonshine? Your daddy? That so?"

"Trust me, Mr. Sweet, he won't be doin' that no more."

The casual smile faded from Wallace's face. "You have money?"

"A little."

The smallest of the Baker girls dug in her pocket and proudly produced several dimes.

"Put those away, I told ya," her sister said. She did.

Wallace searched the back corner of his cheek with his

tongue for a moment. "You got a pen...something to write with...paper?"

After a brief search amongst them one of the children held forth a bible and a nub of blue crayon.

"Well, what do you know?" Wallace said.

"Our mother's," the girl said.

Wallace smiled. "Couldn't ask for better." As he wrote on the inside leaf of the bible, Wallace carefully explained to Richard. "You get to the train. You take it all the way to Corpus Christi. Show the conductor this if you don't have enough for tickets. You get yourselves there, you go straight-away to the First National Bank. Ask for the manager, Mr. Phillip Carlson. Good man. You give him this. He'll see to you. This will get you enough for a few nights at the hotel there, meals, fresh clothes, and then train fare on to wherever it is you all need to go." he said, writing in silence for a bit more before passing the bible back to Richard.

The little girl with the dimes tugged Wallace's sleeve as he did. She motioned him to stoop so that she might whisper. He crouched down and she cupped his good ear in her tiny hands.

"It's the grain," she said.

Wallace pulled back. "What's this then?"

The girl nodded emphatically. "Mother said it's in the grain. Said it's no good. Our flour growed yellow mushrooms. Made Mother mad. She threw it all out. But then, later, Daddy, he said that them mushrooms was a growing in the horse feed too. He got worse mad than Mother." Her voice went small. "Lots worst."

Wallace smiled and gently rubbed her cheek with his

calloused thumb. He longed to console her, but the only words he could find were the thin and hollow words of a mortician. To Richard and the other boy he said, "You do as I told you now. You get and you stay gone...for a while at least. Later, you send along a wire, you let me know your whereabouts. Stay in Corpus if you can think of no place better. You can wire for more money if need be. I'll tell you when it's safe to come back. Your family farms, they belong to you all now." He stood and looked them each in the eye in turn, from the biggest to the small. "All of you. They belong to you. Not me. Not my brother. You all. I'll see to proper care of your folks...headstones...proper Christian burials. You'll come back someday. Soon. As God sees fit. It will be alright. You'll see." He patted Richard's back.

The boy met his eyes with a gaze the old man couldn't decipher. He wasn't sure if he saw anger or pain, doubt or despair. But, regardless, there was nothing more Wallace could think to say or do, and so he left it at that.

"Here," the girl at his side said. In her hand was a large blue button. "It's my good luck," she said.

The old man lifted it from her palm and held it out at arm's length to survey it better. "Yes, yes, I do believe you're right. I thank you." With a pat and a wink he secured it in his pocket.

Wallace gave Richard Worth, Jr. his pistol and stood at the fence to watch over them as the small tribe melted off into the night. Just as they were all but gone, Wallace made out the littlest Baker girl asking how much further they'd need to go. Even across the distance Wallace caught the chorus of shushes that followed. In his pocket his finger pestered the button he felt foolish to find comfort in, foolish to have accepted. He hoped he wouldn't need it.

...

Stillness. It crept up on Abigail Petry and quieted her as the proverbial cat stealing the baby's breath. Death would be a comfort, nothingness a shroud against the cold teeth of life. Oblivion purred at her ear. It kneaded her bosom and cradled into her and she was glad to give it her company, her warmth. But, just as death appeared certain for her, Abigail was rudely snatched away from that dream with just a word.

"Mama?" little Walter called. "Mama?" And so she awoke. She returned to the bed where the Sweet brothers had placed her in their home. She awoke only to know the anguish that her son was not there.

She was not alone, however. At the foot of the bed a man holding a rifle stood with his back to her.

"So they're posting a guard on me now," Abigail said. She chuckled at her own little joke. She was proud to know she could still find humor. The wound to her stomach knotted and gripped her in searing pain, reminding her that it was not part of some dream, that it would hurt her again to laugh.

The man turned to her. His face bore no telling sign that he'd heard or appreciated her joke. Nor was he moved by her agony. Clearly he was in enough pain of his own. His left eye was no more than a raw socket. She recognized him right off. He had worked for her husband one summer. His name was Avery Stolks. She'd not cared for the way he'd looked at her over the course of that summer past and she cared even less for his expression now.

"Hello, Mister Stolks," she said as calmly as she could muster. She could think of nothing more to say and was sure her voice would only crack if she dared.

Avery Stolks was beyond pleasantries. "Where are they?" He tapped the rifle barrel on the bedpost, his one good eye wild and wide. "Where's Wallace Sweet?" he demanded.

...

Evan Evers stood over young Walter Petry. The boy had squeezed tight his eyes, but still, as the man leaned in close, Walter was gagged by the man's rancid breath, the sour of his clothes, the stench of his burnt flesh.

"Where'd it go?" the man whispered.

Walter continued to play possum.

The man came in even closer and knelt beside the boy where he'd tucked himself against the horse's hind quarter. He rested the gun across Walter's shoulder, the cylinder all but kissing the boy's ear. The man's breathing ran quick and shallow. For his own part, Walter was sure that if he'd been able to make water—as his father once joshed—he would have filled his own boots.

"Did ya see? Where'd it go?" the man repeated, his voice lilting with nervousness. Walter felt the man's thigh trembling against his ribs as much as his own. "Tentacles," the man muttered. "Did you see? It had tentacles."

Walter opened his eyes.

The man beside him looked worse than ever. The burn

along his arm and face was so gruesome looking that Walter winced to see how it cracked and oozed. But for his madness—Walter was sure—the torment of it would have struck the man bedridden, if not dead.

"That thing killed my brothers," the man said, his eyes darting about. "As sure as the dawn, killed them...and ate them."

Walter got the odd notion that the man wasn't trying to lie to him, but rather, to himself. Apparently it was a passable performance.

"Poor Merritt," the man said and chewed his bottom lip in grief.

It would have been comical to the boy save for the gun pressed up against his ear and the fact that this delusional man meant to use him as a shield against the demon of his own mind.

"Keep sharp," the man ordered and thwacked Walter's cheekbone with his gun barrel. "Daydreaming will get you killed out here, Gale."

Walter had no idea who Gale was. Weighing the fingers that folded around his nape, Walter toyed with making a dash for it. He wondered if the man's aim might be as addled as his brain. *Not likely*, he concluded.

"Damn tentacles," the man repeated.

And then Walter saw them too, shadowy things, thick as a man's limbs, slithering through the tall grass. They could only be seen by not looking directly at them, but they were there. Creatures in the corners of his eyes, darting ever forward, inching, groping to make contact with the man and boy. All around them. Soon one would brave the cleared earth that seemed to be keeping them at bay. Soon they would come and have them.

"Fortune favors the brave," an old man—the town's civil war hero, Colonel Rembrandt Warren Hawkins, no less—had once told the boy. As they'd met in the town square one bright morning, the wiry Colonel had stooped to press a stone into the boy's palm, and, with those words, "Fortune favors the brave," he'd subtly directed Walter to pitch it at a barking dog, tethered in front of the barbershop. On that occasion, Walter had rebuffed the Colonel's directive. Now, however, with a madman upon his back, little Walter found those words a comfort. Young Walter Petry had no idea how many of the Colonel's men had made the same mistake.

The boy's hands worried at his chapped and cracking lips, then to his eyes, and finally his tangled mop of hair. Amongst the tangles he discovered a clump of sandspurs. He tugged but they were fast and refused to leave the nest they'd made. He remembered his father.

The night before he'd died his father had come to visit Walter in his bed. Still in his work clothes despite the late hour, the man sat heavy on the mattress edge and placed a calloused hand on Walter's chest. In a voice worn and tired from a long summer day's labor, the man did his best to explain to the boy how he'd met with the devil in his own dreams just nights before. How that "Ol' Scratch" had made promises. The man explained how he, William Petry, son of Owen, had made an agreement with the fallen one. He had made a pact. He would trade away those days that remained of his life—many years yet, by his hopeful reckoning—and Lucifer would tack those days onto those belonging to his son, Walter. So then, the boy would get those days of his father's plus his own. In return, the devil would take from Bill Petry the one thing he wanted from all men, his soul.

As he sat there on his son's bed, the man had assured the boy it was a right and fair bargain. No matter what these troubles were it would mean Walter at least would see them through.

Walter weighed the words of that night and found no comfort in them. After all, Mama had long explained Lucifer to be the Lord of Lies.

He tossed off the idea of going for the axe. That would only make a certainty of bullets headed his way. And it was too close to the tall grass and the creatures in wait there. No, he would simply run. He'd run quick, and he'd duck as he went. Duck and weave, like even a baby chick had the good sense to do when a serpent was fast upon them. His legs felt like coiled springs beneath him, ready, but also dangerously close to reaching some disastrous point where they might explode into shards from the tension. He waited until the man's fingers went light in a moment of shifted weight. Walter sprang away.

He'd not made two steps before he recalled the other words of wisdom the Colonel had bestowed that morning. "Fortune favors the brave," the veteran had said. But once Walter had let slip the stone, discarding it with a plunk into the hard earth at his feet, the old man grinned, adding, "But the coward has little need of such generous boons."

As Walter made for the porch, the arrow of time proved to have a curious flight. Every step became its own eternity and with each came a wash of things past. Mama caught in silhouette behind billowing white sheets while she hung them at the clothesline. A scattering of prize marbles on the living room's hardwood floor. Mama sighing now over Aunt Melissa who will never marry and die alone. This she says while spooning scrambled eggs onto his plate. Daddy, rifle in hand, scolding Walter to stay put as he heads off to the barn where old Paint Brush bucks in his stall, pitching screams the boy never knew a horse could make. The old Colonel, head shaking with disappointment, turning away. The rock in flight. The massive plate glass of the barbershop shattering. And then Walter was on the porch.

Walter had gotten much farther than he'd thought he would before the first shot broke loose. The boy wasn't hit, though. Nor did he perceive where the bullet had gone. There were no telltale signs of it striking the house. No wallop of wood or tinkling of glass. That's when he realized that the man hadn't even shot in his direction, but back out over the field. Just the same, Walter would have continued inside save for what the man called out next.

"You get back to your attic! I got you covered," the man bellowed.

Walter reached the door and stopped. He turned back to see the man firing off high into the air out over the tall grass. But he wasn't simply firing haphazardly. Although clearly he fired high of the tentacle-things in the grass, the man nonetheless was carefully drawing a bead on something off in the air. Some new threat?

He fired twice more, and Walter followed the trajectory only to discover the first few stars of the evening. It was as though the bullets had punctured the dome of the sky.

"Stay back, you whores!" the man screeched and quickly fired his remaining rounds.

At first, Walter didn't bother with closing the door behind him. If the crazed man, this interloper, meant to come in there'd be no stopping him. He thought of the tentacles just as he reached the stairs and so he went back and quickly slammed it tight and threw the bolt. The boy bounded up the stairs and was relieved to hear more rounds being fired as the man continued his battle against the heavens. It was a short-lived relief. Upon reaching his room Walter found the hatchway to the attic thrown open and the ladder pulled down. The bad man's directive to get back to the attic had not been a spur of the moment thought then. He knew where the boy had been hiding.

Outside, the gunfire and curses abruptly ceased. And although there was no explaining it, the man was suddenly there next to the boy. He whispered in Walter's ear as he yanked the both of them down behind the bed, "We can't stay here. Not safe. Not the attic. No place. We got to make our break. We got to make it for town."

Walter finally dared look the man in his eyes. He was hideous, a twisting of ruined flesh, like crayons left too close to the hearth. He reeked nearly as horribly as he looked. *Nearly*. Walter closed his eyes.

"I want to wake up," the boy said quiet enough that one might still sleep through it.

"What's this?"

"I want to wake up," Walter repeated. This time a bit louder, but still weak and lost in the pounding drums of their hearts.

"You think this here's a dream? Shut your belly aching, boy, or I'll put you behind me with the others."

"I want to wake up. I want to wake up. Wake up! Wake

up! Wake—"

The barrel of the man's gun smacked the boy's jaw, splitting his bottom lip and chipping one tooth as well as cracking yet another. Walter was knocked senseless to the floor, his skull taking yet another wallop against the boards.

Certain the man would fire up the stove and carve out his heart to eat it now, Walter began to weep, crying once more for his mother.

"Get yourself together, boy. Yer folks are dead. I told ya, we're making for town."

...

Patrick didn't recall being released. He wasn't even aware that he'd been bound in the first place. Mariel had trussed him up and chopped his little toe off, and, most remarkably, he remembered nothing of that ordeal, either. He'd awakened, but powers of reasoning eluded him. His crusted eyes blinked in rapid succession, revealing all the intelligence of a freshly-birthed calf. He threw his mouth open wide in a violent gasp as though while he slept he'd not breathed. Perhaps he'd dreamt of the womb. He'd come up from the deep. Still, he was lost upon a trackless sea.

Beside him in the bed was the town miller. Or, at least, most of the town miller. The truncated torso and head. Patrick and the miller were finally set free, adrift together now upon Mariel's sprawling bed, tossed among a stew of yellow mushrooms. Patrick lolled about dumbly mouthing the sheets and dead beside him. By chance his lips eventually found a mushroom and then another. Soon enough Patrick was gobbling caps and stems, his mind of that single purpose, not pausing even when he came to one of the miller's severed toes. Eating until he retched, Patrick then lapped up that sickness as well.

"Patrick?" his startled wife, Maddie, called from the door where she and Moses Platt stood in stunned disbelief. "My God, Patrick," she cried as he rolled over to reveal himself.

Moses lifted his gun, concerned that the man was mad and would set upon them. Maddie shoved the small man back. "No! What's wrong with you?" And before he could stop her she'd rushed to the bed. Patrick, for his part, simply rolled back among the spread and clung once more to the trunk of the town miller as if he were all that kept him afloat.

It was as ghastly a scene as the two of them had ever known. At first Moses assumed Patrick was drunk. He and Maddie recognized the miller, and, as they wrestled those remains from Patrick's grasp, it became clear that there was more that befuddled Patrick than mere whisky.

Maddie first cleared off the miller's body, with Moses's aid stacking the portions like cord wood by the door. They finished with the gruesome task as quickly as they could manage and then she returned to her husband. She commenced to stripping the bed of the befouled bedding. The remaining mushrooms there might have been cast away then but for Maddie being distracted by the discovery of Patrick's mutilated foot.

"Moses, I need you to look through there and see can you find it," she said as she discarded the bundle next to the miller's remains. Her brow had taken on a sheen of sweat and her cheeks and neck flushed as though riddled with hives.

"Find it? Find what? The damned toe? And for what purpose? Can't put it back on."

The small man was right, of course. But even from the brief contact Maddie's judgment was already soured.

"Just find it!" she seethed through clenched teeth as she fretted over her husband while the old man pitched and moaned in his delirium.

"Shush, now, Pat. You shush and behave. Your Maddie has you. I'll set you right. And after I see to you don't you worry nary a bit. I'm gonna go down there and put an end to that murderous little whore and her barkeep boyfriend. God and his angels as my witness, you've my word on that."

While Maddie tended to Patrick, Moses picked through the mess of mushrooms and violations. Soon enough he'd forgotten why he was doing so and wondered if he'd heard the woman's words or only made them up in his fancies. He wandered to the window and considered the night.

Chapter Fourteen

Evan Evers, seeing double, paused to consider the heavens. A pair of gibbous moons hung there, as did the vast and countless multitude of stars, and each of those points of light closely alongside their similar doppelgangers like the eyes of a thousand secreted nocturnal creatures peering down from the depths of eternity. Evan ground his teeth to know their gaze fell upon his disfigurement.

Though it aggrieved him as well to do so, he kept his burnt hand hard upon Walter's nape, the pain a potent reminder to his easily distracted mind that the boy accompanied him. He was Evan's unwilling crutch of flesh. With his good hand, the man covered his injured eye in hopes of clearing away all the night sky's mirror images. It was not so easy a fix. In his mounting frustration he kicked Walter in the small of the back, sending the boy headlong into the cheatgrass and hard earth. When Walter made to scramble off, Evan dug his boot into the same spot where he'd kicked and drove the child back down. He guffawed to hear the boy's shrill cry die for lack of breath and his laughter kicked away a yellowish brown spume that had collected on the shores and corners of his ruined lips. It was only then that Evan Evers caught the shadowed silhouette of a man—or was it two—regarding him and the boy from the very edge of the night.

Evan whipped free his revolver. Without warning he loosed its entire load on the forms. Like heavy blankets loosed from a clothesline, both shadows fell. Even as they went down, it seemed to Evan that the very earth opened to take them in. The gunman stood dumb as the shadows threw up beseeching arms to the heavens. God chose to grant no mercy, however, and under His and the myriad eyes of the heavens the strangers were received by hell.

The boy chose this moment, certain he'd get none better. The knife he'd kept concealed in his boot found its way into Evan's thigh. The boy had made to stab the man between the ribs but his effort to twist about from beneath the man's boot heel found Walter lacking. Still, five inches of the blade clove into the thick of Evan's thigh and he was only spared the remaining two when the shaft met with bone.

"God Almighty!" Evan roared.

The man drew down on the boy and made to shoot him as well, but naught but a quick burst of ineffectual clicks emanated from the spent revolver.

Walter struggled to find his feet. He failed, however, and Evan fell into him with the two tangling up, the man on top, and thrashing the boy for all he was worth. Evan continued to beat him for a full half-minute even after the boy went limp.

They lay for a good while as one, a heaving mound of broken flesh as might be tossed down by fabled giants for the other creatures of the night to feed on. A stiff wind kicked up to make whispers in the cheatgrass. Evan finally rose up only to rest back on his haunches, his wounded leg still pinning Walter. He surveyed the stillness about them and reloaded. Only after that did he turn his attention to the handle protruding from his thigh. Without thought he yanked almost carelessly to free it. Beneath his denim trousers the flesh puckered around the thin blade, clinging as if to fight the departure. With the knife removed, blood gushed forth rich and quick. So much so that Evan was concerned about bleeding out even though he knew well enough that it wasn't possible from such a wound. He threw the knife off into the dark and struck the boy between the shoulder blades with the butt of his piece creating the *whump* of a rug beater at work.

"That's for good goddamned measure!"

Walter moaned long and low, but nothing more.

A scant few minutes earlier, Wallace had been bent forward in the moonlight taking stock of the two of them. Was this another pair of children? At a loss without his spectacles it was hard for the old man to say. No, one was clearly not a child. Although by the way the larger figure stooped and clung to the back of the other, Wallace suspected a person advanced in years. So then, *a child with one of their elders perhaps*?

Satisfied by that reckoning, he was just straightening to call out when a fury of gunfire from them lit the night. At least two shots were aimed true. Wallace's left shoulder was as though rent from him even as the ribs beneath were slugged with fire. Those figures previously shrouded were suddenly illuminated in the split seconds of repeated muzzle flash. One indeed was a child. A boy. But the other, the one who fired upon Wallace, was something else. At best a man horribly disfigured, at worst, some ghoul clawed up from the grave.

As pain broke him, Wallace was a boy once more with his father watching on as he and Caleb rode the carousel ponies of the boardwalk.

But Wallace Sweet would recall no more. The last he

was aware was of the moon careening about in a wild transit as though he'd slipped from the slick saddle of his brightly painted mount and struck his head. The world conspired with the moon as the sum of all spun about faster and faster, pain the axle on which the world turned. Father and Caleb were not found. Dizziness took possession and sickened him. Just before blackness shrouded Wallace, the ground opened and he and the cast of carousel ponies, teeth bared at their bits as though in fits to fight this last gallop, cascaded down and down, spinning into their shared whirlpool grave all while the unseen Mad Operator kept hard upon the throttle.

"Father," the old man whimpered, his hand almost reaching a frozen, frenzied mane, and then he was gone.

By the time Evan had gotten himself and Walter to their feet he'd already forgotten the incident. His worries returned once more to all the other threats haunting them from the fringe of the night.

Evan ran his tongue over his swollen lips. "You see one of them damned tentacles, you call out. Don't clam up with fear on me, boy. I go, you go. But we won't be going out that way. We understand one another?" As he said this he'd pointed his gun first to Walter's temple and then his own. It was a pact Walter wanted no part of, but he nodded all the same.

Just as they moved off once more, Evan was pleased to find Wallace's prized Stetson lying atop a tall clump of grass. He turned it over a few times admiring it before tucking it onto Walter's head. It floated comically on the boy's ears and dipped too far over his eyes. The boy was too injured from his beating to care. For the ensuing miles it would take all he had in him just to watch his feet. Crossing the old cornfields would prove the worst part of all for Walter. The hole in the sole of his shoe seemed almost to invite the stubs of broken corn stalks to stab him there. Soon enough he was limping as badly as Evan.

"You call out now," Evan instructed repeatedly as the lumbering pair pushed on and on.

Theirs was slow going, but eventually, after all but forgetting their destination, they made it into town and stumbled unnoticed along the quiet streets. Walter felt like a hobbled mule and was sure the man would never stop. He would drive Walter until the town was behind them and then no more, and so they would carry on into the nothingness beyond.

The boy was dreaming of that nothingness when he awoke to discover the plank walk beneath his feet and the damaged and blockaded doors of what some called the public house. Walter knew better. He knew that was just a nicer name for the saloon. Behind him, splotches of blood from his abused foot marked their trail.

A single bare bulb mounted in a ceramic fixture under the entry's awning provided the small island of light they'd found their way to. The upstairs windows also shone, but the downstairs windows were shuttered, and, like the doors, they had been barricaded with tables from within.

Neither Evan nor the boy had much of any real recollection of their journey. It'd been nothing more than a convoluted miasma of misery, exhaustion, and fear; the destination reached only by a mindless resolve. The meager lights of the saloon had drawn Evan from the distant fields as they might lure a moth. Indeed, even as the man and boy stood there struck dumb within the illumination's thrall, they were occasionally pelted by a confused host of flying insects who shared in the same plight. These were mostly thick, dully fluttering moths, but also translucent midges and no-see-ums. A few strange varieties of long-winged termites mixed there as well. Minutes passed. Walter was satisfied to move no further and Evan had lost purpose. Soon enough the man and boy were speckled with the creatures as their number took turns lighting upon them to crawl about momentarily before taking wing once more only to be replaced by others.

Within Walter's arm reach, on the warped facade of the saloon's siding, three spiders, two as large as half-dollars, had slipped out from their places of concealment to dine. His eyes fixed on them and Walter wondered whether or not they might not come to take their meals upon him if he tarried there too long.

Far off along the street, a woman, or perhaps a child, cried out for something or someone before the night swallowed the vain plea. Like sentries charged to disregard all but threats to their post, the boy and the man paid no heed.

Walter was startled then as Evan stomped his boot on the plank walk. The smallest spider disappeared, darting into a seam of the wall's warped slats. The remaining two both stood their ground, threatening in arched stances, forelegs tensed on high and fangs bared. The man slowly scraped his boot back and Walter looked down to see the mess of ground chitin and mucilage revealed beneath, all that remained of what had once been either a cricket or cockroach.

Suddenly Walter felt the smoldering in his back and ribs stoked into flames once more as the man goaded him with two sharp jabs of his gun barrel into his tender side.

"Call to 'em," Evan hissed, referring to those who might be within. "Call," he demanded.

Walter gathered his elbows in as best he could to defend himself. It was a feeble and worthless effort, however, and so after an eternity of just a few seconds, he obeyed.

"Hello," he cried weakly.

"Nobody's gonna hear that." Evan jabbed twice more, harder each time. "You need to—"

A stern voice interrupted Evan from the other side. "Who's out there? Who is it? Speak!"

Walter recognized it to be the voice of Moses Platt. Or, as he knew him better, ol' Mop.

The remaining pair of spiders abandoned their stances and retreated into the saloon's crevices and Evan slid away to the side, pressing against the wall as if to join them. With his gun still trained on Walter, the ruined man made a motion with it directing the boy to answer. Walter hesitated and Evan eased the hammer back with a resounding click. The swollen mass of his disfigured hand rose slowly and he pressed the index finger to his lips. His eyes squeezed tight as he did and Evan shuddered in a bath of pain. The torpor was lifting. His damaged body was waking.

"Just you," Evan Evers said finally, eyes still closed, the words hardly more than the motion of his mouth.

There was a muffled exchange within as the bulb above their heads blinked dark.

...

Abigail Petry had no idea that Avery Stolks had spent the last few hours gunning down innocents in the streets. She'd heard some of the shots, but had no way to know the intention or result of them. Still, as he stood before her bed, his now cold rifle in hand and demanding the whereabouts of Wallace, she knew the man was deranged. She knew without doubt that Avery Stolks sought out Wallace Sweet to do him harm.

"Did it offend you?" she asked, her voice calm.

Avery was put-off by both her demeanor and her odd query. He'd forgotten that his left eye was gone. Furthermore, he'd forgotten that it'd been plucked from his skull by his own hand, just as Abigail had surmised. His remaining eye blinked, betraying his confusion.

The room was sparsely lit by a small lamp on the nightstand. Surrounding that were the untouched provisions Wallace had left her. Being Moses's room it was otherwise spartan, without even drapes to cover the window. The door behind Avery was open but no light came from the cave-black hall. The sole window was closed despite the heat and even so Abigail remained under the thick patchwork quilt Wallace had tucked her in before he'd left. A chill gripped her just the same. She couldn't place whether she was dying or merely as delusional as the man at the foot of her bed.

"Where's the ol' man? Where's Sweet?" Avery Stolks demanded. He couldn't be certain if he'd already asked or not. He stabbed the rifle at her in frustration.

"I'm sure they've got them a cleaver in the kitchen or maybe a hatchet out to the barn if your hands have been sinful as well."

"What? What're you sayin', woman?"

"To cut them off."

"What? My hands?"

"Yes. Isn't that the word of the Good Book? 'If thy hand offends thee, cut it off. Better to enter into life maimed, than having two hands to go into hell.' Isn't that the word? Mind, it's been a while since I studied on it, but I'm fair certain that's how it goes. Looks like you're off to a good start, Avery." Her face glistened with sweat and the quilt shifted over her toes, but otherwise she was serene. She even smiled.

Avery did not. He snapped the rifle to his shoulder, and, although she was only a scant few feet from the muzzle, he lowered his single eye to better sight her down its length. His left cheek swelled up out of habit, squinting closed an eye no longer there. Knuckles whitened. Beneath her quilt, Abigail braced.

The report of gunfire came not from Avery's rifle, however, but from beneath Abigail's quilt. Four muffled shots from the .32 pistol Wallace had left her sent a plume of goose down erupting into the air. As those snow white feathers shot up in a flurry and then slowly began to cascade back upon the bed, Avery Stolks stumbled forward, his jaw dropped open wide like a snake taking on an egg. The rifle fell from his hands and bounced from the bed to the floor with a clatter. Avery gasped twice all while his single eye fixed hard on Abigail's. She matched his gaze with her own cruel expression. He stood a full minute as they went on that way. And then she fired once more.

A trickle of blood found its way out of Avery Stolks's gaping mouth and escaped down his chin. Another flurry of feathers was sent into the air as he pitched into the bed.

With the better part of him sprawled between Abigail's legs, Avery tried in vain to hold himself up. He rocked forward in three protracted and diminishing efforts only to slowly slump and fall back from between her knees a bit more each time like some besotted Lothario. Slowly he slipped from the bed and as he did his feet pedaled at the floor. But they were weak, useless, and the floor slick with feathers and blood. Avery's skittering, skidding boots made nothing save a most macabre dance. His limbs were as powerless as a marionette's without a master, and his legs buckled under the slightest addition of his weight. Abigail kicked against the quilt even as he was at last falling away, sending him off the foot of the bed in a final gale of feathers. He disappeared with a resounding thud.

Abigail moved as quickly as her battered body would allow. She was finished with waiting and pinning her hopes on others. More like Avery would come. Far worse, more like Avery would visit her son. She couldn't bear that thought. She had to save him. *Save him and get the two of them far, far away from this circle of hell.*

She began undressing even as she opened the wardrobe hoping to find something to wear other than the bloody nightgown they'd brought her in. But the gown had no more fallen to her feet then she discovered the meager and far too small clothing of the diminutive Moses Platt. With no other option, she retrieved the nightgown from the floor. It proved not so easy a task given her condition.

Dressed once more as inadequately as before, she removed a pillow case from one of the large down pillows and in it she packed the supplies Wallace had left her. All except for the pistol. That she decided to keep in hand. Cocked.

"Lord, I certainly don't know your plan," she prayed out loud as she went, "but if you could see to help me and my boy, why I...." She stopped abruptly when she failed to think of a promise that meant anything. What could she offer? Her prayers? Her devotion? Those things and any others she imagined all seemed far too insignificant. Besides, were those not the very things she should pledge without negotiation? Without expectations? The briefest notion struck her that she might be better off if she prayed and cast her lot to Satan. All mortals knew what Old Scratch wanted from them. No sooner had that blasphemous thought danced its path through her mind then she was grieved to worry damnation would be its partner.

"Dear Lord...." She began again in earnest, only to fall silent once more.

She padded barefoot down the hall with the idea of searching the foyer for shoes. She realized anything she found probably wouldn't fit. Still, she couldn't count on finding a buggy or horse to borrow or steal and the distance was far too much for bare feet. A quick search turned up nothing, however, except for a pair of massive goulashes—caked with mud, no less—just inside the front doors. Even over other shoes they would have been far too large. She sat and tried them on regardless in her desperation only to throw them off in what became a fit of kicks and tears. The caked mud broke away in showers and turned to spackle where it found her sweat soaked skin.

She didn't have the strength for such hysterics to last long. Soon enough she sat panting against the wall. She scolded herself silently while wiping the dirt from her face as best she could and got to her feet more determined than ever as she pushed back down the hall to where she'd been.

Plodding along and needing the wall to hold herself up at times, she recalled a moment of her childhood. A lifetime ago, as a crooked-toothed girl often mistaken for a boy and living with her aunt and uncle on their meager parcel of bottom land back east, that man had tried to teach Abigail how to hunt. As she stumbled down the main hall of Sweet Wood, Abigail returned to that afternoon lesson when he took up a possum by the tail. It had been shot through the spine, but not killed and unlike what she expected of a possum, this poor creature was doing its best to crawl away from them. It was a pathetic display to see it drag its broken hindquarters through the leaves.

"Ya see here, ya snatch 'em up quick-like," her uncle had said as he demonstrated. Then, with a snap of his wrist, he swung the thing about, and like a woman beating out laundry on a rock, he repeatedly bashed its head into a tree until the ears produced pink foam, until Abigail vomited.

Making her way back down that hall she'd begun to feel like that possum. Pausing, she checked her ears for pink foam.

She hadn't thought previously to search Moses's room for boots or shoes. The little man's feet were undoubtedly a better fit. Following that, and if she could manage it, she might as well go upstairs and rummage the Sweet brother's rooms for a shirt and pants.

As she paused another of many times, she was struck by the décor, or more precisely, the sterility of it. She hadn't possessed the wherewithal before, but now she scrutinized her surroundings. Richly wallpapered walls were otherwise bare. Not a single photograph, or quilted sampler or painting, nor any other artwork or decoration adorned them. The furnishings, though beautiful and no doubt expensive as well, were sparse and placed for utility's sake alone. Peeking into a cavernous den as she passed its open entry, she'd discovered no knickknacks or personal items of any sort out in the open upon the shelves, tables or desk. A framed map—old and appearing to be that of the territory—dominated one wall. Otherwise, except for sconces, the walls were kept bare there as well. Encyclopedias along with what she assumed to be law or some other variety of similar textbooks lined the shelves as orderly as soldiers. Atop the otherwise barren desk that commanded the space, a set of pens stood alone in front of a leather-bound desk blotter. On the other side of the room, before the massive fireplace and its bare mantel, two matching overstuffed red leather chairs shared a table between them.

Nothing more. *Nothing at all to convey family or a sense of home.* It was to Abigail an uninviting, almost business-like place, at best resembling a fancy hotel, at worst, more akin to the funeral parlor the brothers operated.

And then something came over her. A popping sound in her ears. Dizziness. Despite the air being still and warm, Abigail Petry was suddenly overcome by a frigid cold. Her torn-up gut seized with ache and she clenched her whole body around it helplessly bound by chill and pain. She leaned into the wall. All she wanted was to be home, with pain or no. She simply wanted to be home. Why did these men bring her here? Damn any and all of their good intentions.

Minutes slipped by and she'd begun to slump to the floor. *So this is death*, she told herself. *No. What of my son? Oh God*, she thought, finding strength in reviving her panic. *What of Walter? What of my baby?* She couldn't die here. She had to save him. And there was no time to rest. She must hurry.

Where she'd been unaware of its presence before, the unmistakable tick-tock of what must have been an enormous grandfather clock reverberated above the quiet from someplace unknown. She meditated on it, used it to steal focus from the pain, the cold. The ticking clock of all things, she thought. The clock of God. How could she have been oblivious to it? It was as though it had just begun to keep time, as though His hand had just set it in motion. No. No, it had been there all along, steadfastly working. But she had kept it pushed below the perception of her consciousness. *Foolish mortal. Foolish sinner.* Now she was aware. Now she acknowledged it. The report of its mechanism was inescapable. She had yet to move from the wall but still the thing grew louder and louder until it echoed in her skull, brought strobes of light to her tightly clasped eyes. If ever the chimes were to strike—*no, not if ever, but, as soon as*—the chimes struck, then, most assuredly, the world would be ripped apart in that shattering clatter. Her ears would seep pink with foam. This she understood.

Save for the resounding of the God clock, the air

seemed positively charged with the high-pitched whirr of silence. Who could know how little time she had? At what hour and minute were those hands? She choked back a scream and threw herself down the hall.

...

The standoff at the barricaded saloon door was brief. Walter—Evan's gun in his ribs—had little choice. His eyes struggled with the dark now that the light was turned off. He'd made the mistake of looking right at the bare light bulb, just before it'd flicked out, and so what little vision he had was dominated and obscured by a purplish-red orb. He wondered if this might be his last chance to get away. No doubt Evan's eyes were troubled with the sudden change as well. No doubt if Walter simply spun about and—but then the gun barrel stabbed into him again.

Moses bellowed, "I...That is, *We*...we ain't asking again. Last chance. Who's out there?"

There would be no running. Walter offered the only thing his pain and fear-addled mind could produce. He answered Moses with far from the whole truth. "It's me, Walter Petry, Mr. Platt. Bill Petry's boy."

There was a brief pause before Moses hollered back, "Just you, little Walter?"

Walter opened his mouth to speak. He hesitated and looked to Evan. The man had already cocked the gun. Now he cocked his head and tucked in his disfigured lower lip as if to say, *don't be stupid*.

"Jus' me," Walter said. It was a poor performance. Two thin words, thick with deceit.

Nonetheless, the sound of the barricade being dismantled followed quickly. The bulb blinked back to life and then one of the doors—still off the hinges—scraped open just a hint. The gun that had been in Walter's ribs swung up and kissed Moses Platt on the tip of his nose. Evan took Walter by the nape once more, and, using the boy for a shield, drove the two of them inside.

"Nothing sudden," Evan hissed to Moses as he kept the barrel stuck to his face. "Get that piece on the floor."

Exhausted, still a bit drunk and clouded as though he'd fallen back into the opium habit he'd wrestled with years before, Moses complied. "I don't wanna see blood no more," he said. "Especially none my own."

Evan saw that the small man was indeed caked in gore. Moses stooped to drop his pistol and Evan kicked it away even before it had slid completely free of the man's hand.

Evan slung Walter Petry to the side and the boy stumbled to his knees where he remained hunkered in shame when he looked up to meet Moses's hard stare. The little man started to remark on the boy's betrayal. He cut his words short, however, stayed by the boy's badly beaten appearance coupled with the recognition of Walter's hat. The boy wore Wallace Sweet's prized Stetson.

The saloon was quiet then but for the lingering squeaks of the wood floor as Evan directed Moses to reseal and barricade the door before moving the three of them to a table. Earl stood dumbly behind the bar, at the very far end of which sat his call girl, Mariel. She was tucked into the stump of her swollen arm, head bobbing and wrestling a losing match with consciousness. On the bar beside her was a severed arm, clearly not the girl's but a man's. Along the jagged edge a length of twine dangled from makeshift sutures.

Maddie was in the other far corner along the stairs where she tended to Patrick and Caleb, both laid on makeshift beds made from mattresses and quilts brought down from the upstairs. She sat on a chair between them. Right off she appeared not right in the head to Evan, and indeed she was having a good deal of trouble in that regard. She ignored all else as she tended Patrick with a damp cloth while she continued to fail in piecing together the past few hours. She'd found Patrick upstairs, that much she kept coming back to but could get no further. *Wasn't there another man there? A dead man. Strange things. And now they were back down here in the saloon.*

Moses Platt sat as Evan had demanded and quietly returned to his previous pastime of watching the floor at his feet pitch and swell like a body of water. *Yes, just like a body of water*, Moses thought. *Or perhaps just a body*, he decided. *A body heaving its death-rattle breath.*

The little group had been holding out for dawn. Thankfully, it was almost upon them.

"What's your pleasure, stranger?" Earl offered as though it were just another Saturday night.

"What is my pleasure?" Evan repeated back, settling into his chair like a warm bath. He rested his gun on the table before him. The table rocked to him under the weight. Evan repeated the bartender's question yet again. "*What…is…my…pleasure?*" The query had transformed, however, taking on a lurid, if not vulgar tone, and was delivered with much consideration, as if there was no limit to the barkeep's power to fulfill Evan's desire. "Something wet," Evan finally settled. His eye drifted to the dying whore at the end of the bar. "Something living."

It wasn't clear if the last bit was an addition or a correction.

Earl fumbled with a full bottle from the wall behind him. "I got whiskey…or I—"

As the bartender bent to retrieve his second offer from beneath the bar, Evan snatched his Colt and fired in the same motion, bursting the whiskey bottle in the man's hand like a balloon. Instinctively, Earl froze.

Evan hissed, "If anything other than your finest libation doesn't come up from under that bar in the next three seconds, you're a dead man. One, two…."

"Tequila. I have tequila." Earl stammered as he produced the bottle. "It's wet. And there's a worm…but I don't think it's living."

Earl was soaked. Glass shards speckled his face where whiskey commingled with the blood of a dozen or so tiny lacerations. The steady trickling of the rest of the bottle's amber contents running off the bar shrouded the same sound of urine spilling from behind Earl's apron.

It had taken a moment, but following the gun's blast and the bottle's explosion, Mariel roused from her stupor. She blinked like an infant up from its nap and looked about unnoticed by all until she loosed a gleeful squeal. "Yummy! This one's already cooked!"

She lifted the severed arm off the bar and pointed it at Evan. Her eyes shone white all the way around and her smile was just as dramatic.

The room tensed for the stranger's response. Moses, Evan's gun still closest to him, tensed even more so. But

Evan Evers only lifted his burnt limb, sniffed it appreciatively, and coyly smiled. A low, throaty chuckle followed and he eased his gun back down on the wobbly table. "Already cooked.... Ding, ding, ding...come an' get it," he sing-sang and gurgled a little more. He closed his eyes. "Say there, good people. I seen the lot of you is armed. The boy here...the one I come in with, not this whiskered little gnome sittin' with me...the boy, he's going to come around and gather those up. Nice and tidy-like." Evan's eyes opened, the wounded orb only half-way-so, revealing but a sliver of milky white. "Don't make me kill anybody...more today. And I'll have that bottle of Mexican fire water, good sir."

Walter began working his way around the room collecting the firearms as he'd been told.

"Don't forget to fetch me the shotgun from behind the bar, boy," Evan called to Walter after Earl had rushed over the tequila and poured two quickly drained shots. Evan cast Earl a hard stare as he did. The barkeep tried to smile. Evan scoffed. "Bartenders...meh...." he said, and slapped his shot glass down for more. "Oh, just leave me the damned bottle and sit over there where I can keep my eye on you. Hands on the table," Evan barked, losing patience as the man shook and spilled. "And get my little friend here a glass. He looks parched."

Evan leaned back in his chair once more, taking in the room with his focus settling on Maddie. She remained single-minded in her administration of Patrick's care save for the occasional snap of her head every so often accompanied by a flailing of the air as she chased away the unseen things tormenting the corners of her vision. She wasn't going to be any trouble.

"Say, Walter," Moses said, "That's a right fine hat. How'd you come by that?"

Walter paused and looked to the stranger.

"Go ahead," Evan snorted. "You can tell him. We've got us no secrets here."

Walter stood dumb.

"Fella tried to kill us," Evan said. "Tried to kill the boy," Evan lied. "So I shot him. Hell opened up and swallowed him. All was left was his hat. The boy took it as his trophy."

"You murdered him," Walter said. "He did and I swear it so," the boy added when no one acknowledged him.

In the corner, Caleb moaned and tried to rise, but Maddie consoled him and quietly urged him back down.

Evan cocked his head and ground his teeth. "I did not…. What the hell is wrong with this place…you people?" Evan asked. No one acknowledged having heard him. Evan ignored this and shut his eyes once more.

"So you murdered the man?" Moses pressed.

Evan looked to Walter. He shrugged. "From the mouths of babes."

Earl returned with a glass for Moses and the two men regarded one another even as they considered the gun on the table, the threatening stranger with closed eyes. Earl felt a surge of hope to see the small man might be returning to his senses.

"I killed my schoolteacher when I was thirteen," Evan said, still showing them his eyelids. "He was hovering over me just like you're doin' now, bar-tender. And just like you, he had the fool notion of putting his filthy hand on my gun. Bullet came right out the top of his head. Yup, shared his mind with the whole class that morning. I was to have a previous engagement the day of the funeral, so I couldn't attend, but I heard tell that they had to put the pasty bastard in a top hat for the funeral viewing." Evan opened his good eye and stared the man down. Earl stammered half an apology and slunk away. "Just sit down over there like I done told you," Evan said as he did.

"You're hurt," Maddie said to Evan, her previous dementia seemingly lifted.

"Why yes, I am," Evan agreed. "I don't reckon they'll be calling me handsome from here on out, will they?"

"Let me help you," she offered. Wary of the stranger, she made no move, however, remaining crouched with the damp compress on her husband's brow.

Evan sucked at his swollen lip and considered the woman and her offer. After a long moment he said, "What? You gonna help me like you helped them two?" He drunkenly nodded to where the corpses of Deputy Pine and Claudette lay covered beneath table cloths. "Hey, you fellas," Evan boisterously called to Patrick and Caleb, "I'd be nervous if I were you." He laughed long and loud.

Caleb opened his eyes and regarded the stranger briefly, but otherwise the wounded men made no sign in response.

Maddie groused. "Fine. Suffer if you want, mister," she said, and wrung her bony hands all while Evan laughed.

As Walter started behind the bar to add Earl's shotgun to the weapons he'd already collected, Earl spoke up. "Where's your daddy, son?"

He was speaking to the boy, but it was Evan who answered.

"My daddy? Funny you should ask," he said. "Merritt killed daddy the same afternoon I killed that schoolteacher. Yup. Merritt shot the old man right through his cold heart just after dear old Dad had taken an ax handle to me for my schoolhouse mischief. Not that Merritt done our daddy in for that, mind you. No, my brother Merritt never so much as passed a salt shaker on my account. No sir...but he sure settled the old man's hash. I got to...well, I got to give him credit for that. But don't you all go getting weepy-eyed over the demise of ol' Davis Todd Evers. Weren't no great loss. One less drunken beet farmer in the world, that's all."

"I was asking the boy," Earl said. As if the comment alone weren't enough, his beleaguered and sarcastic tone was.

A rage washed over Evan. Even his face changed hue. He leapt up and kicked away his chair as he took up his gun. "Oh now we got us a sassy-assed bartender!" He cocked the gun and strode with murderous purpose to the man. As he bore down on Earl there was no doubt among them that he meant to shoot the bartender point blank in the face.

"He's dead," Walter said. "My daddy. He's dead. And my mama, she's dead, too."

Evan stopped short of pulling the trigger. The gun barrel was gouged into the side of the quivering bartender's nose. All eyes—save Earl's—fell on Walter. Earl remained focused on the gun. As everyone waited for something more, the boy stood quiet. Bundled in his arms were two pistols, Caleb's shotgun and Maddie's Winchester.

"The sickness got Daddy," Walter said. "And I'm pretty sure...I don't rightly know...but, that is to say, pretty sure...I'm the one what killed my mama."

...

Abigail Petry bounded down the hall. Crashing into a small table, she tripped and stumbled to the floor. The hard fall ruptured her sutures and nearly tore loose her bandages. With fumbling fingers she did her best to reaffix them back into place. Failing, and making quite a mess of things, she gave up and in her frustration yanked them off. She was near delirious once more. In her frenzied state she became turned around. She forgot Moses's room and her search for shoes, and instead found herself climbing the stairs. Her mind was bereft of coherent thought. Near the top she was on all fours and laying down a bloody trail. She felt as if she were smothering.

She might have stopped once she reached the summit—or perhaps even turned back around and descended the stairs—had she not heard the noise. First one hard thump, and then, even as she convinced herself she'd imagined it, there came two more in quick succession. The sound was coming from a room at the end of the long hall, the room she'd been in when they first brought her here, she suddenly remembered.

Another thump.

She steeled herself and went to the room. She'd all but forgotten the pistol in her hand. Thankfully, some part of her mind had focused on not losing it, however. With a trembling hand she let the small firearm lead the way. The door was open. The room beyond, quiet.

...

Evan was clearly moved by Walter's announcement. Forgetting the man who'd angered him only moments before, Evan took the gun away from the bartender's face and holstered the massive horse pistol. Earl finally breathed again as he rubbed the red ring left behind and shuddered to imagine what had almost become of his head. He'd already pissed himself. Now he thought he was going to vomit as well.

Evan focused on Walter. "You and I got a good deal in common, kid. This shit for nothing world don't cut no breaks, do she?"

Walter was silent now. His eyes searched the floor as Evan swayed under the spell of drink and exhaustion waiting for some response. But Walter didn't want this man's sympathy and that was a truth best kept quiet.

Moses took his turn to speak. "Little Walter, your mama ain't dead, son. She's been seriously hurt, that much is the truth, but she's in good care out to Sweet Wood with Mr. Wallace. I give you my word."

Walter rubbed his swollen eyes, his matted hair. He was dumbfounded, confused and perhaps more than a slight suspicious. He was confused and not thinking clearly as he tried to remember things. He was suspicious that all of these people had designs of the sort only adults might have. It was like piecing together a puzzle without the benefit of knowing or seeing the whole picture they made.

Once, years earlier, Walter had retrieved a postcard his mother had torn up and thrown away after finding it in his father's toolbox. It'd been the source of a fierce argument between his parents and so Walter was curious to see it. After they'd gone to bed, he stole downstairs and collected the pieces from the trash. By flashlight, under the covers of his bed, Walter arranged them and worked the postcard back together. At first the ragged bits made no sense. Flesh and feathers and hair and fur. A horse's head, perhaps. A woman's breasts. So odd. Only after he had more than half of the pieces in place did he begin to realize what he was looking at. It was indeed a naked woman. Holding—but in no way concealed by—a pair of ostrich feathers. And not a horse, but a donkey. The woman beneath it. Walter understood why his mother had been so angry. He took the postcard fragments back downstairs, returning them to their place in the trash.

He soon learned he could not so easily discard the image, however. It would remain to trouble the boy even in his dreams. *What had Father wanted with such a thing? How did he ever come to possess it? And even then, why keep it? And why would that woman—who even resembled Mother,* he thought—*have done those things? She appeared willing.* For so many reasons Walter would wish he'd never seen it and he would never see his father the same way again.

Yes—Walter thought he recalled—the men from the construction site had been to the house. *Hadn't they? But why had they come? Or had he only dreamt their presence? Did he dream of them wrapping his mother in sheets and carrying her away, or did that truly happen? But then also, when did those other men arrive? The three bad men. Before? After? And why had they come? Angry men killing one another. Father bloated and rotting at the kitchen table. Axes cleaving flesh and bone.*

Walter's mind swam in a clutter of disjointed images. He felt as though he might not even have all the pieces, and, of those he did have, some must be overturned or concealed beneath others so that he could only see the shape or partial image and nothing more. It was all so much. Perhaps, like that postcard from long ago, Walter would regret piecing it all back together. Perhaps he should leave well enough alone.

Someone said something to the boy, but only after the bad man placed a hand on Walter's shoulder did the boy realize it'd been him. The man had called for Walter to sit and now he repeated that and more. He told Walter to lay the guns down at his feet. To have a drink.

Feeling and moving like a piece of machinery soon to be beyond repair, Walter followed the man's instructions.

"The boy don't need him no hard liquor, mister," Moses said. The little man didn't doubt such an argument might get him killed. He didn't care. He'd long lost his patience with the situation, and long before the belligerent addition of this foul smelling stranger, at that.

His argument bore no consequences, however. As so many others had so easily done for all of Moses's life, Evan Evers simply dismissed the small man. More shots were poured after Walter finally nursed the first glass through to its conclusion. Evan, looking something like a salivating dog beneath the table, had watched intently all while the boy had struggled with the drink.

Evan and Moses drank again. They each did so without hesitation or pleasure, as men alone even in company, and with minds forever occupying the end of their lives. When

Walter made no motion to take up the next shot, Evan snatched it up and slurped it down without ceremony. Trickles of tequila ran from both corners of his ruined mouth as he did. Where his neck was blistered he suffered to be afire once more. He chose to ignore the harsh sensation. He was still seeing two of everything, although not quite so severely, with the images now overlapping for the most part and teasing on the verge of uniting whole. He decided more tequila was the solution.

"I used to trap when I was a young man," Moses said. It was not readily apparent whether he was speaking to any one person in particular or merely the room in general. He went on. "Small game, mostly. Not bear. I was too young, too *insignificant*. My father's words. But small game. And not with my father. He had no time for the likes of me. Another story, that. But me, I had my traps and I had me my dogs."

Moses looked up from his story as Evan poured just the two of them yet another drink. The bottle was quickly reaching its end. The pair paused long enough to down their shots. Over in the far corner Caleb let go a long moan, but nothing more. Maddie moved closer to him and whispered consolations unheard by the others.

"And then there was this one day," Moses went on, "I was down by the river and I crossed paths with another feller. Boy really, I should say, not much older than me. Another trapper, he was. And well, he had himself a right bad situation. Dog caught up in one of his traps. One of his own...both dog and trap. And both meant to catch raccoons, not one another. The dog was wailing something fierce, as you might can imagine. Poor thing all caught up by a front leg. Bloody mess. And that's how I come upon 'em. And I said, 'Willem,' that was the feller's name, Willem. 'Willem,' I said, 'Might I can help you and your dog out there? Lend you a hand. Maybe I'll hold the dog while you work to get him free?' But ol' Willem, he was headstrong. Like to call me Runt…and a sight worse sometimes. He was a fella what thought not too much of anybody save himself. 'No,' ol' Willem said to me, 'I don't reckon I need no help from the likes a you.' That's what he said.

"And so I proceeded to sit down under a tree with my own two dogs just a ways off just to watch and see how things panned out. I didn't see me no need to insist. And, right about directly, as Willem was bent down over that dog, trying his best to get that paw free, well, sir, that dog whipped around and bit Willem. Bit him bad. Now this here had been a good dog, mind you, but the animal was in a poor way, scared something fierce and hurt. And Willem, he'd failed to account for as much. Like that!" Moses snapped his fingers. "That dog took Willem's eye."

Moses reached over for the bottle and poured another round, finishing it off. He drank his last share as Evan watched him intently, waiting for more of the story. The little man only smacked his lips and sighed as he slid the empty glass away to the middle of the table. He said no more and closed his eyes and stretched out as if to sleep. Eventually it became clear to all that Moses was finished with both the bottle and his tale.

Evan took the empty bottle in hand and tilted back in his chair. "So…are we meant to glean something profound from that?" he asked. He tossed the bottle in Earl's direction. "That's your cue," he said as the bottle bounced along the floorboards and rolled to the bartender's feet.

Earl stammered apologies as he hurried to get up, and, as if in conjunction, the lights surged and blinked for several seconds. In the flicker the Brazen Head suddenly jerked and clicked to life once more. The unexpected movement startled Evan and he produced his gun in a fast-draw and nearly fired on the fortune-telling machine. He quickly realized his overreaction, however, and, laughing a bit too heartedly, he crossed the room to get a better look at the thing. He kept his gun out and waved it over his head for all to see as he did.

Moses and Walter looked to the collection of guns on the floor between them. Both the small man and the boy were weighing whether they could quickly retrieve one and shoot the man before he knew better. Moses rested one hand down at his side while the other found the table. His fingers began to tap as if he were seated at the piano.

...

Abigail crossed the threshold of the room expecting a confrontation, a target for the pistol in her hand. She found none.

The room, a bedroom, was just as her scant recollection of her time there told her it would be, spartan, very much like Moses's room downstairs. The only thing to really set it apart was the broken window. One of the panes had been shattered. She vaguely recalled the incident with the bird that had crashed through it, a mish-mash of disjointed images all but forgotten.

She was troubled that there was some additional detail she was missing. It teased just at the edge of her awareness. She fought to pull it from its hiding place, only to imagine it eluded her like a frightened cat crouching beneath furniture, all hissing and hackles and pawing claws each time she moved too close. Maybe, she considered, that image was her subconscious warning her to leave this thing be. Long minutes flowed by as her eyes ran in circuits along the jagged edges of the broken window pane all while her attention was turned inward.

The house had gone quiet since she had gone quiet. The grandfather clock downstairs still kept time, but Abigail grew oblivious to the echo of its ticking mechanism once more. Her only movements were those involuntary motions of heart, lungs and eyelids. Sweat ran down her brow and caught up in the shallow lines of her face, the creases of her neck, the hollows of her shoulders. Where her nightgown had failed to take them up, beads of perspiration gathered and streamed to tease and tickle the small of her back, the soft of her inner thighs. The rivulet of blood that had coursed from her wounded stomach finally subsided. The coagulated remnants caked and cracked like the clay bed of a dead, dry stream. She slumped down at the bedside. Nearly an hour passed as the grey dawn began to haunt the window.

Another loud thump shook her from her reverie. Walter, her son, had tried to kill her. *Had that been the thing she'd forgotten? Perhaps. Perhaps not.* And again another loud thump came as something outside struck the side of the house. She struggled to her feet. Before she could think better of it, she moved to the window in search of the source.

A lone tree stood close by. Silhouetted among its branches a flock of mourning doves huddled. They were at least thirty or forty in number and Abigail was struck by their assembly as she'd never known doves to gather in such numbers. *Then again*, she supposed, *like all birds they must. Not so odd, after all*, she concluded.

The source of the strange noises was revealed then as one of the birds took flight only to careen blindly into the side of the house. It plummeted to the earth, broken from the impact, disappearing as it fell from Abigail's vantage. Her eyes followed its descent only to discover a dozen or more doves strewn beneath the tree like fallen fruit. Their soft bodies lay motionless save for one fluttering about in small hapless circles. Another bird dropped lifeless from the tree to join them. Abigail turned away.

She would go home. She abandoned her search for appropriate clothes and shoes. She did not bother to find remedy for her burning thirst. Some primitive corner of her mind registered the pain in her gut, along her arm, her wrists, her ankles, but none of that pain would be acknowledged. She moved slowly but with resolve. She would go home.

At the stairs she was stopped. Not by the prospect of the descent, although in her condition it would be dangerous. She was stopped as she discovered Avery Stolks staring up at her from where he sat on the landing below. But for the heaving of his chest she would have thought him as lifeless as those fallen birds, so pale was his complexion.

"Shouldn't you be dead," she said, her tone matter-of-fact.

Avery lifted the rifle from his lap in response. Abigail Petry clenched her fists. Too late her mind's eye revealed the pistol she'd left on the floor of the room behind her. She could turn but she could hardly run. She looked Avery in his remaining eye. It blinked wildly—hardly more than the pupil surrounded by bloodshot white—betraying the fear of the mind it served.

"Oh, Avery," Abigail said, her words as soothing as a mother's to a troubled child, "We all have to die, sweetie."

She brushed the sweat-damp hair from her brow as if to invite Avery's bullet to strike her there. It did.

Chapter Fifteen

Walter Petry had received the news that his mother was alive at Sweet Wood as something of a mixed blessing. He loved his mother dearly, as all good children should and do, and so he was inwardly ecstatic to hear she yet lived. At the same time, however, he was troubled to think of her. How could he ever look her in the eye again? How, after the horrible things he was sure he'd done, could he face her? He wondered if she still loved him. He was sick with worry that she wouldn't have it in her heart to forgive him. The boy had no idea that he needn't worry himself over such concerns any longer. Walter Petry was an orphan, only he did not know this yet.

Evan Evers stood at the Brazen Head. He was scrutinizing one of the discarded fortunes he'd found in its retrieval slot.

"Be-ware the color yella," he read slowly aloud. His tongue was thick and his vision blurred. He turned the small slip of yellow over and silently considered the opposite side.

"Don't waste your money, mister," Earl Hodges called. "That fool thing's broke. Been broke. Keeps sputtering out that same fortune."

"Idiot," Evan chastised. "Only thing not workin' right is you. This here...this is a modern marvel. Just run down on paper, that's all. Says right here on the back of your little fortune...you're supposed to send off to order more. St. Louis. Hell of a town." With that Evan crumpled the slip and threw it in the barkeep's direction. It sailed wide and fell short by some forty-odd feet. Evan turned back to examine the Brazen Head more closely. As he did, he spoke once more to Moses. "I liked your story, little man. About that fella losing his eye to the dog. You've got yourself a gift. What was that, some kind of what...a parable? You know, you're better than this here whatchamacallit...dire warning...fortune-teller device. Maybe we ought to stick your lil' ruby red noggin all up in there. See if it can spit out fortunes for pennies." Evan laughed and rapped the display glass with his gun barrel, cracking it. He shot a glance to Earl as he did. It was a hopeful look. A look that said he hoped Earl meant to do something about it. The bartender bit his lip and looked away. Evan continued with Moses. "So which is it? Am I supposed to be the dog...trapped dog...or the blind, stupid fella?"

Evan's back had been to Moses and the boy for some time. He was convinced his ears would perceive their slightest movement, however, and, just for good measure, he'd also been surreptitiously watching Maddie for any sign that the boy or the little man might be making their move against him. He was sure the runt would do something stupid...eventually. After all, the guns were piled right there at their feet, and oh how this little man obviously thought so highly of himself. And Evan welcomed their assault on him. In fact, he'd kept his back to them in hopes of goading an attack. He wanted the sport of gunning them down. He wanted them to have it coming. He wanted to kill each and every person in the room. And, he assured himself, before he left, he would.

Behind him, Moses's fingers tapped on and on upon the table. The noise of it ever so annoying, but at least it let Evan know where one of those little hands was. There was no sound from the boy, not so much as a fidget or a peep. Nearest to Evan, and where he could easily watch her, Maddie continued to play nursemaid to the old men laid out before her. She didn't truly care for them, Evan decided. They were merely her prop, her feeble distraction, just like the cowardly bartender had his glassware to polish. Still, Evan noted, her attention seldom went elsewhere, and even when it did, it neither strayed nor tarried for more than a few fleeting seconds. The bartender off to his side continued his act as though nothing were wrong. Unlike Maddie, the saloon proprietor's darting eyes gave him away. Even as he nervously tried his best to pretend to look elsewhere, they always returned to Evan.

Meanwhile, the whore in the corner must have fallen asleep. She'd not moved for so long that Evan was looking forward to the rude awakening he would give her. He would save her for last. *Dessert*, Evan Evers mused.

He turned his attention to Maddie. "You're certainly an angel straight down from Lord…God Almighty…. The way you're looking over them fellas. They your kin? Must be. Or you just Christian through and through?" He slouched back into the broken display of the Brazen Head and the glass crackled a bit under his weight. "Well, my goodly woman, which is it, angel or saint?"

The man's voice had gone sweet. *But too sickly-sweet*, Maddie thought, *more like a mouthful of warm syrup when a body was thirsting for iced tea. An inept salesman.*

"It's my opinion you're the dog in Mr. Platt's story, mister whatever your name is," Maddie replied. She hadn't done him the courtesy of looking up from her ongoing administrations to Patrick. Her words felt empowering to her just the same, to stand up to this bully. Even so, she suddenly knew the tingle of goose pimples prickle along her arms, the back of her neck.

"That so? That so?" Evan said. His eyes blinked with a strange rapidity. "And it's Mr. Platt, is it? What makes me the dog? I'm lowly? I'm a…some kind of thing to be feared? A danger to you sorry people?"

Caleb roused a bit and hoarsely whispered something. Maddie leaned in close to better hear him.

"What's that? Speak up!" Evan demanded and smashed the side of the Brazen Head with his pistol. Glass shards tinkled to the floor. "The dead and dying, what, they want to side with you?"

Maddie ignored Evan. To the bartender, Earl Hodges, she said, "We need us some more water over here." After a pause, she thought to clarify, "Clean, drinking water. Cold's preferable, if there's any left to be had."

"I'm thirsty too," young Walter Petry said.

Earl looked inquisitively to Evan. No one could say if he was seeking permission or waiting to hear whether the stranger wanted for water too.

Ugliness curled up Evan's already terribly disfigured features. "Why're ya lookin' at me for? Get the poor bastards…get 'em some drink…water," he all but garbled. "And for the boy too. Who else? Who wants water? Speak up!" Wincing, he turned to Moses. "How's about you, Jonathan Swift? All that story-tellin' set you parched?"

"I'd be happy for some more...substantial drink," Moses replied.

"You're the dog," Maddie went on, still not looking at him, "because you're hurt, and so much so that you bite the hand that reaches out to ease your pain. I've offered to tend those wounds of yours. But you insist on suffering and snapping back. You got you some bad burns and lost a lot of blood from your leg. You look to be nearing your end without proper care."

"My end? You don't say?"

"It's a pity, is all. I will pray for you. I'll pray and do whatever else I can if you'll let me." The old woman finally looked up at him. "Son, please. Just put the gun down. Or holster the thing, if that's the best you can do. I know you're afraid. But we're not the ones who hurt you. Come sit here and let me look after you."

Evan closed his eyes and sucked in a deep inhalation through his clenched teeth. As he slowly released the breath he opened his eyes once more. He holstered the Colt.

"Good. We can bring another mattress down or—" Maddie began.

Evan cut her off. "Stand up," he directed.

"What? I—"

"Stand up!"

Moses intervened. "Now look here, mister. There's no call—"

"I will kill you...when it is your time. Little man. Until such, shut the hell up. Now you," he directed back to Maddie, "Do like I said and up off your keister."

Maddie rose slowly from her chair.

"Was that so damned hard? Jesus, but you people. Now go over there and pull back those sheets," he said, referring to the corpses of the deputy and Claudette.

Maddie paused long enough to exchange glances with Moses and Earl. Moses nodded and Earl avoided her beseeching gaze. With no other recourse, the old gal tossed her damp washcloth into a bowl by her chair and moved across the room. She kept her back to Evan. She reasoned he was less likely to gun her down from behind. Even as she thought this she was reminded that Patrick liked to call her an "unrepented" optimist.

She yanked the sheet off of the deputy first. His remains were so terrible that she hoped they would be enough to satisfy the stranger's curiosity. They weren't.

"And the other one," he said.

When Maddie slowly pulled the cover from Claudette, Evan attempted a long whistle. Had his lips not been so disfigured the old woman was sure it would have been successful and impressive, but instead all he loosed was a shrill slur of rushed air and spittle. He limped over for a better look. Kneeling down at Claudette's side, Evan brushed the matted hair from her face. The strain on his leg released a fresh fount of blood from the stab wound in his thigh. He was oblivious to it and the sight of the dead seemed to breathe life into him.

"Well, howdy hiddee hee! Looks like I was late to the party. Ain't she a beauty now! Or *was*...until she crossed paths with you monsters. I may not of know'd it to look at you, but you people, you are a pack of cold-blooded killers! Son of a bitch! Damn! And a law man, too. Color me impressed. I got to say...glad I took your guns away.

Murderous bastards! Who knew? You got to shoot straight with me, now...who did what to who here?" He turned back to Moses. "If I was a betting man, I'd wager most of this is your handiwork. Or did the coward get him some too?" he said with a wink of his mangled eye to Earl.

"You got it all wrong," Moses said.

"I do?" Evan said. "Why don't you just skipper-scamp your nervous little fingers away from the temptations of y'alls' arsenal there and sit yonder where you can tell me all about it." With a lolling wave of his gun he directed Moses and the boy to join Patrick and Caleb. "You can get back over there, too," he said to Maddie. "Hell, and you too," he added to Earl. "All of you...over there! You too, Sleeping Beauty. Party's in the other corner!" he yelled at Mariel. "Wake up, lil' doggie! Wake up! Wake up!"

Mariel didn't budge. Her chin on her chest, she clasped the severed limb to her bosom like a beloved doll.

Maddie gathered and replaced the sheets back over the deputy and Claudette before she did as the stranger told her. She was thankful when he didn't protest. Moses stood, but nothing more. Like Maddie, he suspected they were being gathered like sheep for the slaughter. His mind scrambled about with the notion of going for a gun from the pile near his feet. He knew, however, he'd never manage it before Evan could fire at least four or five shots if not every last one he had. If only he could know whether Earl had another firearm behind the bar. And even then he wondered if the bartender would have the stomach to use it if Moses sacrificed himself to give him the chance. There was nothing in Earl's demeanor to offer the small man any such hope. Earl was hesitating, fidgeting unnecessarily with his apron and anxiously watching to see what Moses would do. Evan cocked his Colt revolver. Moses Platt shook his head in defeat and led Walter to the mattresses. All he could do was keep himself between Evan and the boy. When the small man complied, Earl hung his head and did the same. He moved slowly, though, remaining behind the security of his bar for as long as he dared.

"Bring a bottle," Evan growled as the man drew near. He turned back to Mariel. "Hey, girlie, let's move it." He kicked her barstool with his good leg.

And, with that, the lifeless body of Mariel finally toppled from her seat to the floor, the severed arm still tight in her grasp. With that gruesome discovery, it was as though the machine of fate was set into motion.

Maddie gasped and Caleb sat up. "God Almighty," he cried, casting his wounded hand out at Evan, "you murdered my brother! Strike down this demon! Strike him down!"

Evan Evers found his head swimming. Pain and anger. It wasn't Caleb Sweet calling out for his damnation. He looked from the dead whore at his feet to across the room. There was his brother Merritt, bloodied and butchered, pointing an accusatory finger, hissing hate from a frothing mouth.

"He's the devil. He won't let us leave this place. Hell. His dominion. The devil don't let you leave. He'll keep us here. Keep us all here. He's the devil. He's damned us. Strike him down! Lord, we beseech—"

Evan fired four times in all. The first shot struck Caleb on the right side of his lower jaw and the second centered on and just below the nose. Excellent marksmanship given

Evan's condition. He had fired from the hip and meant to shoot the specter of his brother in its mouth. The other two shots came without pause as he pumped them into Mariel. In Evan's deranged state he saw her moving as he fired on Caleb. She was rising up from the floor to pull him down. Tentacles revealed themselves from her torso and now they writhed around her, manipulating her limbs. So then, even as Caleb was blown back into Maddie, Evan was firing into Mariel's still warm but lifeless body.

The second shot to strike Caleb—the one which passed beneath his nose and exited the back of his skull taking the better half of it as it did—ended its trajectory in Maddie, striking her hard and spinning her to the floor. She landed face-down and did not move.

Moses instinctively made two bounding steps towards his old friend and employer only to realize the folly of his movement. There would be no saving Caleb. And now the guns were even further behind him.

Earl Hodges was in most cases a coward. Over the years he'd allowed no less than three deaths to take place in his saloon all because he was too fearful to intervene. On two of those occasions he'd failed to act even with a loaded shotgun in his hands. But he hadn't slept in days. His mind was fractured and agitated and he was more afraid than he'd ever been in his life. He let that fear do his thinking for him. Taking the bottle by the neck, he brought it down on Evan's skull as hard as he could swing. It exploded with a vicious impact and the man was knocked sideways from the blow. He staggered along the bar and struggled to hold himself up.

It wasn't enough. Evan would not go down. Howling as if he were the demon Caleb accused him of being, Evan—his scalp stripped away by the bottle with a good portion flapped back to reveal the baby teeth white bone beneath—turned on the bartender. There was no pause to hear Earl's apologies, his begging for mercy. Evan shot Earl Hodges in the face as well. It was a single shot that ripped away one of the thumbs of Earl's outstretched hands before passing into his forehead to instantly silence his babbling pleas for mercy.

The lifeless bartender was blown back into the bottles and glasses lining the wall behind him. Evan spun about. He trained his gun on Moses who'd only just turned to make a go for the weapons piled on the floor. Caught as he was, Moses stopped short and turned to face the man.

Evan sneered. "I would have loved to have shot that weasel-faced bastard bartender in his mug twice. I truly would. But then I wouldn't have this left for you, little man." He took his time bringing Moses Platt into his sights. Evan meant to place the bullet right between his eyes.

Walter had chosen the shotgun simply because it was at the top of the heap. A mouse darting out from his hole, the boy had made his move and seized the shotgun and returned beneath the table before any of them was the wiser. The boy fired now from that hiding place. Not only did Walter's hands shake as he yanked the trigger, but his whole body convulsed. Needless to say, the shot was not particularly well-aimed. He'd meant to shoot Evan in his torso just below his raised arm. A lung shot, or better. But Walter missed that mark entirely. Instead, the brunt of the blast caught Evan in his extended forearm. In an instant, the better half of Evan Evers's arm, to include his gun hand and the Colt it'd held, was scattered onto the wall behind the bar.

Evan fell to his knees. He began sobbing for his brothers and was still going on that way as Moses approached him. The small man had retrieved Maddie's Winchester.

"Normally I wouldn't want to put the likes of you out of their misery. I much rather enjoy seeing you in it. But you murdered Wallace Sweet. And then you did the same to Caleb. There's no way on God's good earth that I ain't going to kill you myself for either one, you son of a bitch."

Snot was running down Evan's face and he sucked it in and spat at the little man who was eye to eye with him now that he was on his knees. Almost instinctively, the nub of Evan's missing arm worked about as the hand that was no longer there groped for a gun that was equally absent. He held up his other hand to ward off the inevitable.

Evan's eyes rolled back in his head. "Merritt! Dale! Don't you let this little pink-faced demon kill me!" he wailed. "Merritt!"

Moses stopped short, bracing for an attack from the windows or doors. Since the stranger had arrived alone—but for the boy—and been hours with them, Moses hadn't considered that he might have partners. But no one came.

Walter could no longer contain himself. "You killed 'em, mister! They can't save you! You killed 'em! Killed 'em all! And you ate 'em!" He began to cry. "You ate his heart...." he sobbed.

Caught in the crucible of the boy's truth, Evan gave up his fight. His posture slouched and his chin drooped to his chest. He settled and sat back on his calves as though melting. Just when it seemed he might collapse entirely, he turned his face up and brought his good eye into focus on Moses who stood burning to speed him along, but still taking no action. Evan's expression changed. The rage washed away.

"Daddy, Merritt went an' threw my marbles in the sand an' now I can't find my best blue aggie," Evan cried. His remaining hand pawed, palm up, ineffectually at the floor boards. Moses was taken aback and the Winchester eased down from his shoulder as Evan went on. "I don't like the beach, Daddy. I want to go home." His voice fell to a whisper. "Take me home, Daddy." There was only the sound of Evan's arm dripping onto the floor. Evan looked up to Moses. For a moment he seemed confused. The moment quickly passed.

Evan looked about, studying the room as though he'd just arrived. His expression lit up as he did. "Y'all got ya'selves…oh, you ain't no dumb lumber…you sewn up tight as ticks…ticks tucked on a hog's ear," he said. Then, as his good eye lingered on the linen-draped corpses in the corner, his disfigured countenance, pale now from blood loss, twisted up in ugliness once more. "You sorry buncha murderin' bastards." A string of spittle slipped over his lip and ran down his chin. He turned his attention back on Moses. "I'll see you there, mister," he said with a cruel smile.

The small man swelled. "Don't wait up," he hoarsely replied as he brought the Winchester back to his cheek.

Walter had seen enough. He turned away and shielded his eyes with his arm. He could avoid the sight of it, but there would be no escaping the sound of the ensuing carnage as Moses methodically emptied the Winchester. Only after the room grew still again did the boy peek out from beneath the table.

Moses stood over the grotesquely twisted form of the last of the three bad men. At his feet a crimson pool continued to gather even as golden motes of dust cascaded and swirled all about the little man's bald head, he and they caught up and illuminated in a single shaft of the new dawn's light as it broke through a thin gap of the barricaded saloon doors.

...

Consciousness returned to Wallace Sweet in fragments. First he was aware of his dreams. Dreams of falling, falling and falling, pitching head over heels. His was a plummeting descent through an infinite void wherein he suffered a nightmare of suffocation. He flailed his limbs about vainly seeking some purchase, but there was only nothingness. All was desperation and despair until it seemed his dreams had tired of him and he was finally allowed to shake himself from the void's grasp. A jolt shot through him. He startled awake in pain, disoriented and unsure if he were not still part of a dream. Sucking in a great gasp of breath, he gave silent thanks to his God for both the air and the cold but firm earth he found himself sprawled out upon. Still, an inky darkness enveloped him. His old eyes were more useless than ever.

He'd been shot, he remembered that much right away, although any other accompanying details eluded him. In the pitch black he couldn't so much as even make out his hands before him, but a probing of his wounds revealed neither to be life-threatening, merely an entry and exit through the sparse meat of his left shoulder and a similar grazing of his ribs. The knee and ankle of his right leg both troubled him; a result of his fall, he surmised. Thankfully, nothing seemed broken, however.

A bit dizzy, he found his feet.

His ear still ached from being shot. As he gently reexamined that wound he mumbled, "They're chipping away at me piece by piece, Caleb."

He chuckled at his little bit of humor and suddenly knew by the echo of it that he was underground. Looking up, he could just make out a sliver of night sky high above him and then he became aware of the sound of water near at hand. Not realizing he was already at the water's edge, he stumbled and fell into it up to his knees. Cursing, he struggled back out and very quickly deduced he was caught in a narrow sinkhole. The chamber marked where a limestone shelf met with clay and earth, the sides both too steep and too fragile to scale and formed into the shape of a bottle, wider at the bottom and converging rapidly to the small opening some twenty feet above. Wallace understood he was trapped like a fly in a pitcher plant. It would be impossible to climb out. Even if he could, whoever had shot him might still be up there waiting for him. Avery Stolks? No. Not Avery, but clearly someone just as delusional and violent. Wallace Sweet watched the opening above him for a few minutes. Thankfully, his commotion had drawn no attention.

As he watched and waited he supposed his attacker might think him dead. For the time being he didn't want to enlighten them to the contrary. That, or maybe they were wise enough to know that the fissure was too dangerous to approach. Or maybe they were simply gone. There was no way for Wallace to be certain on any account.

Wallace explored his surroundings feeling his way carefully. After he failed to come across his torch, Stetson, or shotgun, he imagined they were either lost to the waters or on the ground high above him.

It was a small space, a grotto. Water had carved it out, apparently emerging as a wellspring in one corner. From there it flowed along the top of the limestone shelf exiting via a small passage it had produced through the earth and clay. It was tight going and a cursory exploration revealed it afforded little more than head space above the waterline. Blind, Wallace also had no way to know how far it continued that way. Whether it remained passable or not, the prospect of following it was hardly desirable. He soon realized, however, he had no choice. He would have to follow the stream and hope the cave eventually led to the surface. Perhaps, he considered, it might emerge in a place unknown to the bastards who'd shot him. "I should be so lucky, he whispered to himself as he crouched to make his way.

The water was swift and cold as death.

He slowly felt his way along until his hand discovered what felt like flesh. He recoiled and then found it again. A growth of mushrooms lined the cave.

...

Dawn found the survivors—Maddie Thompson, wounded but to survive, her husband, Patrick, Walter Petry, and Moses Platt—at Sweet Wood. In a welcome breath of providence, they were met there, much to their surprise and relief, by the remaining members of the construction crew, James, Joseph and the foreman Goodman. What they found inside—Avery Stolks and Abigail Petry—brought Moses Platt to tears. Maddie tried to save Walter from the grisly sight, but the boy had already rushed ahead and so it was too late. The child stood dumbly on the stairs between the corpses before the old woman could collect him to her and hurry him away.

The men braced for the boy's hysterics, but nothing of the sort was heard from him.

Moses and James saw to cleaning up while Patrick was put to a bed. The old man raved between his brief lapses of consciousness. Those close in attendance, hearing his words, shuddered to consider what figments haunted the man's mind. Afterwards—after Moses explained things to Goodman and the others as best he could, given his befouled and befuddled state—the little man and the boy and Maddie were persuaded to take the rest they were in such desperate need of. Moses, a drunken mess, argued against this at first, until the foreman pointed out the newly orphaned child was giving him less trouble. With that, the small man acquiesced. Soon the house was quiet.

The next day, Joseph and James stood watch while Goodman and Moses—at the smaller man's dogged insistence—took Goodman's wagon and spent the better half of the morning ferrying the bodies of the deceased from the saloon back to Sweet Wood. They rode with shotguns in their laps, little doubting that they would cross paths with trouble. Thankfully, however, the streets were deserted and all was still. The bodies then were interred in the barn—for lack of better facilities near at hand—and it was agreed that come the morrow they would be shuttled out to the new funeral home. And so it was.

The following morning, even as the dead were arriving, Moses teetered atop a ladder to hang out the funeral parlor's new business shingle from the front eave. It was a superfluous detail. With the brothers gone, the small man could not truly provide for what would be the first and last clients of the new establishment. But he'd fashioned the sign himself and he considered it his duty to officially open the parlor in memory of his fallen friends and employers.

Then he set to the real work. Embalming was skipped out of fear of accidental desecration, and any reconstruction beyond the sewing shut of the more massive wounds was dismissed entirely. Moses did manage, however, with Maddie's and James's assistance, to clean the bodies and dress them respectfully in their finer clothes. The funeral parlor's crematory was unfinished and so, with no other civilized recourse and no further services to offer, graves were dug and pine coffins constructed. Even young Walter was put to work with a shovel.

After the bodies of the schoolteacher and his wife were discovered, as well as several others following a house by house search, it was decided a mass grave was in order for those and any others to follow. There was no time or inclination to find cause or blame behind so much death. With only a few exceptions all the dead had met violent ends. An unfortunate result was that the survivors assumed the old retired school teacher, Hastings, had been murdered by his own wife. Her body was found sprawled atop his out on their front porch. The old horse pistol she'd used on the two of them still in her hand.

A linen shroud was provided for Evan Evers and he was buried by James in the vacant plot adjacent to the funeral home. He would not rest with the good people of the town. The grave was shallow. It would go unmarked.

As James toiled to break the hard earth, Walter Petry looked past him from the parlor window to watch Moses, Joseph, and Goodman as the three rode off in the wagon to fetch his father's remains from the Petry family farm.

Maddie, who had been charged with keeping an eye on the boy, was none the wiser when he stole out the back in pursuit.

...

Fever and blisters.

Which came first? The old riddle tickled his mind. *Which came first? Chicken and eggs. Fever and blisters. One begetting the other. Alpha and omega. Beginning and end. All things must end but only as the beginning to another. A mobius strip.*

Darkness. Always darkness. The man and the darkness. His mind raced along but always found its way once more to where it'd been. Fever and blisters. Darkness and man. Raw meat and fever stumbling through the spongy darkness. But the man was not lost. He had been. Oh, how he had been lost. But now this was his darkness. His home. *My black bride.* And ever and fully did he love her. To keep her close in a long life spilling over with decades of wealth and privilege was the sum of the sustenance he needed. He threw off his water-logged boots. He pushed on. Soon enough, his clothes he discarded as well. Nude, he squirmed through the dark womb. He had shed his fear. He was being reborn.

In the waters he cooled his fever, gnawed at his blistered flesh. He considered removing his eyes. What good were they in his world of darkness? Maybe he should pluck them out and feast on them. That would make use from uselessness. *But I will wait*, he thought. *Perhaps later. Yes, later.* And so he pushed on.

...

Walter Petry pressed into the tall grass belly-first and only dared steal a peek for a few fleeting seconds before tucking back down again. There was a constant wind that rustled through the dry stalks and the sun shone brightly from a cloudless azure sky. Just far enough away to be out of earshot, the men the boy had followed were busying themselves with the unexpected carnage of the Petry farm. They stood in a circle around the corpses of men and horse, taking quite a bit of time discussing the grim task at hand before finally unhitching the horses from their wagon. It took nearly half an hour before the team managed to free the dead horse from the hole. The carcass was heaved aside and two of the men clambered into the earth to retrieve the broken body of yet another stranger. Walter was sitting up on his knees by the conclusion, confident that he would remain unnoticed by the preoccupied and distracted men.

Only when they'd loaded those strangers' bodies into their wagon and moved to the house did Walter sink back down. He dreaded the sight to come.

They brought Bill Petry out feet first. The wind kicked up as they did and the men stumbled on the steps. Walter gasped when he thought his father was struggling with them. He was not. As they brought the body up into the wagon, it was clear that the man was as dead as Walter's fragmented memories had assured him he would be.

Walter got up and ran. He didn't care who saw him. As he fled he thought he heard them call out for him. Or perhaps that was merely the wind cutting through the cheatgrass. It didn't matter. He refused to look back. As he ran his insides were twisted up and his throat felt as though it had closed. Tears streamed along his cheeks and blurred his vision. Still, he ran. He cleared a rise in the field and just as he did he was stopped in his tracks. He'd almost run into a horse. But like the animal the men had pulled from the hole in his front yard, the bloated thing before him was dead. The head rested upright on the ground, as did the body splayed out beyond it, in a position that seemed almost peaceful. It was as though the horse had settled at rest. A mottle of flies worked the carcass. He'd caught his breath in surprise, and, with it renewed, the stench overwhelmed the boy. His knees buckled and Walter retched as he fell on all fours.

Almost right away a handful of the flies found their way to Walter and began their harassment of his damp cheeks and eyes. They lit on his vomit and searched it greedily. He shooed them away and covered his face in the crook of an arm. He stole a look back over his shoulder. If anyone had seen him, it didn't appear that they meant to give pursuit. The field was quiet save for the ubiquitous flies and the wind.

The horse was saddled and this worried Walter that a rider—no doubt dead as well—must be near at hand. Another of the bad men. How many had they been? He rose to his feet slowly, apprehension weighing down his slender shoulders, but he discovered no one. There was nothing more. There was only the dead horse. Walter stepped closer. It had suffered a broken leg. Bone protruded from one of the forelegs folded beneath it. Worse, the poor beast had been very badly burned. Most of its hind quarters were singed free of hair, as was the face and snout. The flies found this especially inviting. Their maggot offspring writhed there in feast. Walter had seen enough and was prepared to continue his flight.

And then something made him consider the saddle bags. Fancy tooled leather. The initials "E. E. E." stamped into the flaps. Walter just had to look. A large fly flew looping circuits around his trembling, outstretched hand as though the thing shared the boy's curiosity. He unbuckled and turned back the flap nearest him. He couldn't believe his eyes.

A few years earlier, at a time when Walter was having some trouble with an older boy in school—and worse, most of the other boys were siding with the bully or egging on the conflict—Walter's father had sat him down in the barn for a talk.

...

"So's what's the good in cryin'? None," Bill Petry said. "There ain't nary sense in poutin' that the world's set against you. An' ya wanna know why? 'Cause it just is. An' not just you. It's set against every last one of us. You, me and that boy pokin' you in yer eye," his father said. "It is and was and always will be. That's life. Tough."

Walter shrugged and teased at a clump of fouled hay with the point of his boot.

If Walter's mother had been witness to such dire talk that would have been the end of Bill Petry's fatherly conversation and the man would have gotten his own earful of lecture from her later in the privacy of their bed. The man had the good sense to know as much, however, and that was why he was having this conversation with his son out in the barn.

It was the nature of the world, the elder Petry explained, where all things vied for dominance, survival, that each was beset upon at every turn. From the lowliest beast to God's ultimate creation there was and always would be struggle. Even the angels had warred with one another, he pointed out.

If there was any solace to be had, his father provided, it was that Walter could expect to find rare exceptions to this cruel fact of life. Someday the boy would take a wife. And, if theirs was a good and loving bond, why then, she would rise above all else to be Walter's staunchest ally. Yes, there was that. And there would be others who Walter would find from time to time to join him in fellowship and cause. Those who would give aid and comfort, supporting and even nurturing him.

"Brethren soldiers, should you ever suffer to see battle,"

Bill said. "Your own children," he said with a gleam of pride.

But far and away, Bill Petry warned as Walter listened in rapt attention beneath the glow of the dim barn light, the boy could expect to find the world indifferent to him. Indifferent to his pain and suffering. This for certain, or, far worse, in outright conspiracy against him.

Walter asked why it had to be this way. His father could only throw up his hands and admit he didn't know. He doubted anyone did. But what he did know was that it wasn't so important to know. What did matter was how the boy faced this reality. He could choose to bow to it and let it humble him with tears of self-pity, or he could opt to be a man. Meet the hard world with equal and even greater hardness. Show the world and all within it that he was made of stronger stuff.

By the end of his father's talk, although he wasn't certain it was true, Walter promised that he understood, promised that he would be a strong man.

Leaving the barn, Bill Petry paused after securing the doors and took Walter by the shoulder. There was one last thing.

"When life does see fit to offer good fortune or a break of what fools are quick to call lady luck...a good crop, a spot of rain in the drought, a healthy child, even a new day...well then, there's nothing wrong with sharing your joy with the world. A man might be a man to hide his tears," he said, "but never his smile." With that, Bill Petry wrapped his arm around his son and together they crossed as one with the long shadows of the yard to join their mother inside.

...

Walter had collapsed back onto his haunches. His focus remained fixed, nearly bug-eyed, glued on the saddle bags and the incredible discovery of their contents. He smiled.

Chapter Sixteen

They rode out from the town as a small train of six riders on horseback escorting four wagons, a flatbed truck, and a jalopy that likely wouldn't fare too well on the rough dirt road ahead. In all they numbered eleven men, five women, and young Walter. They were the last of the town's surviving populace and none of their number had needed persuading to join the exodus.

They'd discussed the matter only briefly a few nights before. Jacob, feeling the need to play devil's advocate, offered the only suggestion that maybe they should stay on. "Make a go of it." It seemed the worst was past, he'd said. When no one spoke, he went so far as to point out the dogs were gone. They'd seen no sign of them all through the search for the living, the dead. "True," someone muttered. "Maybe," another corrected.

But Goodman finished the conversation then and there. "Look, we've got neither the resources nor manpower to make do here any longer. Was hard enough with a few hundred. Now we got what, less than twenty? Not to mention the age of most. I won't speak for anybody else, but I'm no young pup anymore." Someone else started to speak and the big man ran his booming voice over them. "Besides," he said, "I've not seen a bird of any kind in over four days now. Any of you? Sparrow? Barn swallow? *Buzzard*? I tell you this, friends. You come to find yourself in a place where there ain't nary a fowl, you can be sure it ain't no place fit for man. You best be movin' on. *We* best be movin' on. All of us," he said.

It was settled. The rest nodded in agreement and the talk of their departure began in earnest.

Passing the last edifices of Main Street, Moses Platt was struck by how much the place already resembled a ghost town. Peeled, sun-bleached paint. Dry rot. Warped siding and missing-shingle-pocked roofs. Boarded-up windows. Several long-vacant shells and the handful of burned ruins. For how long, he wondered, had he failed to recognize this sad state of disrepair? It was as though the place had been left behind years before. It had sunk to this nadir by such gradual decline the small man had been oblivious until now. Looking around him, at the haggard and aged faces weighing the challenges of the road ahead, Moses nodded. And maybe it had been abandoned by them long ago, he thought. Only they were just now getting on with the business of getting on.

"Pretty swift kick in the britches you gave us, Lord," said the little man.

...

Three days prior, Walter had been found at the first place they'd searched for him after he'd run off. Of course the boy had returned to his family's farm. With no coaxing necessary they'd brought Walter and his newly packed suitcase back to Sweet Wood. Along the way Moses had promised that soon enough they would all leave that place too. He'd already made his mind up in that regard. After all, Sweet Wood wasn't Moses's home, despite the years he'd spent there. Moses had no doubt that the brothers' will—concealed in the safe under the floor of the study—

would have bequeathed Sweet Wood as well as other properties to him. Except for a slight compulsion to confirm that was indeed the case, the small man didn't care.

For the past several years he'd contented his mind that he would die in this place. For the past several days he'd sworn he wouldn't. Moses Platt wasn't sure where he'd go, but he was certain he would.

With the help of the old fellows that remained of the construction crew, Moses buried Caleb Sweet on the grounds of the new funeral parlor. Unlike the few fortunate who received pine boxes rather than internment in the mass grave, Caleb was laid to rest in a rich mahogany and crushed velvet-lined coffin. The old man had ordered it for himself personally some years prior. Moses had James help in retrieving it from the Sweet Wood estate after the small man spent an hour alone out in the barn uncrating it and giving it a thorough, if unnecessary, cleaning.

Dark clouds threatened rain throughout the entirety of the sober and routine burial.

Before sealing the casket of his former employer and friend, Moses locked the parlor doors and tucked the key in Caleb's vest pocket. Moses would need the keys to Sweet Wood for one more night or he would have done the same with them as well.

There was no priest and so there were no words, pious or otherwise, spoken. Those few in attendance were confident the brothers would have preferred it that way. Nonetheless, the old men hung their heads for a minute or two of silent reverence after the casket was lowered. When the last of them joined eyes once more with the others, Moses nodded and they set to work with their shovels.

When they'd finished, two simple wooden crosses were planted, one for Caleb, and just beside it another was erected in memoriam to Wallace, whose remains were never found. Lastly, as the others filed away, Moses hung Wallace's prized Stetson there.

They'd hastened throughout the burial to avoid what they were certain was inevitable rain, but even as they made their ways home, still nary a drop had come to pass. As Moses was returning back and knocking his boots out on the back steps of Sweet Wood, he noted the clouds had burned off.

The little that remained of the day would at least be clear.

...

As expected, the jalopy broke its axle almost to the minute that they'd put their first twenty miles behind them. Unfortunately, it happened just four miles shy of the hardtop. If the auto had only made it those four more miles, it would have likely been fine for the duration. As it were, Goodman, the owner, kicked the driver's side door shut and declared he was leaving it for dead.

Another man joked that the only good thing about "the contraptions" was that you needn't waste a bullet to put them down. Goodman failed to laugh.

Walter and Moses were riding in the back of Patrick Thompson's flatbed truck. Maddie drove. Patrick had made a remarkable recovery, although he wasn't about to do anything other than keep his wife company from the passenger's side of the cab. Those were her orders and he abided by them.

"Where do you think we'll go?" Walter asked of Moses.

It wasn't the first time the boy had asked. Moses had answered the exact same question just the day before. This time, however, he realized and appreciated young Walter's ongoing and growing concern.

"Oh, most of 'em will head north with us, I suppose," he said, leaning out and squinting to better take in the road ahead. "Others, why they'll likely skitter-scatter off the other way. Depends, really. Mostly on where they come from originally. Where they might have kin."

"And you? Where will you go, Mop?"

"Me? I got no kin. I go wherever the wind blows me. Wherever this here truck wants to shuttle my bones." Almost on cue, the truck jostled hard sending the little man up and then down hard. He thought of scolding the driver, but thinking better of it Moses instead spent his anger by grunting and straining to better arrange the collection of luggage beneath him. "One thing's for sure," he said as he wrestled with his footlocker, "you an' me, we're gonna be sore as the dickens time we get there."

Walter laughed. "Yeah. Sure enough." They were quiet a while before Walter asked, "Hey, Mop?"

"Yes?"

"Do you suppose folks will ever go back?"

Moses paused and rubbed his chin. "I don't know…might. Can't rightly say. What do you think? Would you?"

"Well…. You said these folks here are gonna go where they got family…kin."

"Uh-huh."

"But that's just it. My only kin I ever know'd was my mama an' my daddy," Walter said. Comforted to have Moses's attention he said the next thing that came to him without having given it any thought. "I dunno. Maybe I'll go back and pay my respects someday. Maybe go back and reclaim the farm. I dunno...."

Moses was formulating his reply, something about life being too short to waste on the dead, and maybe something about land was everywhere to be had, but he never got the words out as he was cut short when Maddie slammed the brakes hard. The truck jolted in a violent halt. Moses was still cursing when he got up from the bottom of the truck bed to see the others staring out over the arid land, troubled by something in the distance.

The small man climbed atop his footlocker and shaded his eyes with his thick hand.

Riders. Six men, maybe eight, on horseback. Riding hard, heading their way.

Patrick Thompson stepped down out of the cab with his Winchester. He spat. "Caleb said something about the devil not letting us escape this hell. Be damned if he might not have been on to something."

"You heard that?" Moses asked. He was sure Patrick had been too delirious if not unconscious at the time.

Patrick shook his head. "Told me as much in a dream."

Though the riders were far too distant, the old man propped the rifle across the hood and readied for them just the same.

"Funny..." Moses said, not quite loud enough to be heard, "I had me the same dream."

...

The man had been one with the dark earth for so long he'd forgotten he could see. As if rising from the cold black of an ocean's deepest recess, slowly the world took on color. Then, before he was prepared for it, the man crossed some threshold and light blazed before him. His skin shone golden, bathed with fire but without pain. Should he hide from it? Should he return to his hiding place? No.

Discarding his fear he moved forward. He rose from the earth. Naked. Thin arms outstretched beneath a brilliant blue sky he turned his face up to it and screamed. No words. The man howled and cried out in the tongue of God. For he was God, was he not?

He knew this place. There was a building there. It housed stone wheels used to grind wheat and grain, the food of mortals. The earth had opened recently. It had not always been this way. He knew that much. Also new here was the thick carpet of golden caps, mushrooms. Thousands upon thousands of mushrooms. A myriad of sizes but all cast in various hues of yellow and gold. He knew them well. In his earthen womb they had nourished him. Through them he'd been reborn. The food of God. The golden bounty spilled forth from the broken earth just as the man. And now, like the man, this new world, all of it, would serve as their dominion.

The man strode forth, feet kicking away the bones of both man and animals where they littered the ground before him. These were the fallen who had offered themselves only to be reduced to sustenance for the golden caps when they were found lacking and unworthy of the gift.

And then he remembered the other places of man. Men as unworthy as those at his feet. Men in desperate need of Him. He knew what he must do. Something slid about in his mouth, out from beneath and then over his tongue. He spat into his hand. A button. He shook his head in disgust and hurled the thing away.

The soft carpet beneath his feet squished amber juices between his toes as he began his trek. He wasn't aware of it, but he began to sing.

...

There were only five horsemen. Moses supposed the optical illusion of the horizon's heat mirage had thrown off his estimation of their number. And thankfully, they weren't demons or devils or even bandits. They called themselves lawmen, but the law they worked for was only the law of those who could pay.

As the riders had drawn near, they'd seen the shotguns and rifles prepared for them and so they halted and sent one rider forward to identify themselves.

Maddie could only chuckle in relief as she gave her husband a look he chose to avoid.

"The devil…really now," she teased.

They were dusted ghostlike in the talc of the arid land, the horses caked at the nostrils and stamping clouds as they remained in motion, restless beneath them.

"We're after three men. Brothers. Outlaws," the leader of the riders explained after they'd all gathered together and made introductions. "Used to be four. Killed one of their own a piece back after we chased them down out of the high country." He pointed vaguely to the purple hills that ran as far as the eye could see along the edge of the world. "We lost their trail there and figured they'd made south. That turned out mistaken, so now we've doubled back. Still haven't caught wind of them, however. You folks seen anything? Any run-ins?" No one spoke. "Where is it that you folks say you're coming from? That is, you don't mind my asking," he asked in a tone unfriendly, demanding.

Thompson answered, cutting to the heart of the matter. "Might be we know where you can find 'em. Your three outlaws." He paused. "They're dead. Dead and buried. Back yonder. But I'd advise strongly against you goin' there."

The leader shifted in his saddle, pulling himself tall. He made no effort to conceal his agitation. Later Maddie would say he wore it like he wore the land. "Friend," he said, "I don't recall asking for your advisement. We've been more than four weeks on these animals. You know where the Evers boys are, well then, I'd *advise* you to start talking." He was a handsome man except for the deep pocks that scarred the whole of his face and neck. The dust of the trail had collected there, adding to their prominence.

Patrick wasn't moved by his threat in the least. The two groups waited at this silent impasse.

The lead rider looked from face to face of the caravan and settled on Moses who leaned in the back of the flatbed on his sawed-off shotgun, tucked into the pit of his arm like a crutch. The little man's face was so pink he looked as though he was holding his breath to keep his mind off his sunburn.

"What about you, friend? Care to oblige?"

Moses scratched the back of his neck nonchalantly, looked off first one way, then the other. Finally, self-satisfied with his tactics, he spoke. "Back the way we come." He put a thumb over his shoulder. "Good twenty miles. Little town. Nothing much. A few farms. But you can't miss it. Not a thing in the world else out there."

"You buried them? And what of their property? Saddle bags and the like. What of all that?"

"What *property*? Their guns? The filthy clothes on their backs?" Maddie demanded.

The man fought to maintain his composure. "That was all they had? You folks wouldn't hold out on the law, on those with rightful ownership to stolen property would you?"

"What is it you're implying, mister?" Patrick brought his Winchester up from where it'd slipped to his side. "No, don't answer. I know'd what the hell you're implying. And I'm here to tell you I don't like it one damned bit."

Walter shifted the suitcase between his feet and huddled down over it, feeling like a goose with an egg.

"If anybody has something rightful due to 'em, sounds to me like your people owe my people the bounty on those outlaws' heads." Goodman growled. "Who's that you say has you employed? Who is it bought you your badges?"

A woman called out from the rear of the motley caravan, "To hell and be gone with ya!"

"No one doubts you fine folks for a minute, now," The lead rider said. He directed his words and a calming wave of his hand to entice Patrick to lower his rifle again. "And there may well be some compensation due you." He paused. "For services rendered."

"We don't want your blood money," Maddie said.

"Hey, now. She don't speak for all of us," Moses called out. When Maddie shot the little man a look he grew two inches and said, "You don't." Back to the lead rider, Moses elaborated. "They killed this boy's kin. And he returned them the favor. He's an orphan now. If there's any bounty to be paid, why then, this boy here should be the benefactor."

To this the lead rider let an eyebrow arch. He considered the boy briefly before spitting. "As it should be," the leader agreed when he looked back to them. "And my heartfelt condolences for your loss, son," he said to Walter. Then he turned back to Patrick. "Now if we can just settle the matter of the details."

The pock-marked man called back to one of his men, a scrawny, collection of sticks in a man's clothing who upon closer examination appeared too young to ride among them. At his leader's direction, the young rider dismounted and produced a map from his saddlebags. He hurried with a nervous demeanor over to the flatbed truck and unfolded it across the hood. The others watched on while the engine ticked to let off heat. "Ain't no towns off that way," the young man finally declared.

"This place of yours, is it on the map?" The leader of the posse asked Moses.

"No, not too many, I should hazard to say," Moses said with a solemn shake of his head.

"None that I've ever seen," Maddie added.

The man smiled to the old gal and dismounted. "Ma'am," he said, doffing his hat in a cloud of dust, "we are just humble and tired servants of the law. And on behalf of me and my men here, and the good folks of Western United Insurers, and even more so for that newly orphaned boy you have there, I can assure you we all would be forever grateful if you could kindly show us our way here." He gestured to the young man who stood before her with the map. A wind kicked up and the scrawny young man had to fight to keep the tattered paper from flying off.

Maddie and Patrick exchanged glances over the map across the hood between them. Patrick, in turn, looked up to Moses and then both sought Goodman's opinion. The big foreman hesitated momentarily before shrugging and dismounting his horse. He passed the reins to Jacob who rode beside him and stepped to the hood of the truck. Planting a finger on the map almost without bothering to consult it, he turned to the leader of the riders. "They're here. All three of 'em. They're also dead. And you might end up the same way you go out that way. That's why we're left outta there ourselves."

The man spent a moment scrutinizing the place Goodman was marking. Then he fixed his concentration on the big man. "Not to ruffle feathers or give offense, but that's not really the issue. We can follow your trail well enough. It'd be the finer points, you understand. Dead? All three? And buried? Precisely where 'bouts?"

"Dead," Moses called down.

"I see. And how do you know these would be the men we're looking for?"

"Mister, we never did get us too many strangers," Moses said. Almost as an afterthought, but deviously calculated nonetheless, Moses offered, "Had 'em a room at the saloon, I think."

It was a detail that captured the pock-marked man's attention.

Goodman went on. "Way out on the east side of town, up the rise, you'll find the funeral parlor." His finger slid along the map. "One is buried in an unmarked grave on the lot adjacent and the other two we put in the ground on a farm you'll find not half a mile further on." He tapped the hood with his thick finger. "Can't miss it. There'll be a dead horse carcass marks the grave. We...that is, the boy...killed the one buried out by the funeral home for murder. Don't ask me how the other two died. Don't know. Don't care. We found 'em that way. Buried 'em in the hole they'd already dug for the man who owned the farm there. Boy's daddy."

"Sounds like more than a mess," the lead rider said. "Sounds like the Evers gang."

Moses stepped down to Walter and put his hand on the boy's shoulder. He meant to say something to console him, but once more fate intervened to interrupt his words.

"Hey, Cap'n Lawrence," one of the riders called over from where he stood in his stirrups peering off through a pair of binoculars. Without taking his eyes away, he said, "You folks set fire to the town before ya left?"

As perplexed as the others, Moses turned to see what the man was going on about. He'd missed it before, but now that it'd been brought to his attention there was no mistaking the column of black smoke rising on the far horizon behind them.

...

There were no witnesses to his deeds and so there was no one to stop him. He cackled and screamed and sang as he went, naked and oblivious to the sun as it beat down unforgiving on his aged, pale flesh, his words nonsensical, his actions all too clear. It took the old man the better part of the day—despite working at a devilish pace—but, as all but the last of the fuel was spent, he'd managed to roll four barrels from the barn at Sweet Wood along the length and breadth of the town's plank walkways. Where the walkways didn't run, he'd filled buckets and carried the fuel where he thought it needed to be poured.

He saved his last bit of fuel for Sweet Wood. The great house was already thick with the smoke of the blaze outside as he went to the kitchen where he meticulously filled a pressure cooker with his last half-gallon and placed it on the burner.

His work finally complete, he lit the stove and ascended the stairs in search of his bed and some much needed sleep.

...

The camp was quiet as the boy sat with Moses at the small fire the man had made away from the others. Earlier, Walter had been crying and didn't want anyone to see. Moses couldn't bear to see the boy off alone in the cold and dark and so he'd joined him. After the fire was going well enough, Moses cooked pork and beans for the two of them.

"I don't blame you, you know," Walter said as he finished the last of his beans.

The small man was sopping up the gravy from the skillet with a piece of bread. He handed half to Walter.

"Blame?" he asked.

"Yeah. For lying to me about my mama being alive. I don't blame you."

Moses considered arguing that he hadn't lied. Considered it, but then tossed it off as pointless. They ate their bread in silence. When he was finished, Walter poked the fire with a stick and watched it and the heavens.

"Find any shooting stars?" Moses asked, making small talk in hopes of keeping the boy from becoming too maudlin again.

"What do you suppose those men will do if they don't find what they're lookin' for?" Walter asked.

"Oh, don't you worry. They'll find whatever it is they're after."

"You mean they won't give up."

"Not likely, I don't suppose." He wondered what the boy was getting at. "Those men are all dead, though. So I guess that wraps things up, wouldn't you?"

"You say so."

"Well," Moses said, giving the boy a curious look, "I do."

"Moses, can I come with you?" The question blurted out of Walter before either of them could have expected it.

Moses Platt sighed and looked into the fire, then into Walter's beseeching eyes. "I got to be honest with you, son. I don't even know where it is I'm going. And I don't have any money to speak of and so...well, I'd likely be more of a hindrance to you, then...."

"Then me being alone?" Walter said, finishing Moses's reply.

Moses shook his head. *How could he explain things to*

this child?

While Moses wrestled with their futures, Walter probed and teased the fire with his stick. The tip had taken on a cherry ember and so Walter imagined it was a magical wand. He began making firefly patterns in the air before him. As he did, he crafted silent spells. First came wishes, then commands which quickly gave way to pleas, and finally, inevitably, he bargained. But the stick held no such powers. When all of Walter's mystical efforts failed to deliver, he stabbed the cherry tip into the dirt, snapping it in two and snuffing it along with his hopes.

Across the camp, off somewhere in the dark, a woman began to cry. A man tried to soothe her, but his efforts only coaxed her anger. First she cursed, and then she fell into wailing. That went on for several long minutes until someone—the man who'd tried to soothe her, no doubt—struck her. She resumed her crying and his muffled voice accompanied her tears until eventually silence settled over the camp once more.

Moses caught Walter's eye. "How old are you, Walter?"

"I'll be twelve the first of the month."

"Twelve, eh?"

"Yes, sir. But I can do a man's work. My daddy would tell you as much…were he here."

Moses nodded thoughtfully. "I don't doubt it. Course some men don't do a boy's work, from my experience."

"I ain't no account, Mister Platt."

"No, no. I know it to be a fact that you're most definitely not some no 'count." Moses grunted to pull off his boots. He had to rest a spell between efforts. Walter watched the fire. In a voice thick with reflection, Moses said, "I was thirteen when my old man run me off. He threatened to shoot me iffin' I didn't get. He was troubled from the war. The bottle. And I do reckon you did save my life back there, didn't you?"

Walter tossed a half of his broken stick into the fire and looked up to the little pink-faced man. *Like Rumpelstiltskin*, Walter thought. He tried then, but he couldn't remember how that fairy tale ended. *Probably poorly. Most of 'em do.*

Moses sucked at his teeth for a moment and then said, "Don't be calling me 'Mister Platt.' Mop or Moses will do. Always has. I got no preferences either which way. And if I say we work, we work. And that'll likely be whenever and wherever we find it and on my say so to boot. I don't want no sass. I won't give it, and I won't take it. I'm not your daddy and you won't catch me tryin' to be. But I will have say-so because I'm your elder and I know better. We gonna have some tough times ahead."

Walter smiled. Moses was waiting for the boy's reply. Instead, Walter leapt to his feet and started off into the dark making for the Thompson's flatbed truck parked in the shadows between their fire and the other's.

"Now where is it you're gettin' off to?" Moses asked.

With an impish grin cast back over his shoulder Walter whispered, "I need to get me my suitcase from down off the truck. I've got something I need to show ya, Mop. Something you ain't ever gonna believe."

END

To see the other novels and works currently available or coming soon by J. Eric Laing, please visit:

http://jericlaing.com/

www.jericlaing.weebly.com

Made in the USA
Monee, IL
25 January 2021

58571779R00177